List of Secrets

Book Two of the Vital Secrets Series

D.F. Hart

A Collaboration with

K. W. Branzell

COPYRIGHT

Library of Congress Control Number: 2019910812
ISBN: Softcover 978-1-7330454-4-5
eBook 978-1-7330454-5-2
Large Print 978-1-952008-24-5

Custom Cover Design commissioned for D.F. Hart by:

Rocking Book Covers

Published 2019 by 2 Of Harts Publishing
Arlington, Texas

The Vital Secrets Series

Wall of Secrets (prequel)

Book of Secrets

List of Secrets

Web of Secrets

Path of Secrets – Fall 2020

Carnival of Secrets – 2021

House of Secrets - 2021

Visit www.2ofharts.com to sign up for my newsletter and get a special bonus supplement to the series!

ACKNOWLEDGEMENTS

To my husband Rick, who is my biggest cheerleader;

To my fabulous sister Leah, and my beta readers Carrie and Lisa, who get as excited about all this as I do;

To Mr. John Doppler and Mr. John Robert Marlow, whose abilities to both bolster my self-confidence and talk me down from my ledges never ceases to amaze;

To Anita, whose encouragement never falters and who shoots straight with me when I need it most;

To Mr. Michael C. Miller, Mr. Glen R. Stansfield, and Mr. Robert Keating, for sharing with me their expertise in law enforcement, civil aviation, and criminal law, respectively;

And to all in the ALLi and SPF peer groups, for their support. I thank you all!

Finally, to an amazing woman who had a wicked cool idea for a plot and who trusted me to bring it to life – My collaborator, proofreader, and one of the best friends I have ever had – My mom, K.W. Branzell. It was both an honor and a joy to travel this road with you Mom!

D.F. Hart

PROLOGUE

Just after one a.m. on a typical November 2010 night in Tucson, Arizona, and the target was late. The killer had been given his prey's schedule in advance, a schedule that usually had no variations whatsoever.

Until tonight it seemed.

The Raven, as he was called by those who hired him, was not the least bit bothered by this. One could not be in this line of work and last long at all if impatience or other infirmities could not be controlled. He was among the best at his craft; with over a hundred kills to his credit already, and with zero success of any law enforcement agency worldwide at even identifying, much less catching, him, he deserved both the rating and the respect he held.

He was engaged by his clientele through extremely anonymous means – typically through interestingly worded ads – and maintained a very high moral standard of which jobs he accepted. Only those truly deserving of death at his hand, such as drug dealers and sex traffickers, needed to fear a visit from him. And because he didn't deal out random judgement for dollars, the Raven slept just fine at night.

He was truly ready for this one to be over with, though. The Raven didn't need to take on any new jobs for a while; his financial status these days, unlike when he first started, was such that he could walk away from this career any time he chose. No, it wasn't money that had him ready to go home. He itched to get back to the hobby he'd taken up fifteen months earlier. While that too employed a certain framework of rules and a moral standard, it was much more personally satisfying.

Mentally he ran down the hobby checklist. New York was happening next. It wasn't where she was supposed to be, but evidently something had happened that had drawn her there. No matter. From the research that had been done, it was obvious she was terrified of crowds. That would make her even easier to deal with in a city that size.

He checked his watch. Almost one-thirty a.m. now. At last, the vehicle he'd been waiting on approached. As it swung past him, he slipped on his gloves, verifying a lone occupant as expected. *Good*, he thought. *No collateral damage to worry about*. He moved quickly but quietly toward the car as it came to a halt about ten feet from him.

The driver put the car in park. He looked right, to retrieve his briefcase from the passenger seat, so he didn't notice the approach from his left side. Before he could open his driver's door, the Raven was in the back seat right behind him, pulling the man's head backward with his left hand, his right hand running the scalpel deep across the exposed throat.

Raven exited the car and faded away into the dark, leaving one of the Southwest's biggest kiddie porn distributors to spend his last few seconds on earth gurgling blood and wondering what the hell had just happened.

CHAPTER ONE

The magnificent wilds of Sunburst Lake, Alberta, on a gorgeous late afternoon in early August 2009.

God, I love it up here, Ernest thought to himself. The view from the cabin's back porch, across the lake toward Mount Assiniboine, was worth the trip all by itself. So different from the flat terrain back home. Every year he usually came up with a bunch of fishing buddies.

But not this time. This time was secret. This time was special.

Finally, at sixty-five years of age, he'd found the one he wanted to spend forever with. She was a sweet young thing, only thirty-one, gorgeous, with a lush, full body he planned to thoroughly enjoy for the first time later tonight. He'd been wooing her for a couple of months now, and she'd finally agreed to go away with him for a weekend together. He just knew the beauty of the location and the romance of the fireplace would finally lead to him seducing her.

After all, no one ever said no to Judge Ernest Copeland. It just didn't happen.

As a standing judge in Fort Worth, Texas for over twenty-seven years, he'd become accustomed to his word being law. No one escaped his wrath if they failed to pay proper respect. Defendant, plaintiff, prosecutor or attorney to those accused - even John Q Public simply watching the proceedings - all stood equally targeted in his sights when he became displeased. He'd ruined quite a few promising careers in his time and was universally loathed on both sides of the aisle as a result.

He didn't give a damn at all.

Now he gazed at his prize, this lovely lady standing beside him in the living area of the cabin she'd just followed him up to. She had insisted on driving her own rental vehicle up. *A little power play,* he supposed, frowning. Not that it mattered. She wouldn't resist his charms much longer.

"I'm hungry, baby," she mentioned. "Want me to whip up some dinner for us?"

"Absolutely," he retorted. That was woman's work. He had no intention of doing it.

"Okay, hon," she said, and headed into the kitchen as he sat down near the fire with a newspaper he'd brought.

She busied herself at the stove for a bit, then crept over to the doorway to make sure he was fully absorbed in his reading and wouldn't interrupt her. Good. He was focused. She unpacked the groceries he'd picked up in the little town down the mountain from here, then retrieved the extra special ingredient from her bag, tucking it into her pocket.

"Would you like a drink while you read?" she called out.

"Whiskey on the rocks," he replied.

"Coming up." And grinned to herself as she added the liquid potassium chloride she'd brought along into his glass, mixing it thoroughly with the Jack Daniels before adding ice.

"Here you go, dear," she handed him the glass, then returned to the kitchen. Ten minutes later he called out to her, handed her the empty glass, barked, "Another," then returned to his paper.

He seems fine, she thought. *I didn't mix it strongly enough. Time to fix that.* The next drink she made she doubled the dose, freshened the ice, took it back out to him. She also added some into the beans she'd made; she hated beans anyway, so it was no sacrifice to make on her behalf. She plated his meal, served that to him too, then returned to the kitchen, pulled on the latex gloves she'd also retrieved from her overnight bag, and waited.

Five minutes in, she heard the plate hit the floor as his body finally reacted to too much potassium coursing through him. She came into the living room, sat on the couch, calmly and quietly watching as a massive myocardial infarction laid out Mr. I-Am-God on the floor like a homeless man on the street. He managed to turn his head toward her, whispering 'help' in a paper-thin voice. She slowly shook her head side to side, her eyes never leaving his.

As his heart gave out completely, the last thing he ever saw was her smiling face, watching him go. She gave it a bit, then reached down and checked his vitals with a practiced hand.

Good.

Now to tidy up.

She retrieved the plate and glass, took them to the kitchen, then cleaned up the food spilled on the floor. She proceeded to wash the dishes and all the cookware, taking care to wipe down every single surface she'd touched so no trace of her would remain. She repeated the wipe procedure on the front door handles, the little table beside the chair he'd fallen out of, everywhere she could think of as even a remote possibility of containing her prints.

Just before she made her exit, she pulled a tiny cellophane wrapper out of her pocket, tied it in a little bowtie like she'd seen so many times before so long ago, and placed it into his front pants pocket.

"One down, fifteen to go," she said aloud, looking back at the scene one last time to make sure she'd not forgotten anything. And saw exactly what she'd hoped to convey– a man, sitting alone reading his paper by the fire, had what appeared to be a fatal heart attack, and fell out of the chair to the floor.

It had been her first kill. And she was proud of herself. She didn't panic, she didn't forget anything. She was truly amazed how simple it had all been. *All I had to do was wear low-cut tight shirts and bat my eyes at that bastard,* she recollected. *And he lapped it up like milk*. She'd never had any intention of letting him have sex with her; she'd just had to play along so she could get him somewhere alone. And it had worked.

She walked out into the fading light for the return trip down the mountain. Climbing into her rental car, she took a small notebook out of her purse, pulled out a pen, and marked a line through Judge Ernest Copeland's name with a great deal of satisfaction. She took a moment to breathe, to relive it, revel in it, just for a moment. Then she put her car in drive, circled wide around his car, and started her journey back.

On to the next.

***

Landon Kendal was in his office, checking manifests against current inventory levels. The shipment from Italy was already two days overdue. He'd padded expected delivery dates as a routine measure, to account for unforeseen circumstances like rough seas or customs issues, but he still needed to lock down the cause of this delay.

As he reached for the desk phone to get in touch with his supplier there, his cell phone buzzed. He pulled it from his pocket and grinned. His kid sister Sam. He smiled as he typed a response to her, hit send, put his cell back in his pocket, and continued his quest to find out where exactly his merchandise was.

***

October the twentieth, 2009. District Attorney Hugh Livingston was not having a good evening. He figured he'd hired the stupidest PR man on the fucking planet for this campaign. Who else but a complete idiot would schedule back to back events only two hours apart when the drive time alone from Plano to Waco was almost two hours? And that was in good weather. This evening had turned misty, with thunderstorms forecasted. Fuming, he waved off his entourage in disgust, walked quickly to his car, and slammed it into drive. If he absolutely hauled ass, he'd just make it.

Running for Governor of Texas wasn't worth dealing with all this shit.

Almost, he amended.

To be honest, it was the fruition of a dream he'd had since the 1980's. He'd worked hard, being sure to keep any high-profile cases for himself rather than handing them to staffers; he'd cultivated strategic friendships across political lines. Every single bit of it had paved the way to this point. Currently he was ahead by a large gap in the polls, but he needed to keep this insane schedule to stay out front for another few weeks. Just a few more weeks until the public went to the polls on November fourth and it would all pay off.

He screamed down US -75 heading south toward downtown Dallas and switched lanes whenever possible to try to get an edge. He made his way through the ninety-degree right-hand motion to merge onto westbound I-30, and then on to I-35E South without incident. He was almost in Waxahachie when the tie rod the Raven had sabotaged finally broke under the strain. Livingston could no longer control his car. It snapped hard right on the rain-slicked road, left the elevated freeway and barrel-rolled down the embankment to land wheels up on Solon Road below.

He was pronounced dead at the scene.

As he listened to the police scanner, the Raven smiled. *Nice job,* he congratulated himself. *That worked out perfectly*. This hobby was already way more fun than either one of his day jobs. Absolutely. And when they inventoried the car's contents, they'd find the subtle little souvenir he'd left behind.

He consulted the memo feature on his phone. Time to line up the next on his list.

***

2,121 miles northwest, at her desk in Seattle's police headquarters, Detective Elizabeth Zimmerman finished typing out her case report on the one she'd finally been able to wrap today. A fatal carjacking two months earlier had given her quite the run. But she'd stayed focused, channeled the dogged determination she had inherited from her father, and the hours tenaciously racked up had finally paid off. She not only caught the man she'd been chasing, but she'd managed to hand Vice an extremely handy piece of intel; they had conducted a raid earlier in the evening that resulted in over three million in cocaine taken off the streets of Seattle.

She had just hit ‘save’ then ‘print’ when her cell phone rang. She glanced at the number. “Hi, daddy,” she said.

“Hey kiddo, what’s up?”

“Just finishing up a report.”

“You caught your carjacking suspect. I can tell by your voice. Good work, kiddo.”

“Thanks Dad. What are you up to?”

“Not much, just got off. Gonna go hang with Joe, watch TV.”

“Sounds fun.”

“Yeah. Hey kid, I… I gotta go. Just wanted to check in on you.”

“Thanks, Dad. I love you. Talk soon?”

“Talk soon.” And he hung up.

She smiled sadly.

He just wasn't the same as before. Before, Frank Zimmerman had been one of Fort Worth's best detectives, ever. It wasn't just her opinion as his daughter; he'd had several commendations over his twenty-five years doing detective work. One case, though, had broken him. One case from earlier in his career that haunted him enough to turn in his detective shield and go back to patrol work once new evidence came to light. He just hadn't been the same since last fall, when the real killer in the 1985 case was finally identified through now more sophisticated DNA testing, and Frank realized that the man he'd helped put in prison back then - and who died while incarcerated - was innocent all along.

Now he walked a beat, and spent his off time with Joe Wallace, his former partner in the Detective unit. And, according to her last conversation with Joe a couple of months ago, Dad had become more and more dependent on whiskey to get through his days as a beat cop.

She sighed. She'd have to take some time, travel down to Fort Worth soon and check on him. Maybe over the holidays at some point. Although that was when the crazies seemed to peak around here.

She'd just have to play it by ear.

Her desk phone rang, and with it came a fresh case. She grabbed her badge, jacket, and sidearm, fixed them all in place, and left to go look at the scene and at one very dead convenience store clerk that had made the mistake of fighting back unarmed against a masked robber.

***

New Year's Eve, 2009. Benbrook, Texas.

Jerry Singletary was at home, alone, stoned and drunk out of his mind.

After the papers had announced to the world that he'd been one of the men caught up in an underage solicitation sting five days before Christmas, he hadn't had a moment's peace from the subsequent media frenzy. Being busted had parlayed into his home being raided, and the large quantity of child pornography he possessed had sealed his fate completely. He had been released on a massively expensive bail after some wrangling, and already colleagues had distanced themselves – not a one that he'd called for help was willing to represent him.

That hurt. He'd known some of them for years.

He'd been immediately fired from the law firm as well, and last he'd heard, a lot of the cases he'd worked would now be under review for possible misconduct charges to pile onto him along with everything else.

If that happened, he'd be disbarred right around the time he got sent to prison.

Insult to injury.

He knocked back the rest of the Jameson, cursed and threw the empty bottle, lurched up unsteadily, and shuffled to the counter for a new bottle to continue his downward trend.

Now, sitting alone in his darkened house, no future in sight that he could see, he wallowed in self-pity. He'd have to represent himself in all this. No family – he was an only child, his parents were dead, his wife had bailed back in 1986 – and now, no friends for support either. His addled brain tried to make some sense of what his life had turned into, and just couldn't.

Screw this, he thought hazily. *Hot bath and sleep, and deal with it all in the morning.* He stumbled upstairs to his jacuzzi tub, weaving dangerously, fresh bottle of Jameson in his hand.

He padded over to the counter and, with some difficulty and swearing, finally was able to turn on the radio. Jazz filled the air. He frowned, pressed another button, and grinned sloppily as Drowning Pool screamed at him from the speakers. “Thash better,” he slurred, bobbing his head to the beat.

Jerry ran the water, stripped down, climbed in. He pressed the button to turn the jets on full blast, leaned back and closed his eyes as the water and his music washed over him. He didn’t see the closet door slowly swing open.

The Raven crept silently to the side of the tub, and as Jerry remained blissfully unaware, pressed the rag of chloroform to his face. The resistance was minimal – thanks to a blood alcohol level almost four times the legal limit and massive tokes of some very strong pot not fifteen minutes earlier, Jerry couldn't have fought off a fly.

A tiny shove was all it took to send Jerry Singletary's head under the water permanently. He was so far under the influence from the pot, booze, and sedative that he didn't even struggle as he drowned.

"Happy New Year," the Raven told him as he placed a token of his visit on the bathroom counter. "Oh, and ironic choice of music, bro. But quite appropriate, don't you think?" He crossed to the side of the tub, gazed at the lifeless face under the surface for a moment to make sure it was finished, then chuckled to himself as he left.

As he drove away, the Raven mulled over the night's events. This had been one of those rare times that professional and hobby dovetailed into a single target. Singletary had already been in his sights to deal with at some point, and then the paid contract to end him had been offered. As a result, killing Jerry Singletary had been satiating all the way around.

Doesn't get much better than this, he thought happily as he cranked the radio.

***

New year, new things to accomplish. She'd drilled down into her next target's life for four hours straight and her eyes were beginning to cross. She rubbed them, got up to move around and restore blood flow in her legs, then walked to the kitchen, got herself more water, and returned to her computer desk.

She sighed, stretched again, then resumed her seat and her research. Her eyebrows raised. *Hmm. Made the U.S. Olympic team in 1990, 1994, 1998. Missed making it in 2002 and 2006.* She wondered if he'd be focused currently on making the 2010 squad for Vancouver; if he was, it would be much harder to approach and distract him. Then again, at forty-one, most skiers had already ended their Olympic chase; the average age of the 2006 team was only twenty-seven years old. She decided she'd have to risk it. She'd make sure to cross his path and hope he didn't have training tunnel vision.

This was almost going to be a shame. She did appreciate talent.

She pulled his picture up again. Definite hottie, and only five years her senior. This one she wouldn't mind letting touch her one bit. As she reviewed her plans, she realized it might come to that; it might be the only way to get close enough to do what she had to do. *Hazards of the work,* she told herself, and grinned. *Sometimes you gotta take one for the mission*. She looked at his picture again. *And I am completely okay with that. When they look like this, I'd take several.*

She opened another browser window, pulled up a travel site, made her arrangements. Then she headed off to bed.

***

Frank Zimmerman sat on his couch flipping channels and working his way through another bottle of Wild Turkey at three a.m. after yet another tedious shift at work. *Another year of this,* he thought sourly, referring to his patrol beat. He wanted to hold out until he turned fifty-five to retire, but as miserable as he was, he didn't know if he could stand another year of it.

Dammit, he wasn't meant for this. He'd been born to be a detective, had known all his life that's what he was destined to be. And he'd been good at it. But after what had come to light, he couldn't face the possibility of pursuing and persecuting another innocent. He took a long pull from his bottle and tried desperately to quiet the accusing voices in his head. Every time Frank closed his eyes, he pictured the poor man's face again, drawn and pale, his shoulders slumped in defeat, the way he flinched as if struck when the judge had sentenced him to life in prison and banged the gavel, the way he'd sobbed and pleaded as he'd been led away to his fate.

I helped put him there, Frank chastised himself yet again. *Young hotshot detective out to prove myself, so fucking determined that I was right, I was so sure that it was him… I was so very, very wrong. And he died there.* Tears slid down his cheeks as the memories broke him all over again, and he polished off the bottle in a futile effort to ease the pain. *God, I wish I could take it back.* As he stumbled toward his room, his cell phone buzzed repeatedly, forgotten on the coffee table.

***

Lizzie waited, fingers tapping out a beat, listening to her dad's phone ring and ring on the other end. And sighed. She knew he was on second shift rotation this month, so he should be home. She'd caught another case that just wasn't feeling right to her, and she wanted to pick his brain about it and see if he could help her figure out what she was missing.

She'd only recently made detective, after paying her dues and working her way up the ranks for seven grueling years. When she finally received her detective's badge, she honestly had not been able to tell who was prouder – her or her father. Her mother, on the other hand, had never been supportive of Lizzie's career choice at all. "It's the whole reason we got divorced," her mother reminded her constantly. "I didn't want to have that life, worried sick every time your dad left for work, and I don't want to have to be worried sick when you go to work either."

It had escalated over time into a huge knockdown drag out fight between the two; her mother called her selfish, and Lizzie finally exploded and told her mother exactly what she thought of being ripped from the father she idolized when she was twelve and dragged over two thousand miles away against her will.

They hadn't spoken since that night, which was just fine with Lizzie.

She sighed again as her dad's voice came on, asking her to please leave a message. She did so at the beep, then, reluctantly, she hung up and returned to her latest puzzle.

CHAPTER TWO

February 2010, Vail, Colorado, and a perfect day for snowboarding and skiing. She had made sure to select a bright blue ski suit that was flattering as hell and showed every curve to perfection. And she was delighted to hear that her target was available for private instruction. Although she could already ski well, it would be to her advantage to play dumb in a big way.

Now she giggled and mildly flirted, and Donny Atherton was entranced the moment he saw his shapely student with honey blond hair and emerald eyes. Over the course of their first day together, she managed to get him to reveal that he was not in fact training for the next Olympics. Matter of fact, occasionally taking students was about the extent of his ski time these days. *Fabulous*, she thought. *Means I can have you to myself.*

She paid very careful attention to her footing in this back-and-forth dance of flirty and chaste, and hoped he would follow each step unaware of the plans she had for him. As he showed her the proper way to fasten skis, she fawned over him. As he gripped her hips and rocked her gently through the motions of properly shifting her weight to lean through turns, she made herself blush as she smiled at him. By the end of the day, she'd solemnly announced that she would feel much more secure in her abilities if she had a few more days of lessons with him before trying out any of the ski runs. And he agreed. He asked her out to dinner the first night; she turned him down, by design.

***

County Wicklow, Ireland, and the Raven had been retained once again for some payback. He trained his binoculars downslope from his perch farther up the hillside overlooking the Glendalough monastic settlement. From here, he could pass for watching for birds or other wildlife as he was bringing his target into view. Slowly, he scanned right, then left. "A-ha. There you are," the Raven murmured as he confirmed the man was indeed being a tourist today as he'd been told. He nodded his approval, then began to head down toward the settlement.

There were people around, but not so many as he'd imagined. Peak tourist season for this park seemed to be from April to October. Mid-February was much less crowded, but there were still enough visitors milling about that he should be able to make delivery and then fade away surreptitiously.

He grinned as he made his way down the slope to his target.

He joined the back of the tour group at first, his eyes never leaving the man he sought who stood about twenty feet in front of the Raven. As the man gazed around, taking in the old tower and the headstones, it was clear he was oblivious to just how close to death he was.

The Raven moved closer as his prey took off his jacket; for mid-February, the temperature was a bit over sixty degrees, unseasonably warm. *Good,* the Raven thought to himself. *Less fabric to penetrate.*

As he passed the man on the walking path, he pretended to stumble, slapping his left hand onto his victim's right shoulder for balance – and deploying the tiny plunger he had palmed containing the ricin-laced metal sphere into the flesh of his victim. "My apologies," the Raven said, removing his hand and slipping the now-empty device into his pocket.

"Are you all right?" the man asked, unaware he now had only about seventy-two hours to live.

"Fine, thanks," Raven answered. "Just lost my footing for a moment there." And he continued past on his way down the walking path. Now all he had to do was tail the man for a day or two and make sure the ricin worked as advertised.

***

Day two saw Donny and his pupil on the bunny slopes, her still hiding her true skill set and winding him more and more around her finger. Small talk, noncommittal, most of it fictitious, met his questions about her life. But he seemed to be satisfied with the answers, and she could tell he wanted to get to know her more. Another dinner invitation was proffered at day's end, and, as before, was politely refused.

***

Within twenty-four hours, he had his confirmation. The priest, who had fled the U.S. before he could be arrested on multiple counts of child molestation, had been hurriedly packed into an ambulance outside the hotel they both were registered guests in. The Raven watched silently from his balcony as the man on the gurney was loaded up and carried away, sirens breaking the still morning air. He followed the ambulance's movement until it was out of sight, then sent a carefully worded email to his employer.

A certain priest wouldn't be preying upon the innocent anymore.

***

On day three, Donny asked again, and she said yes. He beamed at her. “Great,” he exclaimed, as their session for the day was winding down. “Pick you up at six?”

“Sounds great,” she replied, and gazed at him with those sparkling green eyes.

He escorted her back to the lodge, and they parted ways to prepare for their date.

She showered, toweled herself dry, and thought about him while she pondered what to wear. “Dammit, I like him,” she sighed. That part sucked. She didn’t often meet interesting men. But he’d been involved, so he had to go. No exceptions. End of story. *Pull it together and get this done*.

Meanwhile, Donny had also showered, and was pulling on form fitting jeans and boots. “She is amazing,” he murmured to himself as he chose and put on a sweater that brought out the gold flecks in his hazel eyes, then turned to the mirror to make sure his hair was perfect. He'd felt the electricity surge between them on day one, when he'd placed his hands on her sides to try to help her feel what she needed to do when traveling down a slope to be able to turn. Since then, the days with her had flown by much too fast. But she'd finally agreed to spend time together as man and woman rather than instructor and student.

He grinned as he brushed his perfect white teeth. He wanted her, badly. And he had no idea what was driving it. All he knew was that he just had to see her, even if only once, out of that blue suit and in his bed. But hopefully more than once. He felt a real connection forming, and he didn't want it to be just another one-night stand. He'd done enough of those, especially with Olympics groupies back in the day.

His conscience mocked him. *After everything you did, you don't deserve a normal life, or a real relationship.*

"No! That is ancient history. I've changed. I'm not that guy anymore!" he told himself out loud as he stared into his own soul in the mirror for a long moment.

Donny broke out of his reverie and glanced at his watch. "Gotta get moving, I'm gonna be late," he chided himself. The fifteen-minute drive back to the lodge left him with exactly three minutes to spare. Promptly at six p.m. she came down the staircase of the lodge. He offered his arm, escorted her to his car, then opened the door for her. She entered with a surprised expression.

"What?" he asked. "Everything all right?"

"Fine," she told him. "Just trying to remember how long it's been since a date opened any doors for me."

He shut her door, walked around the car, and got in. "Well, darlin, that's a damn shame," he smiled and kissed her hand before starting the car. "Do you like steaks?"

She gave him one of her rarely used genuine smiles, and replied, "Love steaks."

"Then I know just the place." He winked at her as he started to drive.

Twenty minutes later saw them seated at a cozy candlelit table for two, next to a window where they could watch the snow falling softly in huge swirling flakes. He noticed her gazing at them. "They make for great skiing. Not too wet, not too dry, and if you fall, it doesn't hurt quite as much. Unless you're hauling ass down the mountain," he grinned. "Then any fall hurts."

She grinned back, sipped her wine. *Dammit, Donny. Why do you have to be so handsome, so charming, so nice?* She sighed very quietly to herself. *That makes this a lot harder. Be conceited or something. Please.*

The cooked to perfection steaks arrived in short order, and she purposely kept the conversation light as they ate. “Hmm, this is fabulous,” she nodded in approval as she savored the first bite. “Yeah,” he answered. “Best steakhouse in all of Colorado, if you ask me. But even better than usual, because of the company.” And he picked up his glass and raised it to her. She blushed, picked her glass up as well, and they toasted.

By the end of the meal, she knew she was in trouble. She really, really liked Donny. And that had been completely unexpected, the total opposite of the Judge.

He'd been a self-absorbed ass since day one; as a result, she'd had zero difficulty following through with ridding the world of him. But Donny was different. Her resolve was beginning to waver in a huge way.

He dropped her back off at the lodge after dinner, and she had fought the urge to invite him up. Instead, she gave him a small kiss, nodded and smiled when he ended their evening with, "I had a great time. See you tomorrow for another lesson?"

Now she paced back and forth in her room. Emotions. She'd not taken those into account in all this. *Dammit.*

She'd call her best friend. Her best friend always had stellar advice, especially when it came to men. She dug her cell out of her purse, dialed, and waited.

"Hey, it's me," she said. "I need your advice." And she told her best friend about

Donny, how cute he was, how nice, that she was starting to fall for him.

"So, what's the problem?" came the reply. "He's single, you're single, have fun with it."

"You really think I should?"

"Look, it's not that big a deal. If you can't decide right now how far you wanna put yourself out there, then don't. Keep it light. You can circle back to it later. It's not like you don't have other things to focus on, you know."

"You're right, that's true."

A laugh. "Of course, I'm right. Go with your gut here, is what I'm saying. No need to make a life-altering decision right this second."

"Thanks. I'll keep you posted. Love ya."

"Love you too, girly."

Yeah, she thought to herself as she hung up, undressed for bed, brushed out her hair. *Don't have to make this decision right this minute. Really not any set timeframe driving all this, to be honest. It's all as fast or as slow as I choose. So, I can postpone for now, see where this goes with him.*

She pulled out her little notebook, considered. "Well, well, Mr. Norton," she murmured with a smile as she erased numbers beside the two names to change the order. "Looks like you'll get to go next instead."

She climbed into bed, turned off the lamp. Her phone buzzed. She picked it up from her nightside table and checked her text messages.

Sweet dreams, beautiful. See you in the morning. – Donny.

She smiled as she faded into sleep.

***

Day four in Vail, and her mood had changed. She'd decided to allow herself to explore these feelings, had shelved her original plans for him until further notice. It was the first day to get off the practice area and hit the slopes together. They chatted companionably as they rode the chairlift up the mountain to the beginning of the ski runs. Given that she'd severely understated her skiing ability, she had to pretend the green route scared her a bit. Donny was encouraging and gentle, never leaving her side, and when they reached the bottom, he gave her a megawatt smile and a big hug.

"You did great!" he exclaimed. "Wanna go again?"

"Sure," she responded, caught up in his enthusiasm. They rode the chairs again, re-ran the green route at a pace that allowed for conversation. She honestly could not recall the last time she'd had so much fun with anyone. When he mentioned dinner plans, she readily accepted.

"Where would you like to go tonight?" he asked her. "Italian?"

"What about your place?" she countered. "If that's okay."

He took her hands in his. "That is definitely okay with me."

As before, he dropped her off at the lodge, with plans to return at six p.m. to retrieve her for their night out together. She headed to her room to make sure her appearance would leave him breathless.

***

Landon secured his overnight bag in the storage compartment then settled into his window seat in row four for the long flight to Turkey. He was very excited to finally be making this trip; he hoped to expand his set of contacts in the region that would give him a huge advantage in importing Oriental and Persian rugs into the United States. Even as a child he'd been fascinated with other cultures. No surprise then that the import/export business was what he'd chosen to pursue, since it allowed him to experience little slices of other lives apart from his own.

He took the few minutes of time available before cell phones needed to be turned off to peruse his email. Nothing new had arrived that he needed to deal with. Good. That meant he could relax and enjoy his travels. Not to say a plethora of messages wouldn't be waiting for him once they landed. But for now, at least, he could wind down and get some sleep.

Veronica popped into his mind. He smiled ruefully. She was beautiful, no question. There just wasn't any spark, unfortunately – not from his side, at least. He sighed. He supposed he could have continued seeing her, but he'd felt dishonest at the mere thought of it. So, he had disentangled himself as gently as possible the previous evening. No point in proceeding down a path that didn't lead to someone he'd want to spend a lifetime with.

Someday I'll meet her, he thought to himself as the plane pulled away from the gate. *Someday*.

***

Donny was once again punctual as he arrived to pick her up for their second date. And as before, he escorted her to his car, opened her door, saw her safely inside prior to getting in himself. As he eased away from the curb, he glanced over at her. “You look stunning,” he told her, and meant it.

She favored him with a bright smile. She’d taken extra time, made sure she looked her absolute best, and was pleased he’d noticed.

“I was serious about Italian, by the way,” he added. “There’s a great place on the way to my house, we can get it to go, if you like.”

“That sounds nice,” she said, and squeezed his hand.

Not far at all down the road, and he turned in to a parking lot. The little mom-and-pop establishment was cozy and welcoming. They placed their orders and settled into a booth to wait.

“So, when did you say you have to head home again?” he asked her.

“Saturday afternoon, at the latest,” she answered. “Why?”

"That means we only have one more full day together."

"Yeah, it does."

"Well, then," he quipped, "we need to make it count. Did you want to be on the slopes tomorrow, or do something else? We could spend the day in town, I could show you around if you like."

"Hmm," she said. "Can I think on that one for a bit?"

"Sure," he agreed. He stood as the owner brought out their food, packaged and ready to go.

"Shall we?" Donny asked. "My place isn't far from here at all."

"Yes," she answered, then as they got into the car, "That smells amazing, I can't wait to taste it."

He pulled into his driveway and parked, went around and opened her door for her before retrieving the food. He unlocked and pushed open the front door to his house, gesturing to her. “After you.”

She stepped inside and looked around as he closed the door behind them, set the food on the kitchen counter, started a fire in the fireplace, then made his way back to the kitchen. “Just let me grab some plates and stuff,” he called out.

“I’ll help,” she offered and followed him. Together they set the little table.

“I’m afraid I don’t have much in the way of drink choices. Iced tea, water, couple of sodas.”

“Iced tea is fine,” she smiled at him as he poured two glasses, brought them to the table, then pulled out her chair for her. “Thanks.”

He passed her the garlic bread first, then took a couple of slices for himself. Their hands met at the chicken marsala container. “You first,” he offered. She scooped some out onto her plate, then reached and traded plates with him. “Thanks,” he grinned.

After loading both plates, they dug in. “Wow, this is really good,” she exclaimed.

“Told you,” he pointed with his fork. “I’ve lived here a while, and I think they’re the best by far.”

“I would have to agree.”

“So, what do you do when you’re not in Vail, Colorado learning to ski?”

“I’m a nurse.”

“Cool!”

“It pays the bills,” she grinned. “How about you? What do you do?”

“Well,” he began, “I’m on the slopes during the season as an instructor. Off season I’m in sales.”

“Do tell.”

"It's boring, but it pays the bills. Insurance. Something everybody needs."

"Huh," she quipped. "I would have thought you'd have picked something, well, ski related. Being a former Olympian, and all."

He cleared his throat as a shadow crossed his face. "Um, well. Let's just say those avenues didn't really work out and leave it at that."

"I didn't mean to pry."

"Sorry, it's not you," he told her sincerely. "It's just, that whole section of my life, I'd rather forget."

His simple, honest statement resonated with her; she completely understood that feeling. "I hear you."

"Oh, the mystery woman has a past she'd also like to forget?" he teased.

She smiled wistfully. “You could say that.”

“Let’s do this,” he said, and reached for her hand. “Let’s not ruin tonight with bad memories. Be with me here, in the moment, and maybe we can make some good ones. Can we try that? I’d really like to.”

“I’d like that too, Donny,” she answered sincerely.

They finished their meal and cleared the table. “Now what would you like to do? Watch TV? Maybe soak in the hot tub? The back porch has an awesome view.”

She reached over for the little bag she’d brought. “I was hoping you had one,” she revealed as she pulled a tiny blue string bikini out of hiding. “I’ve been wanting to use the one at the lodge, but it’s been noisy and crowded every time I go by it.”

"Well, we have this one all to ourselves," he answered. "Follow me, I'll show you the place, and we can get changed."

He took her on a little tour of the place. She admired the no frills and clean lines of his home. Tastefully decorated in blues and tans, nothing flashy, nothing overdone. As they went upstairs, he pointed over to the right. "Guest bathroom is right through there. I'll change in my room, meet you back here on the landing."

They parted ways and she quickly changed into her bikini. Grabbing a ponytail holder and her brush, she swept her hair up into a loose bun before checking herself in the mirror. They stepped back out into the hall at the same time.

Donny was dumbstruck, mouth hanging open, as he gazed at her. "Wow," was all he could manage for a moment. "You look…wow….um, let me grab us some towels." And he stepped around her into the bathroom, reappearing quickly and handing her a thick oversized beach towel. "Here. Amazing, that's the word you made me forget completely just now. You look amazing," and he blushed a little.

"You too," she responded, her eyes meeting his and holding the gaze. She'd noticed the muscular arms and rock-hard torso, and she approved; as a matter of fact, it was all she could do not to run her hands across his chest and washboard abs.

He led the way back down the stairs and they crossed the living room to the back door. "If you want to hang here a minute where it's warm, let me get out there and get the spa cover off, then we'll be set," he said.

"Okay," she replied, winking at him. It only took a couple of minutes and he poked his head back in. “Ready when you are,” he invited. He held his hand out to her. She took it and stepped out onto a back porch that indeed had a stellar view. All three directions she looked – left, right, and straight out – she could see mountain peaks.

“Wow, you weren’t kidding about the view. Donny, this is gorgeous,” she exclaimed as she hung her towel on one of the wall hooks and then eased into the hot tub.

As he climbed in across from her and pressed the jets on full, he answered, “Yeah, it’s the second-best view tonight though.” She turned her head toward him, smiling bashfully when she saw the want kindled in his eyes. “Penny for your thoughts,” she asked him.

"Probably shouldn't share them," he told her. "I really am trying to behave myself, but you in that suit makes them not exactly pure ones."

"Who said they had to be pure ones?" she purred at him, and slowly inched toward him, never breaking eye contact. As she leaned toward him, placing her hands on his firm thighs, she heard the sharp intake of breath as his muscles tensed with her touch. "And who said you have to behave?"

She raised an eyebrow, waited, sensed the moment he too came to that realization, and her smile was slow and wide as he looked into her eyes for confirmation.

"You sure?" he asked her.

"You think I wear this bikini for just anyone?" she answered.

His arms were around her and his lips on hers in an instant.

CHAPTER THREE

"God, I hate this thing," Samuel grumbled.

"Now, now, Mr. Norton, you need to wear this. I know it's not very comfortable at first, but you need to wear this, every night. You'll get used to it and then you'll start sleeping much better," the home health care nurse told him patiently.

To say that seventy-six-year old Samuel Norton was cantankerous was an extreme understatement. The retired heavy machinery operator had always been a handful for those around him. Now, with sleep apnea and advanced emphysema from a lifetime of smoking, his world consisted of being tethered to an oxygen bottle during the day, and beginning today, a CPAP humidifier combination at night.

He barely tolerated the oxygen canister as it was. This new addition had him mad as hell.

"One day. ONE. With no freakin' tubes of any sort. Is that too much to ask?" he thundered at her before another coughing fit took over.

She stood, hands on hips, watching him hack. Once he finally got through it, she said flippantly, "There's your answer right there, isn't it?"

He would have never admitted it in a thousand years, but he appreciated this new nurse's no bullshit approach to it all.

"Oh, all right," he glowered, sulking. "Show me how this freakin' thing works then."

She placed the CPAP mask on his face, showed him how to tighten it, how to set it. "And here," she pointed, "is the humidifier part of the machine. This is where the water gets poured in; I've already filled it for you. These masks are better, they won't dry out your sinuses as much as traditional CPAP machines sometimes can. Okay? And I will be back in the morning."

"Oh, and one more thing," she intoned as she grabbed her bag and coat. "NO smoking. None. Zip. Don't think we're not aware you sneak one every chance you get."

He grinned at her despite himself. "You know what? You're feisty as hell. I like that. Reminds me of me. See you tomorrow."

She grinned back, and headed out the door toward a brisk March evening. *Stubborn old coot. I just know as soon as he hears me drive away, he will shuffle his way to his back porch and have at LEAST one cigarette,* she thought to herself.

And smiled. She was counting on it.

***

The Raven woke to the sound of his phone chiming. Rubbing his eyes, he moved his arm sideways to his nightstand, scooped up his phone, and pulled up the email notification. “Interesting,” he murmured. He yawned, stretching luxuriously before throwing aside the covers and swinging his bare feet to the floor.

The next stop after the bathroom was the coffeepot to pump artificial life into his still half-asleep system. Once his morning jolt was securely ensconced in his favorite coffee mug, he padded across thick gray carpeting to his workstation and fired up the laptop, running a hand over his face to hasten the cobwebs clearing.

He logged into the fishing enthusiast’s website – only one of many that served as a means by which potential clients could hire him – and found a more detailed message waiting for him there. “Coregonus bavaricus,” he muttered as he read the species name mentioned, then cross-checked his notebook. “Indigenous to Germany.”

He grinned. The Raven hadn’t been to Germany for a while. Time to tour there again, it sounded like. He finished deciphering the rest of the message, then carefully typed his reply conditionally accepting the contract and lining out pricing–coded, of course. One could never be too careful.

Next steps were to wait for confirmation, then sometimes a back and forth about price. Usually a client was so eager to retain his services that haggling didn’t even occur to them. For the first timers, however, there was sometimes a naïve belief that top-notch talent would agree to bargain-basement prices. Those he quickly relieved of their innocence.

Bing! "Wow, that was fast," he exclaimed. He sometimes waited three days to hear back once he'd set parameters under which he'd work. "They must really want this done quickly." He pulled up the reply. His hunch had been accurate. Two weeks' time, and not only no haggle, but a healthy bonus payout if completed within the first week. He frowned. That was most definitely not normal. It was either a very high profile and/or very well guarded target, or a trap, he wasn't sure which. Curiosity got the better of him. He typed a couple of questions, hit send, waited.

And nodded in understanding as he saw the answer. One of the world's biggest suspected sex traffickers, who had gone into hiding after police narrowly missed capturing him in Amsterdam. He responded with his standard coded instructions regarding payment – seventy percent down, the rest on completion – and his usual rhetoric regarding wire instructions. Then the Raven opened a second browser window, checked times, and began booking flights to Berlin.

***

She sighed as she pulled her scrubs off and made her way to the shower to wash off a long and tedious day. Eight patient visits in all, and that was just today. She turned the knob to get the water going and moved over to her vanity to take her ponytail down and brush her hair out while she waited for the water to get hot. A few minutes later, she could see the steam rising from the shower stall. *Perfect timing*, she thought, and stepped in.

As she leaned her head back to wet her hair, she found herself thinking about Donny yet again. Her week with him had been epic and had most definitely not ended up the way she'd thought it would. What began as a name on a list to be crossed off had turned into something else. As she massaged shampoo into her hair, her memory drifted back to the first night they'd been intimate. Her lips curled in a smile at the recollection.

Yeah, she grinned to herself now as she lathered her body. *The hottest ever, hands down*. And it had only gotten better from there. Leaving Vail that Saturday as scheduled had been so, so difficult to do; she really wanted to stay and play with him, but the notebook of names just could not be ignored.

She shivered now as she realized the hot water was just about used up. Rinsing off quickly, she barely closed the gap before pure cold could stream down on her. She bundled up her hair in one towel and wrapped her body in another. And noticed she'd missed a text while she'd been daydreaming.

Hello, gorgeous. I miss you. – Donny.

She giggled as she texted him back.

***

Samuel Norton did precisely what she predicted he would, only he waited about ten minutes before making his way to his back yard, just in case she doubled back. When he figured the coast was clear, he shuffled outside and retrieved the pack and the lighter he'd stashed. He sat down and lit up, pausing only to take off the slender oxygen tube off his face.

He closed his eyes and puffed in contentment even though it was a chilly night. *But hell, still in the high forties*, he told himself comfortingly. *Bet my brother is up to his ass in snow right now back home in Chicago.* The thought made him laugh, and the laugh brought on another coughing fit. "Christ, I'm tired of this," he wheezed once the worst had passed again. He didn't miss Illinois winters, that was for damn sure.

He'd been in Texas so long he considered himself a native. *God, when had he followed the job down here? Thirty years ago? Forty?* He couldn't quite recall. But he'd made damn good money running heavy equipment for road construction, and Texas weather wasn't as extreme. More chance for overtime year-round, for the most part. He figured he'd personally helped pave close to a million miles altogether in the fifty-year career he'd had, and probably had seen most every square inch of the state in the process.

Now he was pretty much homebound, on disability, lugging this freakin' thing – he thumped the oxygen canister in frustration – every damn place. *Complete pain in the ass.* But he couldn't deny it, he'd brought this shit on himself. A walking cautionary tale, that's what he had become. He didn't like it, not one damn bit, but it was true. *Ah, well, can't change it now*, he figured. *Damage is done, so might as well smoke 'em since I got 'em.*

Now that damn CPAP machine. That was a whole different deal. He wanted nothing to do with that damn thing, even if the new nurse – *cute as hell, if I were forty years younger, she'd be in deep trouble!* he chuckled to himself – did say it would help him sleep better. But he had to admit, he was tired all the time. Hadn't had a decent night's sleep in years. He frowned as he stubbed out the first cigarette. Maybe he could try it out a couple times, just to see how it went. He didn't like stuff over his face, never had. That was part of his hang-up with that contraption. *Might be why I never cared much for swimming either, come to think of it. Hell, who knows.*

Samuel shivered. "Best be getting back inside," he told himself. These days he got cold more easily. He lurched to his feet, put his oxygen tube back on, placed his nicotine supply back into its hidey-hole before going back into the house, dragging his permanent companion behind him on its little wheels. As usual, the wheels hung up on the doorframe, and as usual, he cussed and heaved it over the threshold.

He made his way to the couch to watch TV for a bit. After ten minutes of that he was thoroughly disgusted. “Nothing good on,” he grumbled, and turned the TV off again. He sighed. “Well, let’s go try that damn machine,” he said to himself, and went to his room down the narrow hallway. He sat on the edge of his bed, eyeballing the machine, remembering what she’d shown and told him. Uncertainly, he picked up the mask, placed it over his mouth and nose, adjusted the fit like she’d said, then turned the knob, and climbed into bed.

I’ll be damned, he thought. *Already feels a little bit easier to breathe. Maybe she was right.* He closed his eyes, relaxed, and fell into the best night’s sleep he’d had in years. When he woke the next morning, he felt great – well, except for the emphysema. *Huh. I wouldn’t have believed it*. For the first time in a long time, he'd slept all through the night. Normally he'd manage an hour, maybe two, and then his airway would close off and he'd wake up. As a result, he was never truly rested. Until last night. He almost felt bad about raising so much hell about the new machine to start with. Almost.

When the new one knocked and then came in, he smiled at her. "Morning."

"Why hello, Mr. Norton. Did you use it?"

"I did, and I slept pretty good."

"Great!"

She went through the usual routine, made him breakfast, took his vitals, gave him his meds. As he watched TV in the living room, she changed his bedding out for him. She heard him start to snore on the couch. *That's my cue*, she confirmed to herself. Pulling a vial from her pocket, she poured the much more potent liquid nicotine into the water well of his CPAP machine, then went to retrieve him for his midday nap.

“Come on, Mr. Norton, you’ll be more comfortable in bed,” she prodded. He nodded sleepily and retreated to his room. She got him tucked in, placed the mask on him, turned the knob. “I’ll get you up in a couple of hours for lunch, okay?”

He gave her a thumbs-up sign, drifting into sleep. She carried on her usual routine of light cleaning, washing the bed linens. Two hours later she crept back into his room to verify that her idea had indeed worked. And it had. Mr. Norton would sleep forevermore. The intense amount of nicotine being absorbed into his system with each breath had proved fatal very quickly.

To be certain, she checked his vitals. No pulse. No breathing. Pupils fixed and dilated.

She turned off the machine long enough to switch out the water tank with one that didn't contain the special additive, only water, as it should. She also switched out the hose and mask apparatus with untainted ones, so that no trace of tampering would remain. Then she turned the CPAP machine back on. To the next nurse coming by in about two hours, it would look like he simply had passed in his sleep. She placed a little bow-tied cellophane wrapper on the nightstand next to the now sanitized murder weapon as her final touch.

She flushed the nicotine-rich water, put the empty tank and the tainted hose and mask rigging in her bag, and left the house. Before driving away, she got out her trusty notebook and crossed Samuel Norton off her to-do list.

***

Both of Raven's flights occurred without incident and he had landed as scheduled at eight p.m. his time at Schönefeld. He'd had to travel first from DFW to New York and spend the night since he'd already missed the daily nonstop to Berlin. The following morning he'd boarded the Lufthansa flight for the roughly thirteen-hour journey.

He gathered his belongings from the overhead bin, strode through the terminal to baggage claim. Upon retrieving his luggage, he stood patiently in line to get through customs. As often as he traveled, he'd learned the value of patience and courtesy in these situations. The search through his possessions was thorough but as expected turned up nothing that would cause him trouble; the weapon he'd chosen for this one looked like a normal bottle of aspirin. The customs agent stamped his passport and waved him through. The Raven nodded his thanks and made his way outside to the train platform. Consulting his watch, he realized it had all timed out well. The next train was due in roughly ten minutes.

He pulled out his cell phone, confirmed his late check-in reservation was still held at the Schoenhouse Apartments in the Mitte District for the whole week. Satisfied, he made note of the train route which would get him closest. *Ah, there it is*, he confirmed. *The Rosa-Luxemberg-Platz underground station is within 500 feet of where I'm staying. That's perfect*.

The cell phone returned to his jacket's breast pocket as the train he sought rolled to a stop in front of him, crouched like a tiger ready to pounce. About forty minutes later, he was walking up the steps to street level at his destination. He made his way across

Schonhauser Allee to his home for the next seven days and checked in with a petite brunette who was very welcoming. She handed him his key and a guide to local attractions and wished him a pleasant evening.

Once he got settled into his room, the Raven decided a meal needed to come before work. He perused the guide the desk attendant had so thoughtfully provided and decided that Fleischerei Berlin was an excellent choice for dinner. He made his way to the cozy establishment, was graciously greeted and seated promptly. He opted for the porterhouse steak with herb butter sauce, selecting cucumber salad and truffle mashed potatoes as the accompaniments. That settled, he delved into the warm bread brought out to him as he waited.

Spreading pale butter liberally over the first slice, he chewed thoughtfully as he mentally reviewed the rough game plan that he'd formed on the flight over. He still needed to fine tune some things, but he felt confident in his abilities to complete the task at hand and be home before the week was out. Getting the bonus mentioned shouldn't be an issue at all. His order arrived, elegantly presented and cooked to perfection. The mission at hand took a back seat to enjoying an exquisite meal after a long day. He'd resume when he returned to his laptop in room 403.

***

She frowned as she made her notes, stopping to take a sip of the amaretto sour she'd made herself after dinner.

If it walks like a bitch and talks like a bitch, well…

This one might present a challenge. She'd come up with an ingenious idea for this name on her to-do list, and the death would be both very public and very accidental looking – if she could pull it off. Gaining access was the key that had her frowning about it all. She flipped back to the beginning, reading through again what she'd learned about one Monica Stewart so far. *Old money, high society, quite the little social butterfly, aren't you, Monica? And you just LIVE to be seen.*

She had to admit. If she could figure a way to get this one done like she wanted, it would be a huge feather in her cap. She'd known Monica Stewart types all her life. It would be so, so gratifying to not just get rid of this one, but to humiliate her target while doing so.

She smiled a predator's smile before she finished her drink.

***

Well satisfied with his meal, the Raven paid his bill, tipped generously, and stepped back out on the sidewalk. He strolled leisurely back to his quarters. In his room, he unpacked, then headed for the shower. He'd slept for roughly half the nonstop flight, and he found that as usual, crossing multiple time zones didn't affect him as deeply as it might other transcontinental travelers. He was wide awake.

Once done with his shower, he pulled on sweats and a t-shirt, then padded across to the little desk and started up his laptop. He brought up the notes he'd made so far. "Now," he said aloud, "let's tweak this a bit." His intel indicated his quarry was holed up about ten miles from here. The Raven pulled up his mail, found the mysteriously worded file his client had sent him through the fishing site. Using the cipher, he translated it, and began to read, scanning primarily for points of vulnerability that would allow for him to strike successfully and get away cleanly.

"There's not many," he muttered as he rose and paced, running his hands through his hair in frustration. *Think. There's got to be a way to get this done*. He mulled over prior missions, looking for inspiration. *Budapest? Nope, that wouldn't work. That wasn't in the middle of the city, like this would be. Tel Aviv? Possibly. That might just work out well, assuming all other factors were static.* He closed his eyes and replayed in his head how that one had gone.

"Yeah. Tel Aviv. Good blueprint for this one," he decided. "Just have to tailor it to this one now."

He typed it all out, plotting the method of delivery, time to contact, possible escape routes. His hope was that in the ensuing confusion he'd be able to simply melt into any crowd that might gather, but he knew from being in this business for so long to take nothing for granted and always have at least one alternate plan. Then he stood up, deliberately walking away from his computer to mix himself a drink from the minibar in the room. He found that if he lined it all out, took a break from it, then looked at it with a fresh perspective, any holes in his planning were more readily apparent and could be dealt with to minimize risk.

Moving to the loveseat and turning on the television, he flipped channels until he found a program that caught his interest. Setting the closed captions feature for English – he knew a handful of German phrases but was by no means fluent- he leaned back and cleared his mind for a while.

CHAPTER FOUR

Mr. Black was his current alias – just one of many. His real name was of no consequence. The man himself was indeed the leading sex trafficker in Europe, as the authorities suspected. And each time police had tried to ensnare him, he'd dodged them, flipping them the bird and laughing the entire way. But in Amsterdam they'd gotten too fucking close, missing him by mere minutes, thanks to that lackey with a loose tongue. Not that the informant was a threat anymore. His loose tongue had been separated from the rest of him as those loyal to Mr. Black had closed ranks and removed the traitor from the equation.

Mr. Black smiled an evil smile when he'd been told the leak had been well plugged.

Now he was tucked away in Berlin, had been for about two weeks. He'd opted against his bodyguard traveling with him this time, a decision that routinely infuriated those paid to protect him and who dared not question his whims, illogical though they might be. He had arrived and settled in comfortably to a hotel that was to his liking, with a five-star restaurant downstairs and everything he needed to stay indefinitely. And he'd fallen into a routine of having breakfast and lunch brought up to his suite, then traveling down to the restaurant nightly for dinner at precisely seven-fifteen p.m. and sitting at precisely the same table.

Another of his idiosyncrasies was that his food could not touch on his plate – at all. If he ordered steak and two sides, each side had to be on its own separate plate. The waitstaff and kitchen personnel had learned this the hard way after his first night as their dinner guest. His entire meal had been sent back, with a sternly worded request that his meal be completely remade, and his wishes followed regarding separate plating. Although Mr. Black did switch up his order nightly, the seating location and the plating request never wavered. And he routinely salted his food multiple times as he ate.

Now, at seven-seventeen p.m. he was being seated as usual at his table, back to the wall so he couldn't be approached unawares. Tonight, he opted for the grilled salmon, potatoes au gratin and asparagus, then leaned back and sipped his wine, watching the room. His waiter, Thomas, brought him his bread and salad as the chef prepared his meal. Twenty minutes later Thomas appeared bearing three plates on a tray, placed them elegantly before Mr. Black, and removed the empty salad and bread plates. "Anything else, sir?"

“No, Thomas, thank you,” he replied, and reached for the saltshaker that had been topped off prior to his arrival. Per his custom, he liberally salted each dish, set the shaker down, and picked up his fork. He was so intent on his dinner he didn’t notice the Raven watching him from across the room. The Raven had just been brought his tab, and he opened the little folder and glanced at it, tucked enough cash inside to cover the bill plus leave a healthy tip, and set it back on his table. He stood and made his way toward the door, pausing at the threshold for a complimentary mint.

Behind him, chaos erupted as Mr. Black began to choke, clawing at his throat and falling out of his chair. The Raven moved swiftly toward the disturbance, acting like any other concerned bystander, and, in the commotion, was able to successfully use his sleight of hand skills to trade out the strychnine laced saltshaker for a harmless one at the now extremely dead Mr. Black's usual table.

The Raven was detained and questioned along with others at the scene at the time of the tragedy, and having determined that he was just an onlooker, the police pronounced him free to go after they took his statement about what he had witnessed. He nonchalantly left the restaurant, discreetly dropping the murder weapon in a trash bin along his route, and casually walked back to his room, where he sent his client a carefully constructed message confirming that the kingpin of sex slavery in Europe had been dealt with. Satisfied with the day's work, he slept peacefully. When he woke, he was pleasantly surprised that not only had the balance owed him been transferred to his account, but the client had thanked him by doubling the bonus previously mentioned for a quick timeframe.

“You are most welcome,” he murmured, smiling at the screen, before he shut down the laptop and began packing up to head home. He checked out at the front desk, walked the short distance to the station, returned to Schönefeld, and arrived at the terminal gate just as first-class passengers began boarding for the nonstop flight to Los Angeles. He stored his laptop and carry-on above him and settled into his window seat. Within twenty minutes he was airborne.

***

Donny was only half paying attention to the sports program on his television when his doorbell rang. He didn’t hear it on the first ring. But his ears perked up the second time. He paused the live TV and got off the couch.

"Coming," Donny called out as he walked to his front door, confused since he wasn't expecting anyone. When he opened the door, he did a double take, then grinned from ear to ear.

"Hi," she said, and flew into his arms. "I really missed you."

He held her tight against him, burying his face in her hair. "God, I missed you too. What are you doing here?" he asked her as she pulled her head back to look up at him.

"I have to travel to Los Angeles for a conference," she said. "But I couldn't resist leaving a few days early and coming to see you on the way there. I hope you don't mind."

He kissed her and told her, "Funny, I've been racking my brain trying to figure out a plausible excuse to show up on your doorstep down there for the last month."

"Great minds," she murmured against his mouth before kissing him again. She started to reach down for her suitcase, but he said, "Let me get that," and then made her shriek with surprise and delight as he scooped her up too, bridal style, and carried her inside. She linked her arms around his neck and sighed contentedly, laying her head on his chest.

Donny pushed his front door shut with his elbow, dropped her suitcase on his living room floor, and carried her all the way to bed so he could demonstrate how much he'd missed her.

***

Monica Stewart lay face-down on a massage table in the most elite spa in the western United States. It was extremely pricey. She was extremely worth it and took it as her due. She was pushing fifty-five but thanks to a stable of excellent plastic surgeons she kept on speed dial, she didn't look a day over thirty-five. She'd come from very, very old Southern money, and Monica Stewart never let those around her forget it. Her lineage on her father's side had been instrumental in joining West and East via train track back in the 1860's. Others in her ancestry had hit big in oil in Texas in the 1890's, and her destiny as a spoiled princess had been all but assured.

"Ouch! Watch what you're doing, incompetent fool," she sniped at the massage tech who was tending to her. "Those are my *shoulders*; it's supposed to be a massage, not a *mauling*."

"Yes, Miss Stewart, my apologies," the young girl replied, on the verge of tears. She hated working on the ‘ice queen’, as Monica had been dubbed by every single worker onsite. Monica’s mistreatment of anyone she viewed as beneath her was the stuff of legend. The tech finished up her work and slipped out to go cry in the employee breakroom.

“Thank God that’s over,” Monica huffed. “She’s an idiot.” And made a mental note to try her dead level best to have that idiot fired. Then, just as quickly, she dismissed the girl, returning her thoughts to focus on her favorite subject – herself. She sat up, wrapped a towel around her body, consulted the printout of today’s treatments she had booked as she sipped her third complimentary mimosa. Total spa time was three days, leaving her three more for travel and presentation prep. *I will be the most fabulous woman at the Gala*, she reassured herself, and the thought made her smile.

She even planned to make a grand entrance, one that would be talked about for ages, one that would have all eyes riveted on her and only her – as they should be. As her due.

***

Donny flipped the last pancake, added it to the stack, and joined her at the table. They filled plates and ate contentedly, smiling at one another. *This feels so right*, she thought as she reached for the syrup, and the thought completely unnerved her. She'd never expected to get close to anyone. Unconsciously she scowled as she cut another bite off her stack.

"Wow. Are they that bad?" he asked, eyes twinkling.

“What?” she responded, breaking out of her reverie, completely confused.

“That face you’re making,” he told her. “That is not a happy face at all. Something wrong?”

“Oh. Um… sorry,” she chuckled, a little self-consciously.

“Seriously, you okay?”

“Well… it’s… I… I don’t know how to describe it,” she admitted.

“Just say what’s on your mind. Maybe I can help.”

“Okay,” she said, exhaling. “Okay. I was just thinking that this is nice. Waking up with you, eating pancakes you made me. And it scared the hell out of me. I never thought I would ever be in…whatever this is.”

“Huh,” he replied thoughtfully. “Okay, I can see what you mean.”

“You can?”

"Absolutely I can. To be honest, been feeling like that a little bit myself. Though on my side it's been more like 'what did I ever do in my life that was so good that I was rewarded with being with this beautiful creature'. I feel like I don't deserve this" – he gestured from her to him – "at all." He took her hand. "Any of that ring a bell?"

"Yeah, kind of," she said. "Mine's more like, I lost a couple of people I loved very much when I was younger and so I told myself I would never let myself get attached to anyone again. Less hurt that way."

The look of concern on Donny's face melted her heart as he told her, "You know you can talk to me about whatever, whenever, right? You can share as much or as little as you'd like to. I am always here to listen, and I will help however I can." And he leaned over and kissed her tenderly.

"Same goes for you, you know," she told him. "I get the feeling you have baggage that you've not shared yet either."

"Most definitely," he admitted. "I just don't think it's the right time yet. I don't want to open up to you and then have what I share make you haul ass."

"Points for honesty," she gestured at him with her fork. "Why don't we agree that when each of us gets to the point where we feel comfortable sharing more, we do, and the other one promises to keep an open mind. Sound fair?"

"Yep."

"Good." Now she smiled. "I only have two days left to spend with you before I have to continue on to L.A., so what would you like to do today?"

***

Lizzie was exhausted. She'd wound up working way past her scheduled shift end time, but it couldn't be helped. Three new cases in a ten-hour period, and she was going on twenty-fours straight of awake and trying to fit puzzle pieces together. All she wanted to do was take a hot shower and go to bed.

As she entered her house, she sensed something was off. At first, she chalked it up to being tired. But as she climbed the staircase, she heard a familiar noise, and she was overwhelmed by the sudden and deep realization her life was about to shift drastically. Creeping silently into the doorway, her world shattered as she saw two silhouettes in her bed, oblivious to her presence, having vigorous and vocal sex.

Flipping on the light revealed the extent of the treachery. It was her fiancé Jeff – and

Jessica, her best friend since junior high school.

“Oh!” Jessica squeaked.

“You back-stabbing bitch. Get the fuck out of my house.”

“Lizzie...”

“Not one word, Jess. You can leave through the door or out the fucking second-story window, your choice. And don’t text me, don’t call me, we’re done. You’re dead to me. You both are.” She spun on her heel, marched to the kitchen, returned with a box of trash bags and headed for the dresser, noticing that Jessica had gotten up and was silently putting her clothes back on in the corner.

“Come on, Lizzie! Seriously? Don’t do this,” Jeff pleaded.

Lizzie remained furiously silent as she wrenched drawers open and threw his clothes into trash bags.

"What do you want me to say? Huh? What? You're never home." He got up and started toward her.

"Not a fucking thing," she growled through clenched teeth. "There's nothing you can say. Get away from me."

"Hey," Jeff started to grab her arm, then let go and staggered back when he saw the barely controlled rage in her eyes. "Lizzie, I made a mistake. It was an accident."

She laughed without joy. "Oh my God. I cannot believe you right now. Really? Really, Jeff? An 'accident'? Oh, I'm sorry, did you trip over a piece of furniture or something and fall into this slut? You're so full of shit. I'm gonna say this next part slowly and use small words so you understand it. *We… are… done,* you cheating bastard," she hissed. "Over. I want you out. NOW." And she threw his clothes at him. "I mean it. Get out or I will have you physically removed."

"Fine!" he shrugged on his pants, worked his housekey off his keychain, throwing it onto the bed. "That's how you want to be, that's fine."

She held her hand out. "Car keys too, Jeff. That's MY car, in MY name. You should have thought things through better before being a man-whore with my now ex-best friend."

"How am I supposed to get to work tomorrow?"

"Well, maybe your trashy man-stealing whore will cart your dead weight around. It's not my problem anymore. Figure it out on your own."

The set of her jaw and her right hand tapping the butt of her still holstered service weapon conveyed her sincerity of speech. Sheepishly he tossed his copy of her car's keys on the bed too, then gathered up his trash bags and left, a pale and silent Jessica right behind him. She closed her eyes as she heard the front door slam. Sighing, she picked up her phone to get a twenty-four-hour locksmith out. No point in putting off changing locks; Jessica still had a key to the place.

But not for much longer.

Hands trembling, she walked back downstairs to the kitchen, poured herself a whiskey on the rocks, sat on her couch, and glanced at her watch. *Locksmith said he'd be here in thirty to forty-five minutes. That ought to give me enough time.*

She downed her drink, then leaned over and placed her head in her hands and cried.

***

Monica Stewart felt like a new woman. She'd been scrubbed, rubbed and pampered to her heart's content. Now she waited impatiently as the limo driver loaded her luggage into the trunk, then opened the door for her and helped her into the back seat. Settling herself graciously on the cushions, she leaned forward to pour herself some champagne, smiling indulgently like a well-fed cat.

As the limo slowly wound its way toward the airport and her family's private plane, she relaxed and began to mentally run through her wardrobe for Saturday night's gala. It all had to be just perfect. After all, she fully intended to command the attention of everyone in the room. And she knew just how to do it. She would make her entrance at the top of the grand staircase, and all eyes would follow her graceful descent in her impeccable gown. After Saturday night the name and face of Monica Stewart would be front and center on every magazine and newspaper that mattered.

***

She had reluctantly left Donny's company again after three days of sweet togetherness. Now she handed the hotel valet her keys while the porter gripped her suitcases and followed her to the front desk. The posh hotel had no way of knowing it, but through a connection with mad hacking skills, she'd managed to figure out previously which suite her target was assigned to and wrangled the adjacent one for ease of access. She checked in, received her keycard, and the porter escorted her to her room. Tipping him generously earned her a sincere smile and a "Enjoy your stay, miss," before he bowed slightly and took his leave.

Once she was alone, she unpacked her things and put them away neatly before turning her attention to the interior door that separated the two suites. She studied the lock mechanism, then took a picture of it and texted it to someone she knew would have advice on how to breach it. A few minutes later, the text she got back walked her through just that.

"Not much to do now until Saturday," she said aloud. "Time for dinner." She changed into something a little more dressed up than what she'd traveled in and went downstairs. As she roamed the lovely and very old lobby, she noticed the grand staircase, with its cool marble steps and elegant antique wrought iron and wood railing perched regally as the focal point of the entire first floor. She gazed up to it for a moment, calculating. *Yes. That could work.* It would require a little dose of luck to achieve the desired result, but this gorgeous old structure would provide the perfect – and extremely public – backdrop.

Smiling, she leisurely walked to the lounge area for a meal and a drink.

***

Lizzie woke suddenly, startled at first by her surroundings. *Oh yeah,* she remembered hazily. *My bed is tainted now so I crashed out in here.* She looked around the guest room as tears filled her eyes. *That's enough*, she told herself sternly. *They aren't worth your time or your tears, either one of them.* She sighed and swung her feet to the floor.

She looked at her wristwatch. “Gotta be on shift in four,” she said aloud. She really didn’t want to go back into her bedroom, but she had no choice. All her clothes were in there. She gritted her teeth and slowly walked toward the place where her heart had been mortally wounded. “I would rather be in a gunfight right now, I swear to God,” she muttered.

Taking a deep breath, she crossed the threshold, refusing to even look toward the bed as she headed straight into the bathroom for a shower. And she realized she couldn’t even make herself do that here. She felt like this whole area was contaminated with betrayal. Steeling her resolve, she grabbed a couple of suitcases from the closet and the empty laundry basket and used them all to transport her clothes into the guest room and her toiletries into the guest bath. That accomplished, she firmly closed the master bedroom door, and started getting ready for work.

As she rinsed out her hair, it hit her that the biggest slice of hurt had been served to her by Jessica, not Jeff. They'd been best friends since seventh grade, and had shared everything together – laughing, crying, learning to drive, proms, failed relationships, crappy part time summer jobs, graduation, college. But it suddenly made sense why Jessica had recently begun casting doubts in Lizzie's mind about marrying Jeff.

"She wanted him for herself," Lizzie realized out loud. The thought shook her more than seeing them in her bed together had. Her knees buckled with the new blow, and she slid down the shower wall to the floor, weeping as the water swirled around the drain.

***

Landon swirled his whiskey and stared at the fireplace. The weather had been depressing lately, lots of rain. He sighed. He needed a break. *Somewhere tropical, I think. Yes, that would do nicely to get me out of this funk.* He wished he had someone in his life to share a beautiful island vacation with. But it was what it was. He launched off the couch and moved to his laptop. With a few keystrokes, he found the perfect spot, and made his reservations. *Ten days in Grand Cayman would cure this, all right.* Smiling, he walked toward his room to pack.

***

Lizzie made it through her shift on autopilot. Her section chief noticed almost immediately that something wasn't right. Although he would never embarrass her by telling her, he thought of her as the daughter he'd never had. He also knew she was a very private person, so he waited until her shift was over before summoning her into his office.

“Have a seat,” he gestured to his visitor’s chair.

“Yes, sir,” she replied and did as requested.

“You all right, Lizzie?”

She sighed. “No, sir. Not really.”

He held up a hand. “You don’t have to share if you don’t want to. I just noticed you’re not.... as sharp as usual.”

“Yes, sir. I’m sorry.”

He picked up a file on his desk, flipping through pages. “You’ve closed twenty cases in the last six weeks. Good work.”

“Thank you, sir.”

“I’d say that calls for a vacation, wouldn’t you?”

“Sir?”

Now he gentled his tone. "Lizzie. I've known you forever. Something is really bothering you. You have more vacation time built up than anyone in the division. Why don't you take some, work through whatever you have going on?"

Her eyes filled despite her best efforts. "Okay."

"Anything I can help with?"

It was out before she could stop herself. "I caught Jeff and Jessica together."

"Oh my," he commiserated, shaking his head. "That sucks."

She blew out a long breath, shoulders slumping. "Yeah." Swiping at the two tears that had escaped custody and were running down her cheeks, she said, "Maybe a break isn't a bad idea."

"Grand Cayman is beautiful this time of year, and not crowded at all. Marge and I went there for our thirtieth anniversary last year."

"I remember," Lizzie nodded. "You brought those pictures back and showed us."

"So, go," he proclaimed. "Take seven days, hell, take ten. Go recharge and let me know when you get back if there's anything you need me to do."

She considered, nodded. "That sounds…nice. I'll do that. Thanks."

She returned to her desk, filled out the vacation request sheet, emailed it to him, and typed a few other emails to tie some things up before she left. Within moments, he'd sent back her request as approved, carbon copying the payroll department. She could leave whenever she liked, she now had ten vacation days to herself to put with the next two she'd been off rotation anyway.

Twelve whole days to rest and figure things out. Lizzie picked up her purse and keys and headed home to schedule and pack for her unexpected vacation trip.

Arriving at her house, she frowned as she saw the envelope taped to her door. “PLEASE READ” was inscribed in Jessica’s handwriting across the front. Lizzie ripped it off the door, scowling, and, once inside, carried it straight to the fireplace. She turned the electric ignition on, the flames burst into existence, and she admitted internally to a great deal of satisfaction as she flung the unopened menace into the fire and watched it quickly burn away. Then she went upstairs to get the ball rolling on her Grand Cayman adventure.

***

Saturday, April eleventh, 2010. The day of the big Gala had arrived. Two women, unknown personally to one another, woke up on opposite sides of the suite-adjoining door, each of them full of anticipation for the night's events.

One of them would never see the next sunrise.

CHAPTER FIVE

The weather was sunny, the waves were gentle and soothing to watch. A slight breeze rustled the palm tree leaves as Lizzie went out onto her private balcony after checking into her room that overlooked the ocean. Her boss had been right. It was gorgeous down here, and right before tourist season picked up in earnest so not crowded at all.

Smiling, she unpacked her things, changed into her two piece and grabbed a plush beach towel from the nearby stack just beyond the doors to the hotel patio. Out by the pool she selected a chair and ordered a raspberry daquiri from the polite and attentive poolside waiter. She sighed and leaned back, enjoying the warmth on her skin. When he returned with her drink, she favored him with a smile and a tip, then sipped daintily through the straw before leaning back again. Warming herself in the delightful sunshine, she closed her eyes and purposely cleared her mind.

***

Monica stirred to the bedside alarm she'd set. 4 p.m. Her appointment for hair, nails, and makeup down in the salon was at four-thirty. She stretched luxuriously before getting out of bed from her midday nap. She was vain enough that even a trip down to the salon to get ready for an event called for a carefully put together look. Dark blue yoga pants with matching zip-up hoodie showed off her curves and resulted in the perfect young, chic look she'd sought. Not to mention ease of changing later. To spend all that time in the stylist's chair, then ruin it by having to take off a pullover blouse?

Comment gauche. She collected her room key and left for her appointment.

***

In the suite next door, she heard Monica leave. *That's my chance,* she told herself, and went to work picking the lock on the interior door. It yielded easily, as did the other one at the far end of the narrow space between the rooms. She pulled on latex gloves and moved forward quietly, hearing and awareness heightened. Turning the corner, she saw that Monica's evening attire had already been selected and pulled into a starring position on the closet rack, matching shoes placed neatly below.

"Thank God," she murmured. That was a stroke of luck. She really hadn't wanted to replicate her activity on – quickly, she counted the contents of the closet floor – *Jesus, who in the hell travels with seventeen pairs of shoes?* she marveled, shaking her head. *Wow.* Yeah, she'd be in here all evening if she had to do that many. She grabbed the shoes slated for tonight, carried them to the bathroom counter and pulled her tools from her pocket.

She picked up the left shoe, held it up in her left hand so that the sole was facing her. With her right hand she very delicately worked the fine blade into the seam where shoe and heel came together, opening it just wide enough for the syringe she pulled out next to be able to deposit a healthy dose of glue solvent into the gap. She set the left shoe down, then carefully returned them to the place she'd found them. She cocked her head, pondering where to leave the bow-tie wrapper, then smiled as she saw the little gold clutch lying on the nightside table. She opened it, tucked the wrapper inside, closed it again, and went back to her room, making sure she'd left no trace of herself behind as she retreated.

And now, to wait. Once Monica stepped into the shoes, the air bubble around the solvent would be compressed and break. The solvent would then erode the glue holding shoe and heel together. On average, it weakened the glue enough to break the heel off quite easily during normal use after seven to ten minutes. She knew that for a fact. She'd experimented with several pairs before even beginning this trip – including another pair that happened to exactly match Monica's selection for the evening in every way except size.

She knew her quarry, had studied Monica extensively. She knew that pompous bitch would want to make the most 'look at me' segue possible into tonight's overblown party. She planned to already be on the ground floor in the middle of the crowd when it happened. No way in hell she was going to miss the spectacle. It would be one for the history books for sure.

She almost skipped her way to her bathroom to get ready, whistling a happy little tune.

***

Lizzie stretched, then rose. *Time to hit the water.* She dove gracefully, barely rippling the surface, then began lazy laps up and down the length of the pool. After four circuits she turned onto her back and floated for a moment, eyes closed, face turned up the sun, blissful and content. Then she began to slowly backstroke her way over to the ladder to go resume her sunbathing. Completely unaware of her surroundings, she was surprised when she reached back for the ladder and her hand closed over human flesh. Startled, she gasped and spun around.

"Hello, there. Ladies first, please," the man whose arm she'd touched said politely, smiling at her. He was handsome, tall and tan, brown hair, with a great physique, she noticed. And his brown eyes twinkled at her with humor as he continued with, "Sorry if I startled you."

"Oh," she managed. "I am so sorry. I didn't notice anyone else had gotten into the pool."

"Well, you did seem preoccupied."

She chuckled. "Something like that," and smoothed her wet hair down self-consciously.

He indicated the ladder. "After you."

"Thanks." She went up the steps, suddenly very aware of just how little her bikini bottoms were.

Landon watched her every movement as she traveled upward in front of him. He'd been mesmerized by her for the last ten minutes, ever since he'd arrived poolside just in time to watch her dive flawlessly into the water.

At the top she turned slightly, smiling and nodding at him briefly before making her way to her chair. She slipped her sunglasses back on, grateful for the way they masked her eyes, and watched how his muscles rippled while he hauled himself up out of the water. He moved lithely toward her seat, seemingly unaware just how sensual he looked as he walked. As he got closer to her, he said, "I'm thinking of getting another daquiri, would you like one?"

"Sure," she answered. "Thanks."

He grinned, and something about him had her grinning back. He strolled over to the bar, returned a few minutes later with two drinks. "I took a chance and got you a raspberry one," he explained as he handed her the glass.

"Happens to be my favorite," she replied, "so, nice choice."

"Mind if I join you?" Landon asked.

"Not at all," she indicated the next chair.

They sat silently for a time, sipping their drinks and watching the breeze play in the palm trees overhead.

"I'm Landon," he started the conversation.

"Elizabeth."

"Nice to meet you, Elizabeth."

"You too."

More silence, and she began to feel awkward.

"So," they both said at once, then, "I'm sorry, you first."

He looked at her and laughed. "Great minds, I guess. Please, you go first."

"Well…um… to be honest, I hadn't planned on what to say if I met another guest…"

"Ah, I know how that feels. Something tells me you're down here to recharge, maybe figure stuff out, and I'm bothering you. I'm so sorry. Should I leave?"

"No, please don't, I'm sorry. And yeah, I am down here to figure some stuff out. Sorry if I sounded rude. I just," she shrugged, "it didn't occur to me that interacting with others while I am here might be a thing." Now she smiled. "I swear I am usually more together than this."

"Hey, you're on vacation, perfect time to not have to be as squared away as usual," he quipped. "I myself found that I was working way too many hours, needed a break, and I heard it's beautiful here this time of year. So, I decided the hell with it, the business can survive my being out of the office for a week. And here I am."

"How long have you been here?"

"Got here yesterday afternoon," Landon said. "You?"

"My flight landed around ten this morning, and it was straight to my room then straight out here. Speaking of which, what time is it?"

"Just after four."

"Well, that explains it."

"What?"

"I'm starving."

"Well, I wouldn't mind a meal. Care to join me?" he asked.

Lizzie smiled at him. "I'd like that. But I'd like to change first."

"Me too. How about we do that and meet back in the lobby in, say, about a half hour."

"Sounds perfect."

They walked together to the elevator, and both pressed the button for the third floor. They looked at each other for a moment. She hummed nervously under her breath as they waited for the doors to open, then said, "See you in a bit," and tried her best to walk nonchalantly to her room. He turned and strode toward the far end where his room was located.

As Landon closed the door behind him, he let out a breath he didn't know he'd been holding. "Wow," he chuckled to himself as he quickly stripped off his trunks and climbed into the shower. He was completely caught off guard by her; to be honest, he hadn't planned on what to say if he met someone on this vacation, either.

Meanwhile, Lizzie worked shampoo through her hair then rinsed it out. That accomplished, she stepped out of the shower, quickly dried off, and used the blow dryer to get her long brown hair manageable enough to pull back into a decent looking ponytail. She realized she was shaking a bit as she pulled on capris and a cute vibrantly colored top, opting for sandals to complete the outfit. *Never thought I would be having company for a meal down here*. She checked her look in the mirror and reminded herself that this was not that big a deal. Was Landon cute? Oh, absolutely. *But it's just food and conversation, Liz. Calm down.*

With much more poise than she felt, she grabbed her room key and bag and headed back to the elevator. Landon rejoined her just as the elevator opened for them to enter.

“Hello again,” she said. “Nice shirt,” indicating the forest green t-shirt that showcased his pecs.

“Um, thanks,” he replied, hoping he didn’t sound as awestruck by her presence as he felt. “Shall we?”

“What are our choices for food?”

“Well,” he began, pointing to the left as they exited into the lobby, “the hotel lounge just through there has a pretty good setup, mostly casual dining -you know, burgers, stuff like that. The restaurant,” his arm swept to the right, “is fancier. Steaks and seafood. The question is, what would you like?”

“Have you tried the lounge?” she asked.

"I have," he told her. "Burgers aren't as great as back home, but still good."

"I'm thinking a burger sounds good."

"The lounge it is, then," and he held the door for her as they entered.

They were seated promptly and handed menus. One sweep told her all she needed to know. "Yep, cheeseburger and fries," she announced, setting down her menu.

The waitress arrived. "May I take your order?"

"I'll have a cheeseburger, well done, mustard, no onions, please. With fries."

"Excellent, and what can I get you to drink?"

"Ice water with lemon."

The waitress turned to Landon. "Make it two of all that, please, but with onions on mine," he stated, and handed her the menus. As she left to get their beverages, he told Lizzie, “You and I order our burgers pretty much the same way.”

“Makes sense, since it’s the best way,” she announced with a twinkle.

“I know, right?” he smiled mischievously. “Why ruin a great burger with mayo?”

“Yuck, can’t stand the stuff,” she agreed.

Their cheeseburgers, with hefty doses of seasoned fries on the side, arrived quickly. Their hands met at the ketchup bottle, and they both blushed. “Go ahead,” he offered, grabbing the saltshaker first instead. Once proper amounts of condiments had been applied, they dug in. Her eyebrows raised. “Not bad for not stateside,” she remarked.

“Told you,” he pointed a fry before dipping it in ketchup. Silence took over the table for a bit as they enjoyed their meal. When they were done, he asked her, “So, where are you from?”

"Originally, I'm from North Texas, but I moved to Seattle when I was twelve."

"Wow, small world. I live near Fort Worth," he said. "From there to Seattle, huh? Must have been quite an adjustment."

"That's an understatement," she agreed. "Yeah, it took a while. But I finally found a rhythm, graduated high school, went to college and got a degree in criminal justice. Then I followed in my old man's footsteps and joined the police force. Much to my mother's dismay, I might add," she concluded with a frown as she sipped her water.

"How long have you been a cop?"

"Seven years now. I worked my way up to detective a little over a year ago now. It's a lot more challenging than patrol but I love it." She picked up her last fry and paused. "What about you? Where are you from?"

"All over, really," he told her. "Traveled a lot when I was very young. Mom and Dad settled in Pantego when I was eight and I have called that home since. Although for business I still travel a lot."

"What do you do?"

"I run an import/export business. I'm based in Dallas but have offices in Houston and Corpus Christi also."

"That sounds cool."

"It is. I have always been fascinated with other cultures," he shared, eyes beginning to twinkle. "Their history, their traditions, their lives. It was kind of a no-brainer for me to have a career that lets me experience all that." He paused to take a drink. "Did you always know you wanted to be a cop?"

"Yep," she nodded. "My dad started with Fort Worth PD the year I was born. He has one of the highest case closure rates ever as a detective. He's my best friend and my role model."

The talk switched to more general topics – music, movies – as they considered dessert choices. "Hmm," she frowned. "I can't decide between the cheesecake and the key lime pie."

Landon laughed. "I was just experiencing that same dilemma! You order one, I'll order the other, and we can split both?"

Lizzie beamed. "Sounds like a great solution to me."

***

Monica stepped into her dress, carefully sliding it up her body, then checked her results in the mirror. *God, I'm gorgeous!* she purred to herself as she admired the view. She grabbed her little handbag – gold lame, of course, to match her exquisite and very expensive designer gown – then slipped her feet into her new shoes she'd just had to have to complete the ensemble. The heels were a bit higher than she usually wore but what a small price to pay for looking fabulous. One more mirror check to blow herself a kiss, then off to the party she went.

As she stepped toward the elevator, she was so excited she could barely keep her composure. She sauntered in, pressed the button for the mezzanine, and continued to admire her own beauty in the elevator car's mirrored walls.

***

Monica's saboteur tapped her champagne glass nervously. The music that had been softly playing as background noise was about to come to a stop. Then, the evening's host would walk up the staircase four or five steps – just enough to be able to be seen by all those in attendance – and announce the

Gala's official start. It was almost time for the special entertainment she'd planned for everyone to happen.

She smiled as she saw Monica Stewart stealthily approach the top of the marble staircase, timing the entrance so that she would capture the attention of everyone below already looking up toward the mezzanine level.

As she predicted, the host traveled up to the fifth step to make the announcement. Thirty-five steps above him, Monica positioned herself to make a splash. *As soon as the idiot quits jabbering, that is*, Monica sneered silently before fixing a megawatt and completely fake smile in place.

A pleasant round of applause as the host began to descend the stairs, as did Monica Stewart. She could hear "oohs" and "aahs" from the crowd below her as everyone watched her carefully orchestrated approach. As she planted her left foot firmly on the third step, the heel separated as designed. She pinwheeled, starting to scream as she lost her balance. Below her on the ground floor, the crowd's horrified exclamations rolled toward her like a wave, camera bulbs flashing as paparazzi captured it all, the host turning and watching her chaotic descent towards him in disbelief. She tumbled helplessly like a rag doll all the way down before landing in a tangled heap at the man's feet. A doctor hurriedly pushed his way through the crowd and raced to her side. He felt for a pulse, then examined her neck, and shook his head slowly at the host. "Her neck's broken, she's gone," he announced quietly. Hotel security rushed forward and began directing onlookers and media hounds away.

Her killer turned to flow with the crowd being moved back from the scene. It was all she could do not to smile; instead she downed her champagne and tried her best to look as traumatized as those around her. Monica Stewart would get her wish. Her name and face would grace the front page of every magazine and newspaper in the morning and possibly for weeks to come – not to mention nationwide on tonight's newscasts.

This calls for room service, she thought to herself as she worked her way to the elevator then back to her room. *It's time to celebrate.* Striding into her suite, she picked up the phone and ordered steak then retrieved her notebook and drew a line through Monica Stewart's name.

***

The cheesecake and key lime pie arrived in short order, and Landon added coffee to go with his. Lizzie opted for tea. “They both look amazing,” she remarked, eyeing the desserts.

He picked up his fork. “Shall we?”

“Absolutely!” she grinned. They each started at one end of each dessert, slowly working their way to the middle of each plate.

“These are both fantastic! I’m glad you suggested we order both, I would have hated to miss out on either one,” she told him before taking another bite of the cheesecake.

“Me too,” he agreed. Finally, they arrived at one bite left of each. “Which would you prefer?” Landon asked.

"Hmm," she pondered. "I really think I'm going to have to finish out with.... key lime."

He scooped up the last forkful of cheesecake and smiled at her as he popped it in his mouth.

The waitress returned to top off the coffee and tea, leaving the bill discreetly on the corner of the table. Lizzie reached out for it, but Landon was faster. "Please, allow me," he said, as their hands met and he turned his over to clasp hers, brushing his thumb over her skin in a gentle caress.

She blushed slightly. "If you insist."

"Oh, but I do." He pulled out his card and gave it to the waitress as she passed back by without taking his eyes off Lizzie, thumb still caressing the back of her hand. And she felt the heat rising within her as she stared back into his dark brown eyes. Flushed, she broke contact to take another sip of tea.

When she glanced up again, she caught the amused expression he was fighting to hide. "What?" she asked.

"Just admiring the view," he announced. "You're cute when you blush and you're trying not to."

Now her eyebrow raised. "Really."

"Yes, really. And I meant it as a compliment. Something tells me you don't get rattled enough to blush very often at all."

"Oh." She relaxed. "Well, yes. You're right. And it's a good thing."

"How so?"

She shrugged. "Kind of undermines your street cred as a detective if you can't stay in control of yourself."

"Ah, yes, I can see where blushing on any sort of regular basis might impede the work in that instance. Do you ever get a chance to just let yourself go, Elizabeth?"

"Not really, no. And the few times I have, well..."

"Well, what?"

She sighed. "Landon, you really don't want to hear my sad story."

He leaned forward, elbows on table, chin propped on his hands. "If you feel comfortable sharing it, I want to hear it. I'd like to know more about you, Elizabeth."

"Please, call me Lizzie."

"Okay. Lizzie. What brought you to the Grand Caymans? You said when we first met today that you came down to figure stuff out. What stuff?"

She sighed, toyed with her teacup. "Well, I was engaged until two days ago."

"Oh," he realized. "But not anymore."

"No. Not anymore. Came home from an extra-long shift and walked in on him screwing my best friend, in my bed."

Landon winced, took her hand in his and squeezed it gently to comfort her.

"Let me guess. Her betrayal stung more." Lizzie found her hand tightening around his.

"It absolutely did," Lizzie nodded. "Which at first surprised me, but when I thought about it, we'd been best friends for what, fourteen years? Since seventh grade. And she threw that away. I only had three years invested in him," she chuckled mirthlessly, and Landon could see the shadows creeping into her hazel eyes.

"I didn't mean to upset you," he told her sincerely.

"You didn't. You're not the one who cheated," she pointed out.

***

She leaned back, contented. The steak had been well worth the cost. She'd heard people milling about in Monica's suite next door. No doubt they had arrived to secure the ice queen's personal belongings. No matter. She'd overhead some conversations downstairs that confirmed this was just a tragic wardrobe mishap in the view of security personnel and police.

Moving to the bedside table, she grabbed the remote and turned the television on and was immediately rewarded with another glimpse of the fantastic results of her planning. After a stern warning by the broadcaster that the video about to be shown could be disturbing to some viewers, they replayed a part of the glory one of the news crews covering the event had captured. *Pity, though, they didn't show the entire thing. Too bad*. She pressed a button and the TV went dark again.

She changed out of her evening wear and into traveling clothes. Time to pack up and go. She'd never planned on staying out here a full week anyway. Not when she had Donny to return to.

CHAPTER SIX

"Well," Landon said once the check was settled. "What would you like to do now?"

"I've heard the sunsets are gorgeous here."

"They are," he confirmed. "The one last night as I walked the beach was phenomenal. I think you'd enjoy seeing it."

"Then let's do that." She smiled.

He stood, offering her his hand. She rose and gently accepted, lacing her fingers through his. They walked casually through the lobby and down the back steps out onto the huge patio that flanked the pool. "Through there," he pointed toward a path that was cut out of the low brick façade surrounding the pool area. "The hotel's property lines extend all the way to the water, so this whole section is a private beach for their guests."

“Nice!”

Lizzie paused where the smooth path met the white sand to take off her sandals. Landon slipped his topsiders off as well. Then they stepped onto the beach side by side and began to stroll. He reached out and gently took her hand again. She smiled at him, then gazed out over the water, listening to the gently rolling waves lapping against the sand. She detoured slightly, gently pulling him with her, until each wave coming ashore met their ankles.

“It’s warmer than I thought it would be,” she noticed. “Oh, Landon, look!” She released his hand and picked up a shell that had caught her attention. Tilting it back and forth revealed a myriad of colors as the sunlight danced across its surface.

“Looks like the perfect souvenir shell if you ask me.”

"I think so too." And she tucked it into her bag, then made him smile by reaching out to resume holding hands as they walked.

"So. You've heard my story. What's yours? Married? Engaged?"

"Nope, and nope," he replied. "Had a few dates with a really nice woman recently, but there just wasn't any spark, so…"

"You're kidding!" It was out before she could stop it. "Um…er…what I meant to say was, hard to believe you're not off the market…" She faltered, and whipped her head toward the water as she turned beet red.

He grinned. "There's that cute blush thing again. You should let yourself go more often, Lizzie, it suits you."

"I get hurt when I do that," she said quietly, trying her best to focus on the waves.

Now he stopped, turning to face her. He brushed back the slender strand of hair that the breeze had playfully pulled forward from her ponytail. "I'm sorry you got hurt. You didn't deserve that. I just hope you don't shut the world out because of it."

She looked up at him, eyes shimmering, and took one hesitant step forward. He closed his arms around her as she buried her face in the chest of a man she'd just met and wept. "Oh, Lizzie," he murmured. "Lizzie. I'm so sorry they did that to you." He gently stroked her hair as she clung to him and let go of some of the pain.

After a long while she pulled away, sniffling. "I am so sorry," she stammered. "Here you are trying to have a vacation and you get stuck with some basket case you just met crying on your shoulder. Literally." She flopped down onto the sand, rummaging through her bag for a tissue to wipe her face. “Landon, I swear to God you are not meeting the normal me, at all. I am usually SO much more together than this…”

He sat down beside her. “Lizzie. You need to give yourself a break. You just got handed a huge betrayal. It is totally okay to not be okay with that.” She gave him a grateful smile. “Besides,” he continued, “crying or not, I am completely fascinated by you. Have been since I walked out on the patio just in time to see you dive into the pool.” He put his arm around her, and she leaned against him as he said, “Seriously nice dive, by the way, almost no splash at all.”

She chucked. “Thanks.”

“Look,” he pointed out over the water. “We’ve got a perfect seat.”

And he was right. The skies above swirled in every imaginable shade of orange and pink, deepening as farther out on the horizon the setting sun seemed to melt into the dark vibrant blue of the water.

“Wow,” Lizzie exclaimed. “That’s just about the most beautiful thing I’ve ever seen.”

“Surpassed only by the company I’m in tonight,” he murmured. She turned to look at him, noticed his intense gaze focused first on her eyes, then her lips as he leaned in to close the bit of distance remaining. Tenderly he pressed his lips to hers. A rogue jolt shot through her system as her arms wrapped around him instinctively to pull him closer. The kiss deepened and she began to feel giddy. Then she came to her senses, pulling away and scrambling to her feet to create some space between them.

"What…What…" she began. He stood, looking at her hungrily.

"I overstepped. I apologize," Landon said, running his hand through his hair. "The sunset, and you sitting there so beautiful, I got overwhelmed with needing to know what kissing you would be like." He stuffed his hands into his pockets. "I made you uncomfortable. That wasn't my intention."

"We just met today," she pointed out. "Like, not even a whole day ago."

"I know," he admitted. "I'm sorry."

"This is crazy." She walked away a few paces, then paced back, flinging her arms wide. "We know next to nothing about each other."

He sighed. "Yeah."

"So why do I want you to kiss me again?"

He did a double take. "Excuse me. What?"

"Kiss me again, Landon."

"Does this mean you're letting yourself go?"

"Possibly."

"Well, I was raised to fully cooperate with any and all police instructions, so..." He moved toward her, a glint in his eye.

She laughed. "Then get over here."

He closed the few steps rapidly and took her in his arms again, mouth devouring hers. She swayed and clung to him, running her hands up his back then wrapping her arms around his waist as he teased her mouth with his tongue. "Damn," Lizzie gasped as he trailed kisses lazily down her throat.

"Indeed," Landon managed as he nuzzled her neck. "You're breathtaking." Working his way up to her ear, he nibbled gently on the lobe, and the little moan of pleasure from her made him smile against her skin. Very reluctantly, he pulled away from her. “I think we should stop now, since as you pointed out, we only just met today.”

“Oh. Good point.”

“Not that I want to. At all. I’ll be completely honest, Lizzie. If it were only up to me, we’d be heading to my room right this minute, and sleep would be the absolute last thing happening tonight. But I don’t want the heat of the moment to sweep us into something you’re not ready for.” He cupped her face gently. “That wouldn’t be fair to either of us. Know what I mean?”

She sighed. “I do know. I’m, well, dealing with stuff, and you don’t want to take advantage of that.”

“Exactly. Don’t get me wrong, Lizzie. I absolutely do want to.” He grinned at her. “You’re smoking hot, and I’m only human, and I’d love to continue this. But not that way. If we spend a night together, I want it to be because that's what we both truly want and are ready for."

"I agree," she admitted. "My engagement ended just a few days ago. Last thing I need to do is hop straight into something with someone else. Tempting as you are."

Landon laughed. "I will take that as a compliment. For now, let's just enjoy each other's company."

Lizzie grabbed her bag and they made their way back to the hotel, stopping to pick up their shoes.

***

Frank Zimmerman frowned as he watched the news with whiskey eyes. Why did that name sound familiar? *Monica Stewart...Monica Stewart... I know that name.* He got up from his recliner, staggered his way into his home office, and turned on the light. He walked over to his filing cabinet and retrieved his copies. Flipping through the pages, he ran his finger down. “Ah hah, that’s what I thought,” he slurred triumphantly. Asked and answered.

He sat back down in his recliner, took another long pull from his bottle, and began to drift off. Just before he tumbled off into sleep, a stray lucid thought – *hey, weren’t there a couple others on there that died recently?...* -streaked across his mind like a shooting star across the night sky and was just as quickly forgotten as he dozed.

***

Lizzie paced back and forth, back and forth in her room. She looked at the clock. Twelve forty-five a.m. She was fighting a battle within herself to stay put in her room. The logical cop side wanted to just let it be and go to sleep; more time with Landon wouldn’t solve anything and besides, it was so risky, what exactly did she truly know about this guy? They hadn't even told each other their last names yet.

The lonely female side of her, however, was extremely persuasive. *He's hot, he's single, he's interested, what better way to clean the slate and make a new start than to hook up? You're both consenting adults. Doesn't mean you have to follow each other home much less start a relationship. He's over 2,000 miles away in the real world. Be daring for once. Have a good time with him and leave it here in the islands.*

She groaned aloud and continued to pace.

Lizzie had no way of knowing it, but Landon was also wide awake, and struggling with a similar battle. His rational business side threw all sorts of warnings up against any sort of intimate physical interaction, and his drive batted each one down with no difficulty at all. But he was enough of a gentleman that he was not about to press the issue; it would have to be her choice. He flipped channels, idly noting nothing on worth watching. “Time for a swim,” he said aloud. He needed to work off some of the restlessness he felt.

Landon changed into his trunks and headed down to the pool, grabbing a towel from the rack on the way to one of the beach chairs. He dove in and began laps at a blistering pace, churning the water with each stroke.

Lizzie wandered out onto her balcony to gaze at the moon when motion down below caught her attention. In the full moonlight she could clearly see Landon swimming lap after lap as fast as he could go. *Wonder what that's about*, her analytical side puzzled. *Maybe he's all worked up thinking about you and trying to redirect it*, her inner vixen crowed. Although she was completely alone with her thoughts, they still made her blush bright red.

She watched him swim, admiring his taut muscles as they rippled with each motion. When he finally stopped, turned onto his back to catch his breath, she could make out the expression on his face. He looked like she felt. Torn. Then he opened his eyes and noticed her standing there looking down at him. She could feel the heat of his gaze three stories up. Lizzie backed into her room, feeling guilty, like a peeping Tom that had just been discovered.

From his vantage point, Landon watched her melt back into the soft shadows past the moonlight. *So, she's still awake too*, he thought. *I wonder what she's thinking about....* "Stop. Just stop," he whispered to himself, and made his way to the ladder where they'd first met. He hauled himself up and out of the pool, dried off as best as he could, then looped the towel around his waist and headed back into the hotel. When he got to the third floor he stopped and looked longingly in her direction. It took all his willpower to go to his room and not hers.

After staring at herself in the mirror, Lizzie had finally decided. She brushed out her hair, slipped into her robe, tucked her keycard in her pocket. She applied minimal makeup and checked the reflection. *Not bad, Liz, not bad at all.* The butterflies in her stomach threatened to undo her; she hadn't been with anyone new in quite some time.

"Well, here goes nothing," she muttered, and quietly closed the door behind her. She traveled to the far end of the hall and tapped lightly on his door.

Landon had just stripped off his trunks and was preparing to turn on the shower when he heard the knock at his door. He quickly put on his robe, walked over and looked through the viewfinder. And grinned.

He opened the door slowly and started to speak but before he could say anything, Lizzie said, “No strings, Landon, and this stays here, in the Caymans. Deal?”

He gazed at her for a long, long moment. “I can live with that.”

She reached around to the interior door handle, grabbed the ‘Do Not Disturb’ sign, and hung it on the exterior handle. Then she placed her hands on his chest and her mouth on his and together they traveled into the room and closed the door behind them.

***

Donny swung open the door and hugged her. “Welcome back! I didn’t expect you so soon.”

“Yeah, well,” she answered. “I got what I needed out of the first three days of the conference. Thought I’d spend more time with you before I headed home.”

He grinned, then kissed her. “I am totally okay with that. Let me just finish up sending this email right quick. Another new client wants a full quote – auto, home, and life.” He ushered her in then retreated to his computer as she carried her bags upstairs.

“That’s the sixth one this week, right?” she called out to him.

“Yep,” he confirmed. “Business seems to be picking up lately.”

“Awesome!” she said encouragingly as she threw a few of her things onto hangers.

“And… done,” he announced.

"Perfect timing," she told him as she headed downstairs toward him. "Now what?"

"Hmm," he said, wrapping his arms around her. "Hot sex, or food?"

"How 'bout food, then hot sex? Let's go grab a bite."

"Deal." He kissed her on the nose.

***

Frank came awake suddenly, fully alert. And that fleeting thought had returned front and center. "I know there were others," he said to himself. He dug out his copies again, booted up his computer, and began to search. Three other names in, his detective's antenna was pinging – *hard.*

"What the hell…" he leaned back, mulling over what he'd gotten so far. "Gotta chart it," he told himself, falling back on a long-used and efficient habit from his detective days. He opened a new Excel file, and listed out initials and dates. When he was done, he looked at the result. He cross-checked some finer data points, added one more column of data, made more of the shorthand notes he was infamous for that no one except maybe Lizzie or Joe could possibly follow or understand. Then he printed out the result and studied it.

"Could be just coincidence," he muttered, already knowing full well he didn't believe that to be the case at all. In the other room his alarm clock sounded. He rubbed a hand over his face, hit save before closing out his computer, and sighed. He would much rather keep going on this, but he'd have to come back to it. Frank needed to get ready for another long night on patrol.

***

Lizzie returned to work all smiles after her impromptu vacation trip, in no small part due to her time with Landon while in the Grand Caymans. They'd spent an incredible passion filled week together; and by her choice, they were leaving it at that when they parted ways at DFW Airport. She got the sense from him that he would truly have liked more, but she had no desire for anything serious at all anytime soon – *if ever*, she amended silently.

But she had to admit, the time they'd shared together had been phenomenal.

Because she was extra perky even for her, she endured some good-natured ribbing from her mostly male coworkers as she strolled in and got situated at her desk for her first shift back. She booted up her computer and began to listen to voicemails while her computer slowly ground its way through its opening sequence.

As her partner, David Lydealea, approached her desk, he was dismayed to see her scribbling furiously, looking like she was about to throw the phone across the room. She had confided in him about Jeff and Jessica before she'd left, and he'd been kind enough to watch her house while she was gone. From the look on her face, he assumed she was about to need someone to talk to. He perched his six-foot six-inch ex-linebacker frame on the corner of her desk and waited.

After a few minutes, she slammed the phone down. "Un-freaking believable."

"Uh oh, Zim. That's not how I expected you to sound after a tropical vacation. What's up?" he asked in his deep baritone.

"David, he left me fourteen messages here at work. *Fourteen*. And that's just here. He left another dozen on my cell phone.

What part of ‘we are through’ does he not get?”

Her computer whirred to life, and she signed into her departmental email, then swore immediately.

“Check this out,” she gestured to her screen.

David leaned over, and stopped counting at twenty-five messages between Jeff and Jessica combined.

“Jesus! Stalker much?”

She sighed. “I know, right? Thank God there wasn’t any crap left on my door while I was gone… You’re kidding me, David. Tell me you’re kidding. Really?” she asked as she caught David’s expression. “How many?”

“Eight.” He grinned, showing white teeth against ebony skin. “Want me to set him straight, Zim? You and I both know he's already scared shitless of me."

She grinned back despite her foul mood. "It would serve him right. And yeah, he is totally scared of you already. Thanks, Tank," she continued, using the nickname she'd given him back when they started the Academy together. "I will keep that in mind."

"Just say the word, SWG," he replied, chuckling. He'd dubbed her 'Skinny White Girl' as a joke between them years ago, and it had stuck. Now his face turned serious for a moment. "All joking aside, Zim, you might tell the boss about this going on."

"Yeah," she sighed. "Who knew Jeff would be stupid enough to harass a police officer?"

"Well, it really isn't that far-fetched coming from him. I mean, look at the wonderful woman he had that he chose to cheat on. Your ex is chock full of stupid, if you ask me," and patted his huge hand delicately on her shoulder for comfort.

Their boss stuck his head out of his office. "Zimmerman, Lydealea, you're up."

"Well, let's get to it," she said. They walked into the boss's office to get up to speed on the case they were about to catch.

CHAPTER SEVEN

"You have a good trip? You look rested," Beth, Landon's office manager, remarked.

"It was nice," Landon grinned. "How much did I miss?"

"Actually, it wasn't too bad," she told him. "Fairly quiet. I caught your filing up, so there's that. Unless you wanted to do it."

He laughed. "I never want to do it, that's why there was a stack of it when I left."

Beth smiled. "You're welcome. Now, let's see," she checked the calendar. "You have three conference calls, one at nine-thirty, one at one-thirty, the last at four. Two half-hour meetings, twelve-thirty and three p.m. Good thing I filed for you, huh?"

"Beth Lorrence, what would I do without you?" Smiling, he walked into his office.

As Landon fired up his computer and waded through his emails, he found it difficult to concentrate. A certain brunette detective that resided over 2,000 miles away was at the forefront of his mind. Not that she'd ever left it completely, if he was honest with himself about it. Lizzie was the most amazing woman he'd ever met, no question. She had no way of knowing it, but her assessment that he would have liked to pursue something more had been spot on. From the first moment he'd seen her, she'd tugged at his soul.

But she'd made it very clear that what had happened between them would not be traveling back to the mainland. He understood her rationale; that didn't mean he had to be happy about it. It was all he could do not to go online and search for her last name or at least the address to Seattle police headquarters so he could send her flowers, or a card. "Get a grip," he muttered to himself. "You're acting like a lovesick teenager."

***

Lizzie and David prepared to join the raid scheduled later in the afternoon. The armed robbery series they were working happened to dovetail with a suspected cocaine ring. As a standard measure they both had donned Kevlar vests under their jackets; they'd be entering the premises right behind the squad members with the battering ram.

"You ready, Zim?" her partner asked.

"Ready as I'm going to get," she confirmed. "Still want to go in high and right?"

"Yep," David replied. "Course I do. You got way less to travel to get low than I do."

Lizzie grinned. "Let's do it."

They'd already gone over the full briefing in preparation for the afternoon's event, but

Lizzie and David talked it over again on their way to the scene, as was their usual habit. They rendezvoused with the rest of the team three blocks from the house in question, waiting for the signal from the weasel inside the premises to begin the approach. A nondescript Ford pickup meandered past, and the team leader made visual verification that his informant was at the wheel. The driver nodded twice as he drove past.

"That's the signal. Move in," he told the team. "Second set, around back. Third set on perimeter. First set, let's get the door once second and third are in position."

They fanned out, moving to their assigned places. Once second and third teams were ready, two SWAT members with the battering ram charged up the front steps, with two other SWAT members and Lizzie and David right behind. Announcing their presence per procedure, they proceeded to charge the front door. It gave way easily. The first team members worked their way through the door, and all hell broke loose.

Two of the home's occupants were immediately cooperative, hitting the floor and holding out their hands. The third, however, swung into the front room from the kitchen with a semi-automatic rifle, and opened fire. The SWAT officer closest to Lizzie took him out, but not before four bullets struck her, propelling her backward; she met the corner of the front door remnants hard with the back of her head, and slumped to the floor.

In a flash David was beside her. He could see two of the rounds had been caught and stopped by her vest. But her right arm was bleeding profusely; one shot had gone cleanly through her shoulder, the other round had entered just above her elbow, with no exit wound that he could see. “Need some help over here!” he shouted as he cradled her. “Now!” Another team member radioed for an ambulance with the phrase no police officer ever wanted to hear: “*Officer down*.”

“Lizzie. Stay with me. I got you, Lizzie. Just stay with me.”

“Aw, hell, Tank,” she murmured.

“What?”

“It must be bad. You *never* call me Lizzie,” she said with a pained grin right before she passed out.

***

Frank got the call around five p.m. that Lizzie had been shot. By seventy-thirty he was in the sky headed toward Seattle, his heart in his throat.

***

Landon was only partially paying attention to the nine o'clock newscast, when suddenly the program had his full and undivided interest. He cranked up the volume as the broadcaster relayed word of a bust up in Seattle, Washington earlier that afternoon that had netted more than seventy million in cocaine seized. As the news anchor cut to an on-scene live feed, where the beat reporter solemnly informed her viewing audience that a female detective had been shot during the raid, his heart dropped.

Don't say it. Please don't say it. Please, he silently begged the reporter, then closed his eyes and cursed softly when he heard, "The detective, Elizabeth Zimmerman, was last listed in serious condition at Seattle Medical Center. We'll bring you more on this story as it continues to develop." With a practiced rhythm the reporter segued the broadcast back over to the anchor.

Landon turned off the television and sat numbly, unsure what to do next. *That's her*, he told himself. *What would the chances be of more than one Seattle detective named Elizabeth*? He wanted to travel up there and see for himself that she was going to be okay, 'leave it in the islands' be damned. She'd probably be pissed off at him for it. He only hesitated for a fraction of a second. He'd take the risk. It was worth it to make sure she was all right. He strode to his laptop, booked a seat on the eleven o'clock flight, hurriedly packed a bag, and headed to DFW Airport.

***

At the hospital Frank sat with David and was brought up to speed on what had happened to his only child. When the nurse came out to the surgery area waiting room and asked, “Who’s waiting for Zimmerman?” ten different people stood, including her boss. “I can only take two back at a time, and it needs to be short visits,” she announced. Lizzie’s boss gestured to Frank and David. “You two first,” he noted.

Frank and David followed the petite blond through the automatic double doors and down a long corridor to post-op Bay One. “Ten minutes,” she told them gently. “I’ll be at the nurse’s station just over there and will come get you when it’s time.”

“Thanks for looking out for my kid,” Frank told her; she smiled at him, patted his shoulder, then stepped out of the room. He walked over to his daughter’s bed, David flanking the other side.

“Hey sweetheart,” Frank said, very gently taking her right hand. “I’m right here, kiddo.”

Lizzie was floating in and out, still reeling from the anesthesia. They'd had to go in and retrieve the second bullet; David had been right, that one wasn't a through-and-through like the round in her shoulder. But a moment of lucidity allowed her to turn her head toward Frank's voice and squeeze his hand before going under again. From the left side of her bed David reached out a massive paw and tenderly stroked her hair. "You got to get well, Zim," he whispered to her. "I don't wanna partner with nobody else." That brought her back around enough to earn him a thumbs up sign from her left hand before she once again slipped into sleep.

In a flash, ten minutes had passed. The blond reappeared promptly and escorted them back out to the waiting area to collect the next two allowed back for a visit. They passed the surgeon who had worked on

Lizzie, and he turned and walked with them back out to the waiting room so he could relay findings one time to all her brothers in blue waiting for news of her condition.

"Shoulder wound was a through-and-through, luckily it missed hitting anything major. The round that went into her arm just above the elbow traveled up her arm a bit; we were able to get it out of there without causing any more damage. She's got some rehab ahead of her to get full use of that arm back, but I see no reason she won't make a full recovery. She's also got a severe concussion, and she's gonna be pretty bruised up for a while since the other rounds hit her vest at close range. All in all, I'd say she got pretty damn lucky," he concluded.

The entire waiting room heaved a collective sigh of relief.

“How long will she be here?” Frank asked.

“Up to a week,” the surgeon said. “I’d rather keep her a day or two longer and make absolutely certain there’s no complications with the wound areas or her concussion rather than turn her loose too soon.”

“Thanks, doc,” Frank shook his hand firmly. “Appreciate it.”

The surgeon walked back through the double doors to go scrub up for his next patient, and the nurse continued cycling police officers through checking on Lizzie. More and more had continued to stop by the hospital on their way to or from their shifts – Lizzie was very well liked among her peers. Frank and David were sitting and making small talk when suddenly David’s entire demeanor shifted and became intimidating.

Frank turned to see what David was staring daggers at, and frowned, starting to rise.

But David was already on his feet, walking with purpose toward Jeff, Lizzie's ex. "You need to leave. Now," David growled.

"I want to see her," Jeff demanded. "I want to know she's okay."

"You forfeited any rights you had regarding Lizzie when you screwed around on her," David warned him in a booming voice. "Now get the hell out."

"You can't keep me from seeing her!" Jeff started to raise his voice.

Frank stepped out from behind David and into Jeff's field of vision. "They may not be able to, but as her next of kin, I sure as hell can," he thundered. Just then the helpful blond came back out into the waiting area.

"Miss?" Frank called her over.

"Yes, Mr. Zimmerman?"

"That man,"- he pointed at Jeff - "is on the no-fly list with regards to my daughter. No visitation, no information. Got it?"

"*I* am her fiancé," Jeff huffed.

"No, you two-timing prick. You *were* her fiancé," Frank bellowed as he got in Jeff's face. Just then Lizzie's boss stepped over. "If I may intercede for a moment?"

Frank glared at him.

"Jeff, it's ironic you're here. Saves the taxpayers the trouble of having to find you to serve you with these," Lizzie's boss stated, and thrust a set of papers at Jeff.

Jeff snatched them, began to read, and looked up in disbelief. "She filed a restraining order on me?"

"She sure as hell did," David confirmed. "You're not too bright, are ya, stalking a cop?" To his boss he said, "Looks to me like someone is in violation of the ‘no closer than two miles’ part of that paperwork, boss.”

“I agree,” came the answer. “We clearly have grounds to take him into custody and book him.”

Jeff retreated slowly with his hands up, but his face contorted with anger. “This isn’t over.”

“Oh yes, it is,” Frank muttered. “Get the hell out.”

Jeff glanced at each of them with hatred before abruptly turning and walking away.

“Never liked that dumbass,” Frank spat out with feeling. “He’s never been good enough for Lizzie.”

The nurse cleared her throat. “Mr. Zimmerman? I will make a note in her chart and in our system that’s he’s not allowed near her. I will also let security know right now. Probably best if they go ahead and escort him off the property altogether, since it's all definitely within a two-mile radius." She winked conspiratorially and smiled before gesturing to two more officers that had arrived to check on their fallen teammate.

David turned to smile at Frank. "That ought to hold him off for a while."

Frank grinned back.

***

By three a.m. Landon had made his way to the hospital. At that point the waiting area had cleared out. He stepped up to the empty check in desk and noticed the instructions next to the phone. He dialed the number shown and waited. His call was answered by Mel, the no-nonsense nurse on overnight shift. "Post-op," she said briskly.

"Elizabeth Zimmerman, please."

"Visiting hours ended at ten p.m., sir."

“I’m sorry. I just… I came from Texas, I got here as quickly as I could…”

“One moment.” A pause, and then he heard the double doors click. “Come on back. Five minutes, no more. I shouldn’t be doing this at all.”

He proceeded through the doors and met Mel at the nurse’s station. “ID please,” she requested, hand out. He handed her his driver’s license, which she checked against the computer screen, then nodded in satisfaction and handed it back to him. “You’re clear. Right this way.” Mel escorted him to Bay One. “I’ll be back to escort you out shortly.”

He stood at the foot of Lizzie’s bed, just gazing for a moment. She looked so peaceful in her sleep and yet so fragile against the swath of bandages covering her entire right arm. He wanted to touch her, hold her, but he knew better. She needed all the rest she could get. Instead he walked around the side of her bed to the little tray table, and left the teddy bear he'd bought her along with the note he'd written on the plane.

Gazing at her face one last time, Landon turned and quietly exited the room. He walked back to Mel. "She's sleeping, I don't want to disturb her. I just… needed to make sure she's okay."

Now Mel softened a bit and gave him a look that let him know she understood completely. "She's gonna be fine, honey. She's tough as they come. And she's in good hands here. Don't you worry."

"Thanks," he said sincerely, letting out a breath he wasn't aware he'd been holding. "Thanks for watching over her. She's… special."

“You’re welcome. Now, you need to go before you get us both in trouble.”

“I understand.” He held out his hand and shook Mel’s. “Thanks again.” And smiled before he walked back out through the double doors.

***

Lizzie was confused. She didn’t know if what she’d seen was a dream or not. Between the anesthesia and the subsequent pain meds, dreams and reality were blurring together seamlessly. She could have sworn Landon had just left her room. *But that’s not right, he’s in the Grand Caymans…isn’t he?...*She spiraled downward again into blissful unawareness.

***

By the following afternoon, Lizzie’s head had begun to clear. She was talking with her doctor when her dad and her partner strolled in. “Hi,” she exclaimed.

“Lizzie! You’re awake! How are you feeling, baby girl?” Frank asked as he moved in to hug her, being careful not to jostle her right arm.

“Well, like I’ve been shot,” she grinned. Then a head nod and a “Hey, Tank,” to David.

“Hey yourself, Zim.”

The surgeon patted her hand. “I’ll make rounds again in the morning, Lizzie.”

“Okay, see you then, Doc,” she replied as he left, then to Frank and David, “Doc says they’re gonna keep me for five or six days.”

“Yeah, we’d heard that last night,” her father answered, pulling a chair close so he could sit and hold Lizzie’s left hand. Then he glanced at her bedside table tray. “Cute bear.”

"What bear?" She craned around to look, then frowned. "Who brought that?"

"No idea," Frank told her. "But it's got a note on it."

"Dad, can you hand me those please?"

He grabbed both and handed them to her. She fumbled the paper open left-handed since it hurt to move her right arm around too much, and in disbelief read the message that had been left for her:

"Lizzie,

I know we agreed to "leave it in the islands", but when I heard you got hurt, I just couldn't. I had to come see for myself that you're going to be okay. Just know you're in my thoughts.

With affection, Landon"

David glanced at it. "Landon? *Oh*. As in, *Tropical* Landon," he stated with a big grin and a knowing wink. Lizzie had glossed over most of her activities while on vacation, but she had finally mentioned Landon by name when her partner pressed as to the reason for the huge smile on her face.

Lizzie flushed bright red. “Yeah. Tropical Landon. How did he ever hear about this? He lives in Texas, for Pete’s sake.”

“Well, the bust made national news, Zim,” David informed her. “Over seventy million in cocaine seized.”

“Who the hell is Landon?” Frank was genuinely confused.

“Someone I met in Grand Caymans who was also on vacation, Daddy,” Lizzie answered, now blushing so hard even her ears were a bright red. “He was very nice, and we had a nice time together, but I don’t want to get involved with anyone for a long, long time after what Jeff pulled, and I told Landon that. So, when we parted ways at

DFW Airport that was supposed to be the end of it. I guess he saw the news about this, assumed it was me – Did they mention my name?”

“They did,” David nodded.

“Okay, so, he saw the news and flew all the way up here to come into my room and leave a bear and a note. Which means I really did see him leave my room at some point last night, I didn’t dream that. Does that strike anyone else as strange? You’d think if he came all this way, he’d at least stick around to come see me when I’m more coherent.”

“Who said I didn’t?” Landon asked her from the doorway, a bouquet of flowers in his hand.

Lizzie’s mouth hung open. Frank and David looked at her, then at Landon, then at each other. “Um. Yeah. We’re gonna go get some coffee, sweetheart. Unless you need us to stay?” Frank looked at his daughter with a raised eyebrow.

“No, Daddy, it’s all right, I’ll be fine. Go ahead and get some coffee, okay?”

“Sure thing, sweetheart.” And Frank made it a point to be extremely obvious that he was sizing up the man bringing his daughter flowers as he walked past Landon and into the hall. Once it was just the two of them, Landon stepped forward uncertainly.

“I know you’re probably pissed at me…” he began.

“I actually am, a little,” she told him honestly. “What are you doing here?”

“Lizzie, I had every intention of honoring your request. Truly I did. I wasn’t happy about it; I’ll admit that. But it was what you wanted, so I was willing to abide by it. Then I turn on the news and find out that Detective

Elizabeth Zimmerman was seriously wounded during a multi-million-dollar cocaine raid. And the only thing I could think about was getting to your side as fast as I could, to make sure you were okay."

Now he sighed, running his hand through his hair. She saw the worry in his eyes, and it touched her. But she couldn't let that sway her.

"Landon," she said quietly. "You have to know what we had in the Caymans meant a lot to me. It really did. But I just can't do this right now. I am dealing with my ex; he's stalking me. To the point I had to file a restraining order pretty much as soon as I got back. Then, not even a full week back to work, and this happens," she gestured to her right arm. "I care about you, Landon, and I don't want to hurt you. But if you're here to try to continue something between us, the answer right now is no. I need to get my life back in order right now."

In response, he silently went to her side table, laid down the flowers, then turned to her, holding out one of his business cards. She reached up gingerly and took it with her left hand.

"Elizabeth Zimmerman, you're who I want. You take as long as you need to. I'll wait, and I won't pressure you. When you're ready, give me a call." He leaned down, kissed her gently, and walked toward the door, looking back at her long enough to say, "Please take care of yourself, Lizzie. You're irreplaceable," before he left the room.

As he strode down the hall, he noticed Frank and David coming toward him. He nodded in friendly acknowledgement and continued toward the elevator. "He didn't look very happy," David mused as they walked the remaining distance to Lizzie's room. Then, "Zim! What's wrong?" as they saw tears streaming down her cheeks.

CHAPTER EIGHT

"Come on, Lizzie, give me five extra ones," the physical therapist challenged. "You can do this."

Lizzie grunted with effort and completed five more push-ups, then rolled onto her back, panting but satisfied with herself. It had been almost twelve weeks since the raid, and she'd busted her ass to get to the point where she could pass the rigorous physical exam that would lead back to full unrestricted duty. Today was the trial run. Tomorrow would be the real thing.

"Nice work, girl," Theresa, the therapist told her. "I think you're gonna do fine tomorrow."

"Here's hoping, Theresa," she confided. "I am so ready to not be riding a desk anymore."

***

Maybe I should retire completely once this hobby list is done, the Raven found himself thinking. *It's not like I need the money.* He'd considered it before, never seriously. But he found as he mulled it over that the idea held more and more appeal. *Besides, best to leave a game while you're winning it.* That much was true. He'd had an amazingly long run of very successful missions as a professional assassin, with zero threat so far of being caught. But he also knew that one day, someday, his luck would turn. Eventually, every mountain was replaced with a valley. It was just a question of when. A Kenny Rogers song his old man used to play continually crept into his head…What was it called? *Oh, yeah*, he remembered, chuckling*. "The Gambler". Fitting.*

He'd begun to think about walking away from it all more and more lately. *Something to think about, for sure*, the Raven told himself as he worked the lockpick. *Just not right this minute. Focus.* He pulled out of his reverie and back into the task at hand, which was to sabotage all the appliances in the home of one Robert McDaniels, formerly of Fort Worth, currently residing in Decatur, Texas. A gas leak had been preselected as the weapon of choice this time.

Luckily, the dilapidated old farmhouse was seven miles north of town on FM 730, and the closest neighbor was over a half-mile away, so the Raven had zero concerns about being seen much less questioned, and no chance of any collateral damage. He put the finishing touches on his work, left the calling card that always accompanied a hobby kill among the sea of takeout containers and beer in the very old and sturdily built fridge. The last step was to very carefully rig the living room's light fixture to make sure the escaping gas would ignite as desired. Then he pulled the front door closed behind him and returned to his vehicle.

He'd noticed on the drive out that a side road had veered off at a forty-five-degree angle not far from here. He decided to backtrack and see where it led and was immensely pleased with the result. The little gravel side road snaked and curved and eventually came out onto a plateau of sorts. From this vantage point, the house he'd just been in could be seen clearly about half a mile straight down the hill and across FM 730.

"And now, we wait," he murmured, as night began to creep in. His patience was rewarded after three hours, when he noticed the bouncing headlights of a Jeep pulling into the drive. Adjusting his infra-red binoculars, he could clearly see his target stumble profusely as he managed to exit his vehicle and saunter in a drunken slant toward his front door. "Wow, he's plowed," the Raven noted with a chuckle. "I'm amazed he was even able to make the drive home."

He watched in anticipation as Robert staggered up the front porch steps, swaying heavily, attempting multiple times to place the key into the lock. Finally, he was successful in opening the door and lurched inside the pitch-black residence.

The Raven quickly pulled his binoculars away from his eyes. He wouldn't need them for this next part. And just in time, too, as his quarry flipped on the living room light and the entire house down the hillside and across from his position blew upward and outward in a large orange fireball. He stayed for a few minutes, watching the smoke from the blaze curl up like a contented cat against the star-filled sky, before his return trip to town.

***

"Hey, Zim," David began when she opened her door the following afternoon. "You ready?"

"Ready for what?"

"To go celebrate kicking ass today, of course! I knew you would. Come on, let's go grab some steaks. My treat."

"Well, since you put it that way…" Lizzie laughed. "Let me get changed right quick."

She got out of her sweats and into jeans and her Seattle Police Academy t-shirt, finishing off the look with boots and her lightweight leather jacket. "Let's go," she said as she came down the stairs and grabbed her purse and keys. They laughed and talked all the way to the steakhouse that they'd agreed long ago was the best around.

They got settled into a booth and once they'd ordered – Lizzie did her usual, which was well done filet mignon, with lobster mac & cheese and sautéed mushrooms – their waiter brought their drinks and warm sourdough bread to the table. David lifted his glass and toasted. "To my partner Zim, who always has my back. I am so glad you're back, SWG. It just ain't been the same with you on desk duty."

They clinked glasses and drank.

"I know what you mean, Tank," she shook her head. "It's been brutal only being allowed to partially be a cop. I know that probably sounds weird, but…"

"I feel you, no need to explain, Zim."

They talked as they spread butter liberally over warm bread slices.

"So, you know, me and Renee have been dating a long time now," he pointed out.

"I know. David, when are you gonna quit dragging your feet and propose to that girl? She's perfect for you."

The big man sighed. "Yeah. She is. I was actually thinking about doing just that come Christmas time."

"Why wait until then?"

He shrugged. "I don't know. Part of it is, I haven't found the right ring. You wouldn't be willing to help me pick one out, would you?"

"Sure, I can help with that, Tank. Happy to, you know that."

"Yeah. Thanks." Abruptly, he changed topic. "When you gonna move on that nice guy down in Texas?"

"What?"

"You heard me, Zim. Man traveled over 2,000 miles just to come see your skinny butt in the hospital bed. That tells me you're more important to him than you realize."

Lizzie frowned and toyed with her water glass. "It's complicated."

David laughed. "No, it ain't, Zim. You're *making* it complicated."

"Come on, Tank. He's there, I'm here. That alone makes it complicated."

He held up his hands in surrender. "All right then."

Her awkwardness was relieved by the presentation of their orders, but only for a moment.

"Zim," he began, then took a bite of the porterhouse he'd ordered and stopped talking, eyes closed.

"Good?"

"Aw, man. Not just good. Great," he grinned. "Now, where was I?"

Lizzie laughed. "No clue, you didn't make it past 'Zim', remember?"

"Oh, yeah. Zim, I will just say this and then I will let it go." Her eyebrow raised but she remained silent and let him talk. "Sometimes you gotta get out of your comfort zone and be open to new stuff. I mean, you're obviously into each other. And I have known you for years, Zim, and you ain't never had as big a smile as when you came back from that beach. So maybe at some point, you know, just feel it out, see where it goes. Just sayin," he finished, then took a big bite of his baked potato.

She cut off another piece of her steak, scooped up some lobster mac to accompany it, and chewed thoughtfully. "Maybe down the road," Lizzie told him. "Not never. Just, not right now." She didn't tell her partner that she had tucked Landon's card in her wallet and carried it with her everywhere. She'd even pulled it out and reached for the phone a couple of times lately; she just hadn't ever followed through. Even though her idiot ex had finally backed off, she just wasn't ready to open that door.

***

The topic of Lizzie and David's conversation was also having dinner with colleagues and was trying his best to stay engaged in the lively talk happening within his group. But as always, Landon's mind gravitated back toward her, and he wondered just how long it would take before she called him – if ever. Reluctantly, he pushed thoughts of Lizzie to the side and retrained his focus on the people sitting around him.

***

Summer gave way to fall, and for the most part, Lizzie's life had settled down. She'd helped David find the perfect ring, and he'd been so excited he'd proposed at the Labor Day picnic they had all gathered at. Renee had burst into happy tears and accepted immediately, and, almost as quickly, shocked and surprised Lizzie by asking her to be a bridesmaid. After some discussion, David and Renee set the date for Sunday December fifth, a mere three months out. So now after shifts Lizzie found herself talking about dress, shoes, bouquet and color scheme choices; it was foreign to her – she wasn't much of a 'girly girl' – but she found she enjoyed it immensely, and Renee's excitement was contagious.

She was flipping through the Seattle Times one day and an announcement she had only half expected to ever see caught her eye. Jeff and Jessica had evidently gotten married in Barbados. Lizzie pondered it for a long moment, took in the fact that she felt nothing whatsoever, and casually moved on to the next page.

***

Ramon Garcia adjusted his belt and rolled his shoulders to ward off stiffness and keep himself awake. He absolutely hated working nights as a security guard, but it paid the bills. Due to a rampant increase of thefts of copper recently, local businesses had taken to hiring the company he worked for at a record pace. Even the local schools' athletic complexes were targets; he'd seen on the TV not three nights ago where thieves had struck in a neighboring county and left a high school stadium completely in the dark. Anywhere copper wiring could be found, there was a risk of someone looking for an easy payout. And due to the rising price copper was fetching, the criminal element was becoming increasingly bold.

He checked his watch. Time to make another circuit. Heaving a sigh, he climbed out of his truck, turned on his flashlight, and proceeded to once again walk the perimeter of tonight's assigned location. He hated the dark, always had. He hated it even more because they wouldn't allow him to carry a firearm, only a baton – *And what good is that?* He asked himself again – and a taser.

Sighing, he continued his route, sweeping his light's beam back and forth, back and forth. Then he saw it. A rather robust set of cables, all severed neatly in two when they shouldn't be. That was alarming enough. Even more alarming was the fact that the cables had been intact on his last circuit not an hour before. Moving closer, Ramon was able to clearly see that a large length of copper wiring was missing. He swore softly as he reached down toward his waistline for his radio, and realized he'd left it behind in his truck. He'd have to go get it. It would mean his job if he didn't call this in immediately. He turned away from the vandalized cables to go retrieve the most important piece of equipment in his arsenal.

Ramon shuffled along nervously, listening intently as he went. He was convinced someone else was still walking around here besides him; he could feel it. He stopped suddenly, moving his flashlight rapidly around him as he checked his surroundings. Nothing.

"Dude. Quit being stupid, they are long gone, there's no one here but you. Get it together," he muttered to himself as he rounded the last corner that led back to his truck. His flashlight hit the ground and he followed, wordlessly, eyes wide and staring, from the three rounds fired through a silencer that hit him in the heart and killed him before his body hit the dirt.

She moved over to him, tucked the bowtie candy wrapper in his front pants pocket, and melted into the darkness. Two blocks over she got into her car, turned the key, and drove into the night, pulling off the brunette wig and tossing it into the back seat as she went. At a stoplight she pulled out the notebook and marked off Ramon Garcia as completed.

***

The Raven poured himself a whiskey and logged into the fishing site; he'd received notification of two new messages. Wading through the code on each revealed one contract offer to take place in Tucson,

Arizona, and another down in Chile. He drank while he contemplated. The Tucson job had the tighter timeframe, so he scheduled it first. The Chile scenario was more open-ended, pretty much at his discretion. He cross checked against the hobby list to see where things stood on that piece. Which reminded him, he needed to update that. He fired off a quick text containing a statement and question, got a terse update and a combative reply. Ears back, he sent another message, this time strongly worded that would make it clear to the recipient his directive was not up for debate. After a long wait, a petulant sounding answer confirmed he'd get his way. He nodded his approval, then set his cell phone aside and resumed planning the next two contract jobs as well as the hobby-related New York trip.

***

There's been another one, Frank realized. He dutifully did his research, then added another name to his Excel spreadsheet. He was up to five now. Logic told him to start digging on the rest, see where they were in the world – if they were still living at all, that is. And it wouldn't be easy; some of them had very common names. It would take time. But he knew in his gut he was on to something big. No matter how long it took, he had no choice but to try.

He really wanted to be able to talk this out with someone, but he didn't feel right sharing it yet, either. *I mean, what do I really have right now? No proof, that's for sure. Just suppositions at this point.*

His train of thought was disrupted by sneezing violently several times. Freaking cedar count had been through the roof lately. He grabbed his bottle of over-the-counter allergy medicine, took a big swig. It was taking more and more of that stuff to keep his allergies down to a dull roar. Or so he thought. If Frank had been more honest with himself, he would have realized that the ever-increasing alcohol consumption wasn't helping things, either.

He glanced at his watch. *Dammit. Gotta be on in two hours*. He reluctantly saved the file additions and left everything out on the table until next time.

***

Just as he'd planned, the Raven was in place precisely at midnight waiting for his victim to arrive home so the contract could be fulfilled. His client had been very specific about this contract; the atrocities that had landed this person in the Raven's crosshairs were vile, to say the least. Although he'd never tell a client as much, the Raven was so disgusted by this target's line of work that he'd have gladly taken him out for free. Now he checked his watch and waited. He'd been told that the monster hiding in plain sight in Tucson was extremely anal retentive regarding his daily routine, arriving home promptly at twelve-thirty a.m. like clockwork.

Twelve-thirty came and went, and the Raven grew restless. He had no intention of walking away, however. This needed to happen whether he was getting paid or not. He whiled away his time mentally setting the stage for the New York event. Selma Frazier wasn't supposed to be in New York. All the research indicated she'd rarely traveled more than an hour from Fort Worth, Texas her entire life, so the fact she'd left had surprised Raven a great deal, and as soon as tonight was over, he'd dig deeper and find out why.

At one-thirty, a very tired businessman came rolling down the street and pulled into his drive. The flat tire he'd had to change had soured the jubilant mood he'd been in after closing a deal that would expand his child porn distribution lines all the way to Brazil. He threw the car into park, turned his head and reached over to the passenger seat to grab his briefcase so he could review the finer points of what had been agreed upon. Suddenly his dome light came on, and before he could question why, he felt a rough hand tangled in his hair and pulling backward sharply, then a searing line of pain deep across his exposed throat. Blood gushed forward, coating his chest, his hands, the steering wheel. He tried to speak but could only gurgle, wide-eyed and completely confused, until his world faded to black.

***

"Hello?"

"Hey, gorgeous. What's up?"

"Hey!" Donny smiled. "I was just thinking about you. Where are you?"

"At home. I just finished up a shift," she said, sighing. "I'm actually about to turn in for the night, it's been a really long day. I just wanted to hear your voice."

"I meant to ask you what your plans are for Thanksgiving," he told her. "I'd love to spend mine with you. Only question is, up here, or down there?"

"I can come up," she offered quickly. "It's more festive up in Vail with the snow and all. And I'd really like that, to be with you on Thanksgiving."

"It's settled, then," he announced, and she could hear the smile in his voice. "Can't wait."

"So, let me call you in a couple of days, and get the timeline ironed out, okay?"

"Sure," Donny answered. "You sound tired, so, I'll talk to you later?"

"Yep. Night."

"Night, sweet dreams," and he hung up.

She smiled. Her list and timetables getting rearranged without her consent had turned out to be a good thing. Now she could spend more time with Donny.

***

Thanksgiving 2010 was less than two weeks away, and Landon Kendal had no one to spend it with. He sighed, swirling his whiskey as he stared into the fireplace. He knew exactly who and what he wanted. But he'd already told Lizzie he would wait and wouldn't push, and he meant it. Keeping his word on that score was slowly killing him, but he meant it.

Beth, his secretary, had sensed his melancholy mood lately, and made it a point to invite him over to her house during the upcoming holidays to eat with her and her husband and kids. Landon appreciated the offer, but didn't want to impose, so he told her he was planning a short getaway trip. And his little sister Samantha was in her own little world lately; he doubted he'd get to spend time with her before New Year's Day got here.

He was ashamed he knew it so readily, but it had been exactly 207 days since he'd walked out of Lizzie's hospital room, hoping to hear from her. Every single time his phone rang, his heart leapt, just knowing it was her. And every single time, it broke a little bit more because it wasn't. Every night his dreams took him back to the Caymans, where they'd laughed and loved and been happy together. Landon downed his drink, hoping to shut out his sudden realization she was never going to call. She'd made her choices, and they obviously didn't include him.

He got up, strode to his bar and made himself a double this time.

***

Donny was slightly confused once they'd ended the call. She didn't seem to want him to come down to her place in Texas at all. He'd mentioned it several times now, and it sure seemed like she was quick to either deflect or offer to come to him instead. But he wanted to visit her world for a change. He wanted to see where she lived, what her day-to-day was like, get to know her hometown, her friends, her family. He paced, thinking. Why would she be resistant to his coming to see her for a change?

She'd always been very guarded about her past. Now that he thought about it, she'd never really shared much detail about herself or her life at all. And a nagging thought crept in. No good reason she should do that… unless she had something – or someone – to hide…He stopped mid-stride. *What if she was involved with someone else? Jesus – What if she was already married to someone else?* Now he sat, absorbing the theory, becoming increasingly uncomfortable with the implications.

***

Lizzie finally gave up and put down her book. She'd reread the last two pages several times and hadn't retained any of it. Her mind kept drifting south to Texas and a man named Landon that had gotten on a plane at a moment's notice to check on her. She sighed.

She went to her purse, pulled his card out of her wallet, and stared at it, as she had a hundred times before. She reached for her phone, then hesitated. "This is pointless," she muttered to herself. "What are you doing, Liz?"

He had said straight out that he wouldn't press her, but some part of her had been hoping he'd break his promise and reach out first anyway. Especially since there seemed to be a deeper connection formed than just an island fling. Right? Why else would he have rushed to her side the way he did back in May? No contact since then. And she wondered if she'd waited too long now to make contact.

Only one way to find out.

She drew in a deep breath, punched in his number, then hit send. It rang once… twice… then Lizzie's nerve failed her, and she disconnected, throwing her phone onto the couch in frustration at her cowardice.

***

Landon raced across his room to catch the call, but his cell stopped ringing before he got to it. He unlocked the screen and scrolled to missed calls. The last inbound call, time stamped two minutes past one a.m. CST, was from a number he did not recognize. He pondered for a moment, then called it back and waited as the phone rang.

***

Lizzie's phone buzzed loudly on her couch cushion and made her jump. She looked at her phone. *It's him*, she thought in a panic. *What do I do?*

Duh, be a normal person and answer the freaking thing, she answered herself. She took a deep breath to calm her nerves.

"Hello?" she said tentatively.

A long silence on the other end. Then, "Lizzie?" in an incredulous voice.

"Hi, Landon," she replied softly.

CHAPTER NINE

Two days after Thanksgiving, and her daughter's condition wasn't improving. Selma Frazier wrapped herself up warmly for the trek to the subway for her daily visit to see Louisa in the hospital. She shivered at the mere thought of being out in this weather today. But she loved her daughter fiercely, so she would brave both the temperatures and the crowds to do right by her. She tucked Louisa's apartment key safely into the purse she wore cross-body to ward off any purse-snatchers, then pulled on her gloves and headed downstairs.

The tall buildings on either side of her funneled the wind so that it whipped down the street like unruly children. It almost took her breath away. She tucked her chin, shoved hands into warm pockets, and trudged the three blocks to the nearest entrance to the subway platform. Behind her the Raven fell in, maintaining a casual distance.

Selma descended the stairs and passed through the first turnstile, then turned right and kept moving toward the platform. She glanced at her watch. The train she needed would be along in roughly three minutes, not long to wait at all. Selma was grateful for that. She hated crowds, had feared them all her life. She always felt like she couldn't breathe when surrounded by more than a few people. Coming down below the ground and squeezing into cars packed with strangers every day was almost panic attack inducing. To cope, she always closed her eyes and said a small prayer as she waited every morning. And this morning was no exception.

Silently the Raven worked his way through the throng so that he stood just behind and to the left of her, close enough to hear her morning supplication as he slipped the token left at every hobby kill into her coat pocket. The train could be heard as it approached, its progress along the electrified track reverberating through the narrow subway tube to announce its impending arrival. The crowd swelled to the edge of the platform in anticipation, a sea of humanity all trying to be first in line, and the Raven found it so very simple to let the wave roll forward through him and imperceptibly push her over the edge to the tracks below.

Selma's scream was swallowed by the train horn and the high squeak of braking as the conductor tried vainly to stop in time. As the crowd that had pressed forward now surged backward in horror, the Raven again let the flow carry him away from the site of her fall. He blended into the retreating crowd and was back up at street level and walking away before Transit Police arrived on scene.

***

Bella Thomas stretched luxuriously, then eased herself off the couch, padding down the hallway to see what Nathan was up to. "Hey hon," she called out.

"In here," came the reply from the kitchen.

She yawned as she moved past his seat at the table to get a mug out of the cabinet.

Nathan looked up from his laptop and smiled at his wife. "Good nap?" he asked as he stood and moved to take her in his arms.

"The best," she replied, almost in a purr. With a little over four months to go until the baby arrived, she'd begun taking little naps whenever her class schedule allowed.

He laughed and kissed her forehead, then started to lean in and taste her lips when the doorbell rang.

"Are you expecting anyone?" she asked him.

"Nope," he said.

Since Mikel Metzger had fled the country things had lessened in intensity but only by the slimmest of margins. Nathan knew in his gut that it wasn't a question of *if* the psychopath obsessed with Bella would return, but *when*. He quietly moved to the door and peeked through the viewfinder they'd installed, his service weapon drawn and ready.

Then he relaxed. "It's Max," he called to Bella. He opened the door for Bella's godfather.

Max Jones's eyes twinkled. "You two have a minute? I've got some news you are going to want to hear."

***

It was four days until the wedding, and Lizzie found herself caught in an increasing flurry of activity between work and being a bridesmaid. She'd stood in the gap Thanksgiving Day so that a co-worker with family could have the time off. She didn't mind one bit. Her dad was working the holiday too anyway, and Lizzie honestly preferred working to dealing with her mother.

As she moved laundry from the washer to the dryer before leaving for her next shift, she reflected again on her first conversation with Landon in months. After the initial awkward silence, they'd both started to speak at once. He had laughed. “We did it again,” he pointed out. “You first.”

She had filled him in on the events of her life since April, and he brought her up to speed as well. Small talk complete, there was a meaningful pause, then Landon said, “Lizzie, I really want to see you. Would it be all right if I come up at some point?” She had stood in her living room and done a silly little happy dance before solemnly replying, “Yes, I'd like that.”

He'd mentioned coming up for Thanksgiving, but she had already committed to covering the rotation. They talked some more about it, and before the conversation ended, they had ironed out details. Landon would be Lizzie's ‘plus one’ to David and Renee's wedding on December fifth, and was flying in Thursday night – *tomorrow night*, Lizzie realized.

Better get a move on getting this place presentable, she thought to herself. Luckily there wasn't much left to do.

She still had not been able to bring herself to walk back into the main bedroom. The door she'd closed firmly all those months ago after retrieving her belongings had stayed shut. Lizzie sighed, frustrated with herself. She felt foolish about it, but she just couldn't get past it. And she honestly didn't know if she ever would.

***

She'd come up to Donny's place, as they'd agreed, and they'd spent the entire Thanksgiving week together. Then she'd returned to Texas. And the nagging question that had vacated Donny's mind when she was beside him returned in spades once she left. Donny found himself more and more unsettled by her seeming unwillingness to let him further into her life. He wasn't sure what to do about it. He wanted to respect her privacy. But he also was beginning to realize this one-way avenue couldn't continue for long.

Maybe we need to have a talk about this the next time we're together, he mused. *Maybe if I share first about my life, she will do the same. If she doesn't run screaming, that is.*

***

Lizzie finished her shift on time, which was not common at all, and headed to the airport. Landon's plane was due to land around seven forty-five p.m. Glancing at the clock glowing in her dashboard, she calculated she'd arrive at the baggage claim area with about ten minutes to spare if traffic held. And she realized her palms were sweaty. Which was also not common at all.

It was a point of pride for Lizzie Zimmerman that not much at all rattled her nerves, so feeling this way was out of character.

She turned in to the multi-level garage, following signs for arrival pickups, and found a one-hour spot close to the terminal entry. Locking her car, she strolled across and entered, then looked at the arrivals monitor. "Alaska Airlines flight 667, coming in at gate B-nine," she noted, then proceeded to the corresponding baggage carousel and settled in to wait; as she'd predicted, she had a few minutes to kill before his plane even landed, much less unloaded.

To pass the time she pulled out her phone, scrolled through emails, then aimlessly surfed until she heard the 'ping' of an incoming text message. Switching over to her texting app, she smiled as she read what he'd sent: *We're here, beginning to work toward getting off this thing – Landon.* She texted back *I'm in baggage claim area, see you soon!* then tucked her phone into her pocket and began watching for his approach. After several minutes, she spotted him as he came through the security exit and into baggage claim, his focus sweeping left then right, and he smiled when he saw her.

Willing her heart to stop skipping beats, she tried her best to look nonchalant as she strolled toward him. "Hi," she said.

"Hi," Landon returned, his eyes never leaving her face. He gazed at her silently for a long moment, then closed the distance, cupping her face in his hands and kissing her tenderly before wrapping her in a tight embrace. He realized he'd missed having her in his arms even more than he thought. The carousel beginning to turn and bring forth bags from his flight finally got their attention, and he released her but took her hand as they wandered closer to the mechanism to retrieve his luggage.

"I've missed you, Lizzie," he announced solemnly, squeezing her hand as they waited for his bag to appear.

"You know what? I've missed you too," she told him, squeezing his hand in return.

"Ah, there's mine," he pointed, and stepped forward to pull his suitcase off the merry-go-round. "Shall we?"

"You hungry?" Lizzie asked as they made their way to her car.

"I could eat," he replied with a grin.

"Burgers? Italian? What sounds good?"

"Know any good places for a steak?"

"I know just the place," Lizzie answered. "You'll love it."

Half an hour later they were in a booth at Lizzie's favorite steakhouse. As was her custom she opted for the filet, lobster mac and mushrooms. Landon raised his eyebrows and told the waiter, "That sounds really good, make that two please." As they dove into the warm bread brought to them, Landon raised his glass and said to her, "Here's to celebrating."

"Celebrating what?" she asked.

"The phone call I really wanted to get and thought I never would."

She smiled and clinked her glass against his. "Sorry it took me so long."

"Yeah, what was that about, anyway, making me wait like that?" he teased.

Lizzie laughed.

***

Frank was working his puzzle again. Another death that, to him, just didn't seem coincidental – that made six now that he had discovered as he continued to dig. He'd found two more apart from that one but those were years ago; one from cancer, the other a victim of a drunk driver. His gut told him those two weren't a part of what he was currently chasing, so while he listed those two, he noted in his weird shorthand his inclinations about them as well.

More than ever, he felt the need to share his suspicions with someone, but he felt no one except maybe Joe or Lizzie would listen and take him seriously. And even if they did – how in the hell to gather case files, most closed, of multiple deaths all over the damn place? Even when he was a detective, he'd have been hard pressed to pull off getting access to them all since multiple jurisdictions were involved. Now he was just a beat cop, and the chances had dropped from slim to none.

***

Nathan sat snuggled up to his bride and relished the moments of hearing her laugh as they watched a comedy on television. He had not realized how much strain she had been under until Max dropped in to visit. She'd kept it hidden from him – *didn't want me distracted while I was trying to catch him. So, she just suffered alone,* he mused.

The look of relief that had washed over Bella's face when Max told them Mikel Metzger was dead spoke volumes. Since then she'd been able to let go of a lot of what had haunted her; no more nightmares about her ordeal that wrenched her from sleep screaming and sobbing. She was on her way back to her usual free-spirited and happy self.

And Nathan pulled her closer, kissed her hair, closed his eyes, and was grateful.

***

Dinner over, Lizzie and Landon wound their way through the Seattle night back to her house. He followed her in, looking around. “Nice place,” he said.

“Thanks,” Lizzie responded. “Would you like a drink?”

“Sure, whatever you have,” Landon answered, setting down his suitcase just inside the living room doorway.

Lizzie poured two whiskeys, handed him one, and they settled side by side on the couch.

“So, I remember you told me about what happened with your ex,” he began. “Is it hard, staying here?”

"Yes," she admitted aloud for the first time, and sighed. "To be honest, I haven't even been back in the master bedroom since then. I went in long enough to grab all my stuff and moved into the guest room." Her gaze wandered up the staircase where the room in question's door could be easily seen from her vantage point. She took a drink, then continued, "I know that probably sounds really dumb. But I just can't make myself go back in there. Not yet, at least."

Landon shook his head. "It's not dumb at all, Lizzie. It's human nature. When someone experiences a traumatic event, they usually have difficulty returning to the place it happened."

"I know," she replied, running a hand through her hair. "I still feel stupid about it. It's just a room, for God's sake."

"Anything I can do to help with that?"

"Like what?"

"While I am here, I could go in, strip the bed, get rid of the sheets for you. Things like that – if you want."

Lizzie pondered it.

"Think about it and let me know."

"I will. Thanks, Landon," Lizzie told him as she laid her head on his shoulder.

They sat in companionable silence for a while.

"How's your import business going?"

He grinned. "Really well, actually. After this trip, I'm on and off a plane for the next three weeks traveling through Europe and South America. If it all goes like I hope it does, you might be sitting next to the sole U.S. importer of a few really cool things soon."

"Exclusivity? Nice."

“I know, right? The import world can be very cutthroat, but I’ve worked hard to always under-promise and over-deliver, and it’s paying off. I’ve got a strong reputation built up in the industry now, and it’s opening a bunch of doors.”

“Landon, that’s great! And you really sound excited about it. It’s awesome you have a work life that you’re so passionate about. Not many people get the chance to do something for a living that they love.”

He sighed happily. “Yeah. I know. I feel very fortunate.” Setting his glass on the coffee table, he adjusted his position to face her, and took her hand.

“So now, I guess, the big question,” he changed topic, looking at her. “What is this” – he gestured between the two of them - “and where is it going? I know it might be a bit complicated, since your life is here, and mine is based 2,000 miles away in Texas. Still, I think it's worth taking a shot and seeing where this goes." He paused and squeezed her hand. "But I need to know how you feel about it all, Lizzie. How you feel about me."

She took a long drink, and for Landon, time seemed to stop completely as he waited – and wondered- what her response was going to be.

Finally, she spoke.

"Landon, I have thought about you – about what happened between us – for months now. And I think there's something good there. Something warm, and positive. I don't see how we're going to do it being so far apart like we are. It's a logistical nightmare. We won't have all the little things that other couples do together that help them grow. Like waking up together on a regular basis. Even silly, small stuff like going grocery shopping together so you know what kind of jelly I like, and I know what kind of cereal you like. We can't do any of that in a long-distance relationship."

She took a breath. "But, I still wanna give this a try. That's what took me so long to call you. I was trying to apply logic to it all, and sometimes…" she shrugged.

"Sometimes, you just can't," he finished, and she nodded in agreement. "But Lizzie, if you want to try, and I want to try, I think we owe it to ourselves to see what happens." Now he leaned in and kissed her tenderly. "And we will figure it out together as we go."

***

The day of David and Renee's wedding had arrived. Lizzie and Landon arrived an hour early since she was not only a member of the wedding party, but also wanted to check on David.

She went to the bridal quarters first, to see and hug Renee, who looked positively radiant in her long flowing wedding gown. Then Lizzie traveled down the foyer and tapped on the door where David and his best man were in holding. David opened the door, saw her, and grinned. “Hey Zim, come on in!”

She entered and her eyebrows raised. She honestly could not recall ever seeing David in formal attire before. He wore it well. “Tank, you look amazing! Nice threads.” His grin turned into a megawatt smile.

“Aw, thanks, Zim. Got to look sharp for Renee.”

“Well, you nailed it, Tank.”

He scooped her into a big bear hug. She patted his back then smiled as he turned her loose, still beaming.

"You nervous?"

"Nope," David said immediately. "I am a hundred percent in love with Renee. I'm not nervous, I'm excited. How much time we got?"

Lizzie checked her watch. "About a half-hour. I will see you out there, okay?"

"You got it."

Lizzie stepped back into the hallway and retraced her footsteps to the main foyer, where Landon was tending to some emails. "Almost time for me to find a seat, I guess," he remarked.

"Probably," she nodded. "I'm sorry we don't get to sit together during the ceremony."

"No worries," Landon replied. "Besides, you're a vision in that dress."

Lizzie blushed slightly as she glanced down at the floor-length Windsor blue tulle with delicate lace sleeves. "Thanks."

"See you afterward?"

"Yep," she confirmed. "I will meet you right back here once the ceremony is done, and we'll head to the reception hall."

"I'm holding you to that," Landon told her, before kissing her gently and making his way into the chapel. Smiling, she turned and retreated to the bride's room. It was only about ten minutes later that the wedding coordinator appeared, sweeping elegantly into view. "It's time," she announced with a big smile.

Renee smiled back. "I'm ready. Let's do this!"

Lizzie and Carla, Renee's sister and matron of honor, helped Renee with her train as she maneuvered out into the hallway. The coordinator allowed the photographer a couple of very quick shots before pairing off the groomsman with Lizzie and the best man with Carla. Renee calmly placed her hand on her father's arm and gave him a quick peck on the cheek; his eyes were already brimming with emotion. Through the closed doors they could hear the swell of music that announced the ceremony was ready to begin. The coordinator nodded at the ushers, who swung the doors wide, and the pastor's voice could be heard clearly as he instructed those in attendance to please rise.

Lizzie and Chuck, David's youngest brother, walked slowly down into their positions at the front, followed in short order by Carla and Stephan, David's older brother. Carla's adorable four-year-old son Joshua arrived at the front with his pillow bearing the rings and stole the show in the process with his equally adorable tiny tuxedo.

Lizzie glanced at David's face as Renee and her father began to walk into the chapel; he was smiling, and his eyes were welling up with joy as he watched the love of his life come toward him. Renee's father escorted her to David, kissed her gently on the cheek, then took her hand and put it into David's. With everyone in place, the ceremony was underway. Lizzie glanced out into the audience, met Landon's unwavering gaze, and her heart fluttered in her chest. Blushing slightly, she returned her attention to those she was standing beside.

Twenty minutes later, with hardly a dry eye in the house, they were pronounced husband and wife, and David finally got to kiss his beautiful bride. The chapel erupted in applause as they proceeded back down the aisle hand in hand, followed by their wedding party. As promised, Lizzie met Landon in the same spot in the foyer as before to head to the reception.

"Shall we?" he asked, offering his arm.

Lizzie tucked her arm through his. "Lead the way."

CHAPTER TEN

Christmastime tends to mostly bring out the best in people – cheerful music, colorful lights, gaily wrapped gifts, a spirit of goodwill to all. Then again, most people don't work in the police or fire department, an emergency room, or ambulance service. Those people usually have a front-row seat for the outright insanity that also tends to peak during any major holiday season.

Christmas 2010 was turning out to be no different. In the roughly three weeks since David and Renee's wedding, Lizzie had logged an insane number of hours. The past twelve alone had been filled with festive scenes, like a shopper who'd been trampled to death by those around her desperate to possess one of the few remaining "Zhu Zhu Pets" available in the entire state of Washington. Or the drunken Santa who'd stumbled out into traffic and been hit and killed by a speeding motorist that barely braked and certainly didn't bother to stop.

Or the shopkeeper beaten within an inch of his life for the twenty-seven dollars and forty-two cents in his cash register. The store had mostly credit card sales all day, it turned out, and Lizzie assumed that realization sent the robber into a fury. He'd done quite a number on the frail old man, who had been rushed to the hospital in critical condition. She made a mental note to call and check on the victim's status. But first, she needed to clean up – she had blood on her pants and shoes. Lizzie stripped off her clothes, looking at how much blood there was. *Damn. No salvaging these*. Sighing, she shrugged and threw the pants and shoes in the trash can, then climbed into the shower, letting the hot water wash away the layer of grime and despair the day had brought her.

***

FBI Agent Nathan Thomas's workload was light by comparison. Mainly it was the odd cold case that occupied his time. Not that he minded. After the past year he and Bella had experienced, with all its grief and danger, he was perfectly okay with quiet and normal for a while. He left his office at the BAU at a sensible hour and drove home to the love of his life.

***

Donny Atherton screamed silently down the mountain on the black diamond trail. He didn't get the chance often these days; when on skis lately he was teaching newcomers to the sport and his days were filled with the bunny slopes and the green trail, maybe the blue on occasion. When the opportunity presented itself, he relished being able to take on a course more suited to his years of expertise. He cleared his mind of her and settled into the sensations of moving at speed, wind whipping his hair, the feel of his skis, shifting his weight as he traveled down the slope with a grin. When he reached the bottom, he chuckled. He'd forgotten how good running a black diamond could feel. He scanned the skies. "Just enough light for one more run," he said to himself, and began working his way over to the lift again.

As the lift carried him skyward, she crept into his thoughts again. This woman, who could make his heart race with a simple look. Donny had fallen head over heels in love with her -something that once upon a time he'd made serious strides to avoid and later thought would never ever happen for him. But it had. And he knew next to nothing about her. He'd never met someone so emotionally closed off and unwilling to share about herself.

That's not fair to her to think that way, his psyche chided him. *You haven't exactly been forthcoming about your past, either.* He sighed. There was that great big hurdle still to overcome before he could even consider offering her the engagement ring that he'd bought this week on impulse. The click-click of lift chain cable against post housing as it reached its destination pulled him back to reality. He hopped off the lift, made his way over to the drop-in point for the black diamond again, adjusted his goggles, and started down the mountain.

Donny again raced down with a megawatt smile on his face. *Man, I miss doing this all the time*, he thought as he carefully navigated the last sharp curve before arriving at the bottom once more. Feeling exhilarated, he released his boots from his skis, gathered his equipment and left the slopes.

And he had decided. She was coming up next week to spend a few days with him for Christmas. He would sit her down then and bare his soul. If she stuck around after that, he'd plan out the best surprise wedding proposal known to man.

And if she bails? he asked himself. His shoulders slumped as he wrestled with this one. *Well…. If she bails, I won't blame her,* Donny told himself honestly. *I just hope she doesn't.*

***

Lizzie had dressed and was putting on shoes when her cell phone rang. She snatched it up, answered, listened intently for a moment. "Thanks for telling me, I'm on my way back to the office now," she said, and she disconnected from the call. Sighing heavily, she pulled out her pocket size notebook, and adjusted her case notes. The robbery and aggravated assault case involving Andrew J. Timkins, the elderly shopkeeper, was now an active homicide investigation. He'd been pronounced about an hour after arriving in the emergency room.

It made her mad.

No. That's wrong, she amended. *That doesn't even begin to adequately describe what I am feeling right now*. It made her blood boil. A sweet little seventy-seven-year-old man, who had served with honor and distinction in both Korea and in Vietnam as a chopper pilot, beaten to death by some thug who had no freaking concept of what honor even meant.

Someone who would do that... sometimes she wanted to take off her badge and set it aside and beat them into a bloody pulp with her bare hands – *let them see how they like it*. She wouldn't, of course. She respected her badge and what it stood for too much to taint it that way. But she was still human, and the cases she worked, especially senseless cases like this one, occasionally got to her.

"I will catch this little bastard," she promised herself in her mirror before she gathered up her gun, badge, and keys and headed back to the office. She needed to update the case in her computer, and she wanted to review the security footage recovered from the scene as soon as possible.

***

Eric Nibless. That was the next name on her list. She'd begun her research once she'd come back from Thanksgiving with Donny. Drilling down into Mr. Nibless's life and accomplishments had proved quite entertaining to say the least. She honestly could not recall ever coming across someone so bigoted in her life. Although he hid behind pseudonyms and his keyboard, she'd managed to follow his internet trail down into some very extreme anti-Semitic website groups; ones that made the KKK and other established hate groups look tame by comparison. And Eric was by far one of the more vocal participants in these groups.

Well, that explains why he was so eager to take part, she thought disgustedly.

As she continued to dig, however, she found even more things that raised her eyebrows. For someone so hateful toward, so unaccepting of others he sure was a hypocrite. Although everything she'd found about him indicated he'd been married to a woman for the past fifteen years, she uncovered active and heavily used solicitation profiles in chat rooms that catered to arranging hook ups for gay men – and all the evidence she'd found confirmed his wife had no clue at all. The trifecta was stumbling across some data that led her to believe Eric might be involved in embezzlement as well – from his father-in-law's company, where he was the CFO.

She considered for a moment that maybe revenge would best be served on this one by printing out everything she'd found and mailing it to his wife. She picked up her phone and texted exactly that suggestion, then waited to see what the answer would be. She didn't have to wait long.

"I like it. Let's do both," was the reply. *"All that coming to light will definitely make it look like a hate crime."*

Smiling, she began to print out pages for compilation as she continued to research Eric Nibless.

***

Lizzie smiled wolfishly and paused the video feed to take a closer look. Right there, plain as day, was an excellent picture of her killer. He wouldn't have looked a day over eighteen had he not been so obviously strung out; whatever he was using had aged him. He also looked like he'd completely embraced the thug lifestyle. *Well, good for you. You're about to get a real up-close look at its consequences,* she thought grimly.

She emailed it to the lab so they could cross-check against known offenders in the database, saving a copy to her computer in case a media blast needed to happen. But first she wanted to show this picture around the neighborhood in person, so she also printed a copy. With a little luck, she'd have this jackass in a holding cell before her shift was up. She grabbed her gun and badge and nodded to David. Time to go hunting.

As they walked to the car, her phone rang. She answered, not looking at the caller ID. "Zimmerman."

"Hey there," Landon said. "You sound so serious. You in the middle of something?"

"Hey yourself," she replied. "We're heading out to show a suspect's picture around, see what we can find out."

"Ah," he replied. "That explains your tone. I won't keep you. I just wanted to say I miss you, and I should be back in the States in a few days."

"Sorry if I sound short," she told him as she buckled her seat belt. "This case I'm on is getting to me. Tell you what. I can call you when I get off shift, if that's okay."

"Talk to you then. Be careful, Lizzie."

"I will. Catch you later."

Immediately after Lizzie hung up, she heard a chuckle from the driver's seat.

"So.... how is Landon?" David teased.

"He's fine," she sputtered. "He just wanted to say he misses me."

"Aw. Now ain't that cute as hell."

"Don't start, Tank," Lizzie told him as she began to blush and grin at the same time.

He chuckled again but cut her some slack. Parallel parking in front of the store, he indicated through the front window at the young man behind the counter. "I think that's Mr. Timkins' grandson."

She looked. "Yeah," she confirmed. "That's Mark. Let's go see if he knows this creep."

They walked in and up to the counter. "Mark, right?"

He looked at her with sad eyes. "Hello again, Detective," he greeted her as an older man came forward from the storage room in the back. It was Mark's father Lucas.

"Detective Zimmerman. Any updates?" Lucas asked.

"We got a really good still picture off of your security footage," she answered, and showed him the picture. "Do either of you know this guy?"

Lucas went white with rage and Mark gasped.

"That's Bullet," Lucas sneered.

"Come again?"

“That’s his gang name,” Lucas said with derision. “Real name is Alfred. I don’t remember his last name.” He turned to his son. “Do you?”

“His last name is Winnamaker. We used to be friends in elementary school,” Mark explained with sorrow. “Got into junior high and he started running with the wrong crowd. I haven’t really talked to him much since then. He dropped out sophomore year.”

“How old is he?”

Mark frowned, thought a moment. “He’s, like, eight months older than me, so, twenty-four.”

“I don’t suppose you might know his general location.”

Mark sighed. “Not a clue. Like I said, he got in with a bad crowd and we split ways. And after graduation I went down to Texas for my bachelor's. I'm only up here for the holidays. I start med school at Johns Hopkins in January."

"His mom and dad lived about four miles from here," he continued. "But Alfred's home life was…rough. His parents were drunks. It would surprise me if he'd stayed around them. If they're even still there." But he grabbed a pen and paper and wrote down the street, then handed it to Lizzie. "That's the last address I know Alfred lived at. Like I said, it's been forever ago. But just in case."

"Thanks," Lizzie told them sincerely as she shook Mark's and Lucas's hands. "And again, I am so very sorry for your loss."

Lizzie and David returned to the car.

***

The Raven settled into his room in Valparaíso's Hotel Boutique Acontraluz to look over the dossier he'd been sent for this mission. Although his target was a little over an hour away by car in Santiago, the Raven preferred Valparaíso's seaside charm as a nice balance while he went over his plans again. This time the man he hunted was the purported leader of a terrorist cell. He re-read each detail sent to him, then closed the file, wandered out onto his room's balcony and sat, watching the fishing boats return and moor up in the harbor while he mulled over the finer points of tomorrow's scheduled activity. He had decided the best method before he had even packed for this trip. Now he just needed to go over it all in his head to make sure he'd not forgotten anything. "Yes," he murmured. "That should do nicely." He rose and went downstairs for dinner, then returned to his room to get some sleep. The next morning, he woke lazily, had a late breakfast on his balcony and watched the local fishermen as they prepared to battle the ocean once again for their livelihood.

At around three in the afternoon the Raven started at a leisurely pace on the road from Valparaíso to Santiago, enjoying the sunshine on his face and the wind rustling his hair. He'd opted to rent a motorcycle, slinging his hard-shell guitar case across his back. His guitar, of course, was waiting patiently back at the hotel for his return. His AWSM-F .338 Lapua Magnum fit in its place nicely after he'd adjusted the case's interior a bit and collapsed the gun's stock. Getting the rifle through airport security and customs hadn't been as bad as he'd thought either; sections of Chile were quite a draw for big game hunters, and he'd surpassed TSA standards in securing his rifle for the trip in the cargo hold.

He gauged that he was about a half-hour outside of Santiago. Pulling over, he consulted the map he'd printed and made notes on last night. Yes. The hillside he'd chosen would work very well, and he would have the sun behind him, so no worries about glare on the scope to impede his vision – or give away his position. He tucked the map back into his shirt pocket and continued toward his goal. At five-thirty p.m. local time he was skirting the city's outer regions to the right, working his way toward a road he'd seen on the map that led up into the west flanking mountains. By five-fifty p.m. he had parked the bike, hiked roughly a quarter mile on foot to an ideal spot in the tree line where he could clearly see the structure he was after through his scope but not be seen himself, affixed the silencer and sighted in, and settled down to wait. The dossier had indicated that the target enjoyed a regular evening ritual of a cigar on the back patio after dinner. Raven had no worries about taking out the wrong man – because the dossier had also indicated the person he was after was missing most of his right ear.

By six forty-two p.m. the cigar-loving terrorist leader had stepped outside, lit his cigar, turned his head to the left – and fell dead, courtesy of a whisper-quiet single shot fired from a half-mile away. Just after seven p.m. the Raven was back at his motorcycle and heading back to the main road leading to Valparaíso. This time he moved quickly once away from Santiago, arriving back at his hotel to a late supper in his room by eight-thirty.

***

Alfred Winnamaker was terrified, Lizzie could tell. She could also tell by the way he twitched and ran his hands across his face that he was deep in the middle of withdrawals. She'd gotten the call about four-thirty a.m. that he'd been pulled over for a busted taillight and taken into custody once the BOLO had been confirmed. She had let him simmer in holding for an hour or so before having him brought to her in interrogation room one. Now she and David sat across from him and reminded him of his Miranda rights. His bloodshot eyes darted back and forth from her face to her partner's, but he nodded his understanding as he shivered.

It took all of ten minutes before Alfred confessed to beating up the old man. Lizzie had been right. Twenty-seven dollars wasn't enough to get Alfred the fix he craved, and he'd been furious. "But, that dude's gonna be all right, right?" he asked her, sniffling.

She gazed at him levelly. "You killed him, Alfred. You beat him to death. Over twenty-seven dollars."

It took a moment, but Lizzie could see in Alfred's expression when it registered with him what she had just said.

"I killed him?"

"You killed him."

Alfred put his head on the table and sobbed like a child.

CHAPTER ELEVEN

Christmas week.

She said she'd be there by four p.m. Donny looked at the clock hanging in his living room. Three forty-seven. Nervously, he paced back and forth like a caged tiger in the zoo.

"Man, I don't want to tell her this," he muttered, raking fingers through his hair. But he realized he would have to for them to move forward and hopefully for her to be more open about herself too. That didn't mean he had to like the idea. He'd done such a good job of distancing himself from the person he used to be. Donny was truly worried that once he told her about his past, she would leave and never return. But he felt like to be authentic, he would have to risk it.

Suddenly, she was on his doorstep, then in his arms. Holding her felt as natural as taking a breath. He kissed her long and deep. “Hm,” she murmured against his mouth. “I missed you too.” He smiled solemnly and reached down to take her hand and lead her to the couch.

“I need to talk to you,” he told her as they sat down. “Remember when we first met, and we agreed that when one of us was ready to share stuff in our history, the other would listen and keep an open mind?”

“Yes, I remember that,” she answered slowly and cautiously.

“Well.” He took a deep breath to steady himself. “I feel like I – like we – are at a point that it’s time I share with you why I walked away from skiing professionally.”

“Okay. Tell me.”

Donny took another deep breath. “It started right after I made the Olympic team that was going to Nagano in 1998. I had a horrible practice run crash the day before I was supposed to fly to Japan. I jacked my right knee up to the point they had to completely rebuild it. I worked my ass off to overcome the injury. What I didn’t count on was getting addicted to oxycontin in the process.” He stopped. “I need some water, be right back. You want anything?”

She went with him into the kitchen. “I’ll get some tea. Please, continue.”

He poured himself a glass and she noticed his hand shook as he drank.

“Okay,” he said. “So, I was a functioning pill addict. Kept it hidden, for a long time. Found ways to get around the drug testing. Then after a while oxy wasn’t enough, so I added other things into the mix – for me, my supplemental drugs of choice were alcohol and cocaine. Back then I'd been seeing a girl for a few months; her name was Mary…" he broke off, hung his head.

She reached across the counter separating them and took his hand. "Go on. It's all right."

His shoulders heaved as he continued. "There's really no way to pretty it up, and I shouldn't try. You deserve to hear it straight. I purposely dragged her down with me, got her addicted to pills and coke too. One night, we were both high out of our minds, we had a huge fight, and I went for a walk. When I got back, Mary was unconscious. I couldn't wake her up. Then I noticed the needle sticking out of her arm. When they pronounced her dead in the emergency room the doctor told me she'd overdosed on a speedball. She was only twenty-three." He took a long drink of water.

"I called my coaches and my agent while I was standing in the middle of that emergency room lobby, and told them everything, and I checked into rehab that same night. I've been clean and sober since February seventeenth, 2000. Turned my life completely around. But I've never been able to shake the guilt about what happened to Mary. To this day I close my eyes and I can still see her in my bed, dying. If she hadn't gotten involved with me, she might still be alive today. I have to live with that."

Now Donny looked up, tears in his eyes. "And I didn't want to tell you, because I was afraid that you'd turn around and leave. I really hope you don't. But I won't blame you at all if that's what you feel like you need to do."

She walked around the edge of the counter to reach out to him. “Donny. We all have ghosts, and we’ve all screwed up at some point. I’m still not ready to share mine yet, and I hope that’s okay. But I’m not going anywhere.” And she pulled him close.

She felt and heard his sigh of relief as he buried his face in her shoulder. After a long moment, Donny lifted his head. “I do have one question, and I really need to know this now.”

“What’s that?” she asked.

He gazed into her eyes again and asked, “Are you involved with anyone else? Seeing someone? Married?”

She pulled back, a little surprised. “No. Why would you think that?”

His shoulders slumped. “Because I got the impression that you don’t want me to come to Texas. At all. You always come here. But I have been hoping to get to see your world, meet your family, your friends…" he trailed off sheepishly. "It sounds stupid now that I say it out loud, but I just started thinking, why doesn't she want me to come down there? And another guy was the most obvious answer."

"Okay, I can see where it might look that way," she admitted after mulling it over for a moment. "Donny, I am so sorry about that. To answer you, no, there's no one else. Not for a long time. I don't know why I hesitate about you traveling down there sometimes. I guess…" she looked down, frowning, searching for the right words. "I guess it's because that's my safe space." She lifted her head again and looked at him. "When I do get to the point that I am ready to share, that will make a lot more sense to you. In the meantime, just know – you're the only one

I'm seeing, and you're the only one I want to see." And she kissed him tenderly.

***

Landon climbed into his rental car and set the GPS for Lizzie's house. After three weeks of travel, he was ready to take a break, and with her is where he wanted to be. Before leaving the Avis lot, he called her. She answered after two rings.

"Hello?"

"Hey, Lizzie."

"Landon! How was your trip?"

"It was long. But very productive. How's work been going for you?"

She laughed. "It's been full of Christmas crazies and then some."

"Well," he told her, "If you're off work, how about a meal? You hungry?"

"You're in Seattle?"

"Yep," Landon answered. "I came hoping for a dinner date with you as a surprise… did I overstep?"

"No, it's just, I'm on call tonight," Lizzie told him. "But if you don't mind the possibility of my having to eat and run, yeah, let's do it. We can order in. There's a great Chinese place not far from here and they are pretty quick."

"Sounds good. I'll be there in about a half-hour."

"You like Governors chicken?"

"Very much."

"I'll get it ordered. See you soon."

Forty minutes later they sat at Lizzie's kitchen table, passing containers of fried rice and the chicken dish and filling plates. "So," Lizzie asked, "how did the trip go?"

Landon grinned. "Remember when I said that if it went like I hoped, I'd be the sole distributor of some things?"

She smiled. "You said, '*of a few really cool things*', if I am remembering correctly."

Now he laughed. "That is exactly what I said. Well, that's what happened. Everything just kind of lined out perfectly, and yes, now you ARE sitting next to the *sole* U.S. distributor of some very, very exclusive really cool things."

"That's wonderful!" Lizzie exclaimed. "I'm happy for you!"

Her cell phone rang as they were clearing the table. She checked the number, and he watched the cop come to the surface as she took the call.

"Zimmerman." She listened, then responded, "I'm on my way. ETA twenty."

Landon murmured, “You have to go,” as she hung up her phone and hooked it to her belt.

“Yep,” she confirmed, walking into the living room to grab her badge and shoulder holster. Lizzie affixed both to her person, then grabbed her keys. “I don’t know how long I will be. How soon are you going back?”

“That depends on you,” Landon answered honestly, watching her from the kitchen doorway. “I’d like to spend some time with you. But I also showed up unannounced, and I don’t want to get in the way of your work.”

“I’m off the next two days,” Lizzie told him, “and I’d really like you to stay. I’ll be back at some point.” She kissed him and headed out the door. He smiled as he watched her go.

***

Another one confirmed. That made - Frank consulted his notes – *seven*. "Seven out of eighteen total, all in under two years," he muttered. "I know I am right about this. No way this is coincidental. No way in hell." But his instincts and his years of experience told him to keep going, rule as many in -or out- as possible. "Build a solid case, Frank, don't half-ass this," he scolded himself. He refilled his glass with whiskey, glanced at the next name he wanted to track down, and resumed his searches.

***

Nathan and Bella's plane touched down right on time in Dallas the day before Christmas. They were met in baggage claim by Jandy, Faith, and Rick, and made the trek out to Jandy's house in Argyle, Texas for a weeklong visit. Bella was still getting used to having a larger family to belong to, but she liked it already.

***

Donny felt like a huge burden had been lifted off his shoulders. He was humbled by and grateful for the moment he was in – her head on his shoulder and her body snuggled up close to his as they watched TV. He'd confessed his deepest darkest secret – and not only had she stayed but it had brought them closer together. He was dumbfounded.

As she sat beside him, tucked in close, she realized that he'd never shared that with anyone before. It meant a lot to her that he confided in her that way, but it scared her too. *Not what he shared, that wasn't it*, she thought to herself. *It's being close enough to someone that they confide in me that way.*

New territory for her. And unexpected. And a little nerve-wracking.

But she found that although it scared her some, she didn't want it to ever end.

***

The Raven had some planning to do. The next name on his hobby list had turned out to be a package deal – two of them in one location. And after researching Jeff Hartford and Crystal Lee-Hartford in depth, he knew exactly what the approach should be this time. There was not a way to truly ensure no bystanders would be caught up in this one. But it was a calculated risk and based on some data he'd uncovered, it seemed like a minimal one.

Whistling to himself, he logged on to a very select website and began to read all the technical data he would need to know to execute this exactly as he intended.

***

He jerked heavily in his sleep, and it woke him up. Frank lifted his head from the table, rubbed his eyes, and looked blearily at his watch. Three-thirty a.m. He didn't have to report for duty until seven p.m. He stretched, yawned, and shuffled toward his bed. His last semi-coherent thought before drifting off to sleep again was one of jumbled names and possible causes.

***

The entire women's rights group chat was in an uproar, and Eric Nibless was directly responsible. He relished it. Even among the most peaceful and tolerant members, he had crossed a line – and he'd done so intentionally. It thrilled him to no end to hear the 'ping' of new post notifications coming so closely together it resembled machine gun fire. Suddenly a new message in his inbox delivered the news – he'd been banned and blocked from any more participation in that website.

"Ah well, fun while it lasted," he said gleefully. "Now. Who can I stir up next?"

He liked causing trouble. He got off on it. It made his day when he was able to rile people up with a few select phrases and was rewarded with chaos. No group was off limits to him, but especially not minorities or Jews. He hated them most of all.

Eric Nibless, the living breathing definition of a 'troll', opened a new browser window and searched for a new place to spew his venom. A knock on the door interrupted him.

"Mr. Nibless?" his secretary, Katie, opened his door just enough to poke her head in through the crack. "Your nine o'clock appointment just arrived."

“Thanks, Katie, I’ll be right out,” he answered with a smile, sliding into his good guy image the way someone else would a suit jacket. Once she’d shut the door again, he muttered, “there’s another one that doesn’t deserve to be let outside!” to himself as he reluctantly closed out his browser windows and stood up to go keep his appointment.

***

By ten a.m. Lizzie was home again. The look on her face told Landon it was quite a case she’d been called in for almost eleven hours earlier. She looked haggard and haunted, and it hurt him to see it. She moved to him without a word and laid her head on his shoulder as he wrapped his arms around her.

Landon already knew exactly what case she’d caught. He’d watched the six o’clock newscast and the story was front and center. A family of five, found dead in their home two days before Christmas. The children had ranged in age from eight to three. He could only imagine the horror Lizzie had witnessed walking into that house.

"You want to talk about it?" he asked her.

"Can't, really," Lizzie sighed against his chest. "But it was bad. Kids involved."

"Ah," Landon murmured. "I'm so sorry."

"Me too, Landon. Me too."

"How do you do it? Deal with cases like that?"

"I just do. Part of the job. Some are easier to deal with, and some…." She lifted her head, shrugged her shoulders. "Some you carry with you the rest of your life."

"This case sounds like one of those."

She sighed again. "I truly hope not, but I think it is too."

"You want breakfast? Coffee?"

"Yes, to both," she said. "But first, I need a shower."

"Go ahead. Both will be ready when you get out."

"Okay," Lizzie replied, and headed upstairs. She started the water, wearily undressed, stepped into the shower. As she stood under the stream, she began to allow herself to grieve for three innocents swept up in the aftermath of a marriage gone horribly awry, mere babies that would never see another Christmas.

***

The start of a new year felt, for Donny at least, like a truly fresh start – something he'd not experienced in a long time. 2011 would be the best year yet. But he had work to do.

A marriage proposal as big as he envisioned would not come together at a moment's notice. He wanted to do it right.

He smiled to himself as he waded through romantic getaway destinations on the travel site he'd found. *She's going to be so surprised,* he told himself gleefully.

***

Landon yawned, stretched, and glanced at the clock on his home office wall. *Wow. It's after seven already.* Last he'd looked, it'd been two-thirty. The new exclusive contracts he'd landed took more energy than expected to get lined out. But he knew the end results would be worth paying attention to the minutiae at the beginning. He rose and went to the kitchen in search of a quick meal. As he retrieved the bread, mustard, cheese and cold cuts and began to build his sandwich, his mind wandered as it often did to the

Northwest, and a certain very lovely police detective. The time they'd been able to spend together over Christmas week had been all too brief, and he wasn't sure when he'd be able to get back to Seattle; he already had a very full schedule lined out for the next month and then some.

He carried his plate back to his desk just in time to see the new text notification. He picked up his phone and grinned broadly as he read, "*Hi there. Is it too soon to tell you I miss you? – Lizzie.*"

***

The subject of his latest crush was Evan. Eric Nibless had landed a major hottie. He could feel it. They'd met in a chat room, and sparks had flown immediately, with extremely heavy flirting back and forth. Eric had even broken one of his own rules and made contact during the day using the computer in his office at his father-in-law's company. But he didn't care.

He sat, jaw slack with surprise, and read the latest message Evan had left him. *Get out. Really? That's perfect!* he thought to himself as he drafted his response. He'd been ordered to go to Rapid City for that damn conference next month, and he wasn't happy about it– until he got Evan's message. His new love interest only lived about an hour from Rapid City. Eric could sneak away for an overnight rendezvous and no one would be the wiser. He smiled as he finished up his message and hit send, then shut down his laptop for the evening.

Eric's smile faded as he made his way to the master bedroom. *God, I hate this life*. It had been necessary to marry Madeleine, to have the access to her father's fortune that he felt he deserved. But he did not love her, never had, never would. Fortunately, he was one hell of an actor when circumstances called for it.

He crept into the room, the hall light filtering forward over his shoulder and caressing her still form as she slept. *Vapid cow,* he thought bitterly. *Not worthy of breathing my air.*

Patience, Eric. You knew going in that this could be the scenario for a long, long time, he reminded himself. To date he'd managed to siphon away a bit over three million dollars from good old Dad-in-law's business. The goal he'd set for himself was four. *Almost there, fifteen years in. Not a bad pace. Speed it up, you could get caught. And then no frolicking in Europe for you!*

He stripped off his clothes and climbed into bed as delicately as possible. God forbid the cow awoke and wanted sex; she was so impossibly high maintenance that way. Luckily for him, Madeleine only sighed, and stayed asleep.

As he drifted off, he comforted himself by thinking of Evan, and how hot that overnight rendezvous would be.

***

She logged in to the account she'd set up and immediately noticed a new message. Her smile grew wider with each line she read. *Perfect. He'll never see it coming.* Eric Nibless had taken the Evan bait hook, line, and sinker.

CHAPTER TWELVE

February 2011 arrived in Seattle with its usual mercurial mix of rain, gray fog, and sunshine – sometimes occurring all in the same day. But the daily highs and lows remained level; for the most part, residents enjoyed high temperatures in the mid to upper forties and overnight lows only occasionally reaching the twenties.

In Fort Worth, February 2011 was marked by extremes – the lowest temperature recorded in decades at the beginning of the month, offset by a few highs of eighty-two degrees as March approached.

Rapid City, however, remained resolute, supplying constant proof that winter wasn't over yet. Eric Nibless checked into his hotel room in downtown Rapid City after braving the day's welcoming high temperature of seven degrees.

"Ridiculous!" he announced aloud to an empty room as he immediately reached out to turn on a very hot shower. "They couldn't have this conference somewhere that *doesn't* have single-digit highs?" And he answered his own question. *Sure, they could have, but then you wouldn't get to finally meet Evan in person.* The reminder his psyche so thoughtfully provided mollified his irritation and incited his lust.

Now, now, let's not get ahead of ourselves. Check the conference schedule. Thawed out from the shower, he wrapped a towel around his waist and picked up the printout he'd received. *See it? Right there,* his inner voice directed. *Not signed up for any modules between Tuesday at one pm and Wednesday at eleven am. There's your window. Almost twenty-four hours all to yourself to spend with Evan.*

He flung open his laptop, grinning as he reached out to Evan to confirm their meeting around four p.m. Tuesday afternoon. Within a few minutes, he had the confirmation he craved- along with an address to navigate to for the hookup.

Whistling, Eric Nibless got dressed, styled his hair, then left to head downstairs for the kickoff mixer that always preceded a week-long industry event.

***

The Raven checked ownership records again, just to make sure he had the right data pulled up in front of him. *That's what I thought.* Jeff Hartford and Chrystal Lee-Hartford were the proud owners of a private plane. He also verified once again the brand and model – a Cessna 172. Satisfied, he returned to reviewing the technical data for that plane, studying intently for a way it could be covertly sabotaged when the time was right. An hour in, he'd noticed and made note of four different ways to accomplish this. *Good. A nice selection to start with.* Now, he needed to further research each one, to determine ease of access and everything that would be required to pull off what he had in mind. Depending on where they warehoused their property when not in use, he might or might not have a large window of time to complete his activities without being seen.

He spent another hour digging, diving in further, pulling up deeper data on each of the four methods he'd first identified as possibilities. By the end of the second hour, his initial list had lost a member; his more in-depth of that possible method had reached a dead-end. *No matter*, he told himself. *That one was the most obvious and most likely to be found and fixed prior to flight. Still have three strong choices.* And each one would have the same effect – subtly rendering the plane incapable of returning safely to earth once airborne.

It was with a twinge of sadness that the Raven realized the hobby list would be complete soon. In his mind he ran a finger down the page – there would be only five names left once he handled the Hartfords.

What would he do then?

Sounds to me like that's the perfect time to walk away, from all of it - the paid gigs too - and just live life, man. Just live a normal life, his mind answered.

***

Madeleine Nibless walked back into her house from her morning jog, tired but pleased. This morning was the first time she'd taken the longer route of four miles she'd previously tried and *not* been completely exhausted when she was done. *Building up the stamina! You go, Maddie!* her inner cheerleader crowed. And she did feel good about it. She'd only taken up jogging about five months ago; the first two months had been excruciating – she'd had no idea until she started just how out-of-shape she had become. But Madeleine had stuck with it, and now, the rewards were becoming more apparent every day. *Might even work up to a quarter marathon before summer gets here, who knows?*

As she made her way into the master bathroom to clean up, she stripped down, checking her body out in the mirror. *Looking good Maddie,* she told herself, flipping back her light brown hair with a twinkle in her emerald eyes. She could really see the difference that exercising was beginning to have – and not just on the scale display. Yes, she'd already trimmed about ten pounds from her weight, but she'd been more delighted to discover that inches were coming off in strategic places – most noticeably her waistline and thighs. *Keep this up you're going to have go get smaller clothes!*

She grinned at her reflection. "I definitely don't mind having that problem," she announced to the mirror before stepping into her shower stall. As she lathered shampoo into her hair, she considered calling Eric, just to make sure he arrived at the conference safely. And she immediately decided against it. *He can be so snarky and hateful to me sometimes, but it's even worse when he's working…I probably shouldn't bother him.*

She sighed. Truth be told, he wasn't just snarky, and it wasn't just sometimes. He could, and did, cut her to her core with just a few venomous words, and lately it happened more and more. She couldn't understand it. When they'd first met in college, he'd been so… attentive, loving. It had shocked the hell out of her that he'd chosen her, a pudgy bookworm, over all the other women on campus he could have pursued. For her part, she'd fallen in love the first time she'd seen him across the quad – five feet nine inches tall, sculpted features, blond hair and serious, questioning blue eyes.

Now, fifteen years later, she sighed again as she rinsed out her hair. *It seems like we've drifted so far apart,* she thought mournfully. *And I have no idea what to do to fix it.*

***

The package, compiled and ready to go, sat on the passenger seat of her car. She'd already made sure that every single page contained zero physical trace whatsoever. Now she drove up to a U.S. Mail drop box, sighed heavily, and slipped the roughly half-inch thick manila envelope through the chute. Madeleine Nibless would receive it sometime in the next three to five days.

As she pulled away, she sent a silent apology through the universe in Madeleine's direction. *Woman to woman, Madeleine, what's in there is gonna cut you deep, and I'm so sorry for that. But you deserve to know exactly who and what he is.*

***

It's finally here, Eric thought to himself with glee as he checked his watch and saw it was twelve fifty-five. *Five more minutes, then party time can start. I just hope no one asks any more questions.* Part and parcel of these conference modules was a brief 'question-and-answer' session at the end of each one. So far, there had only been a couple lobbed at the speaker. Eric fidgeted in his seat, willing the event coordinator handling this module to announce its end.

Suddenly he saw movement from his left; realizing who it was that had their hand up made him want to scream. *Lucy. Son of a bitch*. This pain in the ass had been around the industry for years and had long ago earned the reputation of asking drawn-out and complicated questions that were a hundred percent guaranteed to make any event run longer than scheduled. Subtle groans around the room let Eric know he wasn't the only one tired of Long-winded Lucy.

It was a small comfort.

Precious minutes ticked by and they were all finally released from the module at ten minutes past one. Eric was furious as he tried his best to walk, not run, to his car. Once he was tucked safely inside, he took a few cleansing breaths, regaining his composure. It wouldn't do to meet his new lover while in a foul humor.

He programmed the motel's address into the rental car's GPS and got underway, his mood lightening with each mile.

***

Around two, she pulled into the parking lot of the little 'no tell motel' she'd found for this event. Its exterior appearance upheld the one-star rating the place had been given on the travel sites, and she doubted the interior would be much better. But it was cheap, off the beaten path, and given the way it looked she felt certain that no one would be overly nosy so long as the room was paid for. She'd already paid online for the unit – number three – that Eric would die in, using Evan's profile and a ghosted credit card also in Evan's name. Now she just needed to get settled into the adjoining room. She felt she had a good shot at being successful on that point – it wasn't like people were clamoring to stay in this dump.

She squared her shoulders, walked in, and paid cash. The attendant barely bothered to look at her, much less take any of her personal information, as he thrust a worn-out key fob her direction and grunted, "Number four."

She returned to her car, grabbed her backpack as she made note of absolutely zero security cameras anywhere, then let herself into number four. As she expected, the interior was awful. She subconsciously wrinkled her nose in distaste and made a mental note to not sit down on anything in this place – no telling what fluids were where.

But it was edifying to see that in the wall separating units three and four was a sliding door, with a lock so simple a kindergartener could get around it. She worked it open in under thirty seconds, and staged unit three for Eric's arrival.

***

At three fifty-five, Eric Nibless turned into the parking lot in his rental car. Shifting the transmission to park, he took a moment to check out the ratty conditions his sex drive had led him to. And shrugged. *Not ideal, but I damn sure didn't come up here for the atmosphere*. He checked his appearance in the mirror. *Gorgeous, as always,* he reassured himself. *Evan is in for a treat.*

He went in to see the attendant, as instructed, and asked for the key to number three. The man behind the counter looked at a scrap of paper the owner had scrawled directives on, nodded, and handed over the key, then went back to watching his mini television set.

Eric walked slowly to number three, anticipation building. He turned the key and stepped into a dark room. "Hello?" he called out.

A voice from the bathroom, deep, masculine, sexy as hell. "Hello! I'm just getting into the shower. Care to join me?"

Eric began stripping, eagerly casting off his clothes as he began to meander toward the closed bathroom door. He was so focused on the excitement of being physical with Evan he failed to hear the sliding door between his room and the next one opening slowly.

Finally, he rid himself of his underwear. Stark naked, he called out, “Ready or not, here I come,” before taking another step forward toward his prize. Suddenly a sharp pain exploded in the center of the back of his head, and he went to his knees, dumbfounded. Before he could vocalize any surprise, another massive burst of pain, and the world went black.

She knew the second blow had crushed his skull and most likely killed him. She didn’t care. Her research of him had exposed everything about him, and she despised him with every fiber of her being. She kept swinging the lead pipe, again and again, as hard and as fast as she could, until finally her energy was depleted. Then she dropped it next to his body, stepped around him, opened the bathroom door, and retrieved the sound-activated playback device she'd set on the bathroom sink next to the bowtie candy wrapper.

She knew she'd leave footprints in his blood; that's why she'd purchased size eleven men's shoes. A trip to a painting supply store had netted her the hooded Tyvek suit, latex gloves, and goggles she wore, as well as the expanse of drop cloth that she now stepped onto to get back to unit four without telegraphing the escape route. That accomplished, she slipped off the bloody garb, set it all on the drop cloth, and began to roll it all up toward her, backing her way into her room. When she was finished, she stood in the narrow doorway between the rooms and visually confirmed that no blood trace pointed out her exit into unit four. Satisfied, she re-locked the adjoining door. Retrieving the baby wipes from her backpack, she scrubbed her face to rid herself of the fine spray that had landed on a fraction of her exposed skin as a direct consequence of wielding the pipe.

The last step before she left was to put on new gloves, get the fifty-five-gallon lawn and leaf bag out of her backpack, and stash the rolled-up drop cloth and used baby wipes in it. Tying it securely, she headed out to her car and drove away. About five miles down the road she spotted a large dumpster and threw her trash away properly like a responsible citizen before peeling off the gloves and returning them to her backpack. Then she headed to the airport. She parked her car in the rental return lot, crossed Eric Nibless off her notebook list as completed, and before she went through security the gloves found a new home in the women's rest room trash can.

She settled into her seat for the return flight and made a mental note to buy her best friend dinner to say 'thanks' for providing such an outstanding — and effective —voice recording.

***

The following afternoon an equally surly and inattentive office worker arrived on shift to find that the gentleman who had collected the key for number three the prior afternoon had not returned it, and the overnight clerk had not bothered to follow up. Determined to not have the extra day's room rate deducted from *her* measly check, she retrieved the master key and headed to the door.

After knocking loudly and receiving no response, she used the master key to enter and was immediately taken aback by a horrible stench that threatened to render her unconscious. Right hand over her mouth and holding her breath, she fumbled around for the switch with her left hand, then gathered up a huge lungful of noxious air to scream with all her might once the florescent light flickered to life and the carnage was revealed.

Within twenty minutes the entire two-man police force of Sleepy Hollow – a town of less than 1,000 but the closest to the motel's location - were onsite, with the county coroner on his way, and crime scene techs summoned from Gillette. Eric's identity was tentatively established from the driver's license still tucked in his wallet with his credit cards. By the next morning, fingerprinting confirmed the victim's name. The news was relayed to the police department in Eric's hometown of Flower Mound, Texas, who sent a detective and police chaplain to his address of record to make notifications.

By Thursday afternoon, the two law enforcement members were being welcomed into the Nibless household by a pleasant but extremely confused Madeleine, who invited them to sit down. Her devastated reaction to the news they delivered her was instant and deep. At her request the police chaplain called her father and relayed the news; her parents arrived quickly, took up station on either side of their only child, and held her as she wept.

On Saturday morning, a manila envelope postmarked from Wyoming arrived addressed to Madeleine, who opened it in view of her parents and her best friend Kathy. The police were summoned immediately to review its contents, and Madeleine, only tenuously grasping coherence as it was upon learning of Eric's death, shut down completely when his true nature came to light.

Flower Mound PD sent a copy of the envelope's contents up to the Wyoming authorities investigating the murder, where it was all duly logged in as part of the case. Before the month was out, the case would be labeled a 'hate crime' by regional press, which caused it to become a nationwide topic of discussion– but committed by who, no one could say.

CHAPTER THIRTEEN

It was the first Sunday in March 2011, and Frank had uncovered what happened to another person of interest; his findings were dutifully recorded in his spreadsheet. That left seven people to track down. Until he saw on the news that one Eric Nibless had been found bludgeoned to death. Once he cross referenced his case files, that name too joined the list.

Six left. Out of seventeen. *Sweet Jesus.*

He finally realized at that moment that he too was probably a target. The thought unnerved him. Based on what he'd found so far, he had no reason at all to believe he would be spared; whoever was behind all this had tenacity, plentiful resources and excellent intelligence about each victim's location and habits. They also knew precisely how to hunt, kill, then vanish - and leave no trace, if they chose.

Reluctantly, he added himself to the list, and hoped like hell he'd be able to see them coming in time. Then he saved and closed his file and headed to work, a heightened awareness of his surroundings in place, and a resolve to tell Lizzie about everything he had pieced together – just in case it turned out that he *didn't* see them coming. As he drove, he dialed her number; it went straight to voicemail. *Right after work,* he told himself. *I will talk to her right after work.* Just before he signed in for his shift, he fired off a text to his daughter.

***

Lizzie's phone had gone to voicemail because she'd turned it off. What she had shrugged off as a mild case of bronchitis had become walking pneumonia; her doctor had given her a shot, plus pills, cough syrup, and a lecture about not taking adequate care of herself. Her second lecture came from her section chief, who took one look at her when she'd brought him the doctor's note and then tried to take a case, and banished her from the roster for a week – the same amount of time the doctor's note recommended she rest.

She'd snarled about it but had gone home, taken a hotter than usual shower, dutifully swallowed the first round of antibiotics and cough syrup, and collapsed into bed. Her body twitched in sleep, warring against the fever the illness had brought with it. But when she drifted into wakefulness fourteen hours later, Lizzie begrudgingly admitted to herself that she was starting to feel better. She stretched slowly, her mind already considering food.

She made her way to the kitchen and after consulting her pantry decided to keep it simple – chicken noodle soup. *Simple, filling, low fuss. Good choice.* While it heated up on the stove, she turned her cell phone back on and noticed two missed calls – one from her dad, one from Landon – and two text messages.

Hey kid, the one from Frank began. *I need to talk to you about something. I'm on overnights this week but let's find time to talk, okay?* Lizzie's eyebrows raised as she read. The cloak-and-dagger tone was not his usual one at all. It would be interesting to see what he wanted to talk about. She checked the time; eleven thirty-seven p.m. He'd already be on patrol. She made a mental note to reach out tomorrow around eight a.m. Texas time if she had not heard from him. He'd be off his shift by then.

The rapid steam rising from the small saucepan caught her attention, and she set her phone down long enough to pour her soup into an oversized mug and get a spoon out of the drawer. Then she sat at the kitchen table and resumed reviewing messages, smiling at the one from Landon that began *Hello, gorgeous.*

***

The Raven reviewed the notes he'd made and nodded in satisfaction. He was ready. The only thing left to do was get to West Palm Beach and make it happen. He checked his watch. One a.m. He hummed softly to himself as he went to shower and then pack for his seven-a.m. flight.

***

"Nathan."

"Hmm?" he responded, not looking up from his laptop.

"*Nathan,*" Bella hissed, and now he could hear the try-not-to-panic undertone. He looked up to see her bracing herself against the doorframe. Her eyes were huge.

"Contractions?" he asked, rising quickly to get to her side. She nodded, visibly focused on trying to level out her breathing.

"Like before?" She'd had the Braxton-Hicks variety over the past few days.

"Nope," she managed, sucking air in through her nose and blowing it out through her mouth. "I think…" another breath, "we need to go."

Nathan raced up the stairs for the hospital bag they'd prepacked, then all but carried her to the car. He drove as fast as he dared and could tell by the way her tone shifted with each new contraction that the big day had arrived. He was grateful for zero traffic to contend with at two a.m. On the drive, he called Max, who was delighted to hear the news and confirmed he'd meet them at Prince William Medical Center.

It seemed like forever to him but at last the sign for labor and delivery entrance came into view. As soon as he pulled up to the drop-off point, he set the car's flashers and raced around to help Bella out of the front passenger seat. She leaned against him, moaning softly as the biggest contraction so far washed over her. Once it passed, Nathan gently guided her through the automatic doors, where a polite and attentive clerk promptly offered a wheelchair for Bella to sink into.

"Baby, I gotta move the car, I will be right back."

"I… know…" Bella answered, still breathing strategically. "See you…. In a bit…".

Nathan felt like he'd set a record for moving and parking a vehicle. He was back at her side before they'd even had a chance to wheel her into a birthing suite.

The nurse helped Bella undress and get her hospital gown on. Once she had Bella lying down, she hooked up the monitoring equipment to measure each contraction, patted Bella on the shoulder, and told her, "I'll page the doctor. Just keep doing the breathing, okay? You're doing great!"

A tech stepped in a few minutes later to start Bella's IV. There was a pause in that activity while a contraction measuring off the charts temporarily seized up Bella's ability to focus on her breathing. Nathan's face was shadowed with worry as he held her hand and stroked her hair. Long seconds passed as she writhed and moaned before it finally subsided.

Thirty minutes went by before Dr. Long poked her head in the door. "Hi guys," she said, stepping forward to check Bella's progress. "Let's see where we are." A physical examination confirmed it. "Well, Bella, this is it, hon. You're almost at ten centimeters already."

"This is it," Bella repeated, a thin sheen of sweat on her face. "How long, do you think?"

"To be honest, no idea," the doctor told her and Nathan both. "I've had first-time mothers only be in hard labor for a few hours, and I've seen others in labor for several. There's really no set pattern here. It varies."

"That is not very…comforting…" Bella's eyes went wide again as the next wave of pain began to build. But a new alarm sounded as well among the rhythmic beep-beep already in play. Dr. Long's attention whipped around to the screen showing the readouts from the monitors, and she scowled as she scanned the data.

“What’s wrong?” Nathan asked her.

“The baby’s heartbeat is erratic,” she answered, frowning. Her eyes didn’t leave the screen as she went over to the wall, hit the intercom button for the nurse’s station, and barked, “I need a sonogram tech in room four. *Now.*”

Within minutes a portable sonogram machine had been brought into play, and the tech was trying her best to give Dr. Long a clear picture of what was happening. When the next contraction descended like a dark cloud, they saw the cause of the distress – the umbilical cord had wound itself around the baby’s neck.

Dr. Long shouted orders to Marianne, the nurse that had just reentered the room, and before Nathan had fully grasped what was happening, Marianne had deftly adjusted the end of the bed downward and tilted the top half to bring Bella into a more upright position. With the next contraction came the overwhelming urge to push. Dr. Long coached Bella through it. As the baby's head emerged, she deftly unwrapped the cord, then encouraged Bella to push with all her might.

Twenty minutes later Nathan stepped out into the waiting room to find Max. "I have a son," he beamed, eyes welling. "Would you like to see him?"

"Absolutely," Max replied. They walked together back toward Bella's suite. "Is it okay for me to go in yet?" he asked.

"Yes," Nathan confirmed after peeking his head into the room. "Everything's been squared away." As the two men entered, Marianne walked over with a tiny bundle snuggled into a soft blue blanket and placed the infant into Nathan's arms. "Here you go, Dad," she announced.

Max went to kiss Bella on the forehead. "Hey, kiddo," he said to her.

"Hey, Uncle Max," she managed. She was happy, but exhausted.

Nathan looked down at the little miracle he held and was overcome with emotion. "He's perfect," he managed to say through his happy tears. Max strolled over and gazed at the sleeping child. "I agree," he returned, a bit misty himself.

"We'd like you to be his godparent," Nathan told him. "We talked about it, wanted to surprise you."

"I'd be honored," Max stated, choking up a bit. He cleared his throat to mask it. "What name did you two choose for a boy?"

"He's named after Nathan's father and mine," Bella revealed, smiling softly as her husband gently passed their son to his godfather. "Charles Daniel Thomas."

***

Six o'clock signaled the end of his shift, and Frank made his way home to shower before meeting Joe at seven for their Monday morning breakfast routine. He felt a little lightheaded in the shower, and again once he dressed and was tying his shoes, but the feeling passed rather quickly, so he dismissed it as being tired and continued getting ready to go visit with Joe over pancakes and coffee.

He'd just hooked his phone onto his belt successfully after two tries and was reaching out toward the table for his keys when he realized his right hand wouldn't cooperate; he couldn't get it to grasp the keychain. He frowned, tried again, and the lightheadedness was back in spades along with a bright blossoming pain in the left side of his head. He had a flash of horrific lucidity streak across his consciousness like St. Elmo's fire against a night sky– *something's wrong with me* – and then oblivion as he slumped to the floor.

At the diner, Joe Wallace glanced again at his watch. Seven forty-two. In the twenty-eight years they'd known each other, Frank had never once been late. His gut twisted as Frank's phone rang and rang then once again went to voicemail, just as his first three calls had. *I'm sure he's fine,* Joe told himself. *Just to be sure, though, I'm gonna go check.* Frank's house was only about eight blocks away. He called the fifth time from his car on the way and again got no answer.

When he pulled into the driveway and saw Frank's car still sitting there, Joe knew for certain something was amiss. He walked up onto the front porch, knocked, and called out to his friend. A low moan on the other side of the door had him whipping out the spare key Frank had given him for emergencies and letting himself in. His heart fell at the sight of his best friend collapsed in a heap on the living room rug. As he raced to Frank's side Joe pulled out his phone and dialed 911, shouting the address so they could send help.

***

Lizzie glanced at her watch. Six-twenty in Seattle, so eight-twenty in Texas. *Dad's home by now.* She dialed and waited and was surprised when Joe answered the phone instead of her father.

"Oh, hey Joe! I forgot you guys do breakfast on Mondays. Dad around?"

"Hey, Liz…" Something about his tone had the hair on the back of her neck standing up.

"Joe... What's wrong?"

A pause, then, "It's your dad, Lizzie. We think he's had a stroke. I am following the ambulance to the hospital right now." She could hear the waves of worry in Joe's usually smooth and level voice as he spoke.

"I'll be there as quick as I can, okay? As quick as I can," she told him, and hurried off the phone to pack a bag. She called her section chief and filled him in as she loaded up a small suitcase, then scrambled to her car for the trip to the airport. Time seemed to stop as she parked, ran into the terminal and then to the ticket counter, and got through security. Lizzie arrived at her gate at eight-fifteen, coughing a bit from the exertion. She boarded, settled into her seat, and fired off a quick text to Landon before her nonstop flight to Dallas left the gate as scheduled at eight-thirty.

***

Landon was on a flight of his own and didn't receive Lizzie's text until he was on his way to baggage claim. He scanned it quickly and replied, knowing she wouldn't see it until she landed. Then he checked his calendar to try to see how quickly he could get back to Texas to be by her side.

***

Lizzie wasn't hampered by waiting for baggage claim once her flight landed; she'd only packed a small carry-on. She walked as quickly as she could to the car rental counter, and within fifteen minutes she was in route to the hospital, just south of downtown Fort Worth. The traffic gods smiled on her and she arrived in the hospital's main parking lot within forty minutes. Lizzie raced into the emergency room entrance and spotted Joe waiting for her. "He's in bay seven," he told her as they walked up to the counter for Lizzie to be assigned a visitor's pass.

"What happened, Joe?" she asked as she placed the sticky label on her jacket and the clerk buzzed the door for them to continue down the hall into the triage area.

"We were supposed to meet for breakfast like we always do," Joe began as he held the door for her. "And your dad is always on time. Until this morning. I called him four times, no answer, called again on my way to the house. I get there and knock on the door and I hear him moaning. So, I let myself in and he was on the living room floor." He gestured ahead of them. “Seven is down and to the left.”

“Have the doctors said anything?” Lizzie asked.

“Not yet,” Joe told her. “They were just taking him back for another CAT scan when I walked out into the waiting area to watch for you. That was about an hour ago, and I let them know his family was on the way from out of state.”

They paused at the nurse’s station, and Joe asked, “Is Frank back from the CAT scan? Bay seven.”

“I believe so but let me check,” the on-duty nurse replied, and typed on her keyboard. Then she looked back up at Joe and Lizzie and started to speak. But a tall, lanky man in a white coat walked up at that moment. “Zimmerman?” he asked.

"Hi, I'm Elizabeth, Frank's daughter. This is Joe Wallace, his best friend," she answered as she extended her hand. The man shook their hands and responded, "I'm Dr. Adamal, the neurosurgeon on Frank's treatment team. Let's talk about where things are right now." And he gestured to a small room just off the hallway.

Once they were seated and the door was closed, the doctor cleared his throat and said gently, "Ms. Zimmerman, Mr. Wallace, I'll be honest. It's not good. The CAT scan revealed a hemorrhagic stroke in the left frontal lobe. That's when an aneurysm in the brain bursts or leaks. In Frank's case, it's a rupture. And it's causing swelling and pressure, which is multiplying the damage. We are prepping him for surgery right now to try and clamp off the bleed and relieve some of that pressure. We won't know exactly how things stand until we get that pressure taken care of."

Lizzie reached out blindly for Joe's hand as her eyes started to fill. Her voice quavered as she asked, "What can we expect, if he survives this?"

"Most usually, a stroke in that region of the brain brings with it partial or total loss of movement on the right side, and at least some impact to memory and speech processing and recognition," Dr. Adamal told them. "He was found around eight a.m., correct?"

Joe nodded.

"And when was the last time anyone saw or spoke to him before he was found?"

"I called dispatch and asked," Joe replied. "He left the station at six-ten."

"Okay. There's not really a way to pinpoint when the stroke started. I can tell you, though, that hemorrhagic strokes are the most severe type, and with each minute that passes during a stroke chances of full recovery are diminished," the doctor informed them. "I'm not saying there's absolutely no chance for full recovery." Now he leaned forward with kind, sympathetic eyes. "Hope for the best, always. But I also wanted you both to be completely informed and prepared, in case the best doesn't happen." He stood. "I need to go scrub up. The surgery waiting area is one floor up from here. My head surgical nurse, Rebekah, will come out midway through the procedure and give you an update. And I will come back out and talk to you more once surgery is over."

"How long will surgery take?" Joe asked him as he guided Lizzie to her feet.

"Two hours, maybe a bit longer," the neurosurgeon replied. And he left the room. Lizzie held it together until the door closed again before she let the tears flow freely.

***

CHAPTER FOURTEEN

When Landon's return flight landed at ten p.m., his first and only thought was getting to Lizzie. He dialed her number as he left the airport.

"I'm in the car, on my way to you," he said as soon as she answered. "How's he doing?"

Lizzie sighed. "Nothing's changed since this morning."

"Hang in there, honey, I'll be there in about a half hour. Okay?"

He could hear the raw emotion in her voice as she whispered, "Okay, see you in a bit." As the call disconnected, he pressed the gas pedal even harder.

When he arrived, he paused in the doorway to just watch her for a moment. Lizzie looked exhausted and weighted down with worry, head in her hands, seated next to her father's hospital bed. The only sounds in the room were the occasional chirp of the monitors and the rhythmic rasp of the ventilator.

She sensed his presence and slowly lifted her head. A smile briefly traced her lips then was gone as the tears came again, and she stood and worked her way over to him, her face contorted with grief as she walked into Landon's outstretched arms.

"Oh, Lizzie," he murmured against her hair as sobs racked her body. "I'm so sorry." And he just held her while the machines monitoring her dad in the background continued their mournful song.

After a bit her breathing became more regular. But she didn't lift her head from its resting place on his chest when she said bleakly, "Dr. Adamal says there's a lot of damage, Landon. He told Joe and me to start thinking about service arrangements, just in case."

Landon tilted her face up gently so he could look her in the eyes as he responded. "I'm here for you, and I want to help, in any way I can. Just tell me what you need, and I'll do it." She nodded.

"Now," he continued, "have you eaten at all today?"

She shook her head.

Joe appeared in the doorway. "Lizzie," he urged. "Go eat something. I'll stay here with Frank. Okay? And I will call you if anything changes."

"Okay," she sighed. "Joe, this is Landon. Landon, this is Dad's old detective partner and best friend, Joe Wallace."

"Nice to meet you," Joe said, extending his hand.

"Likewise," Landon told him. "Although I wish it were happier circumstances."

"I'm going to the nurses station to let them know I am stepping out for a bit," Lizzie announced. She went to Frank, kissed his cheek and whispered, "Daddy, I'll be right back." Then she left the room.

Joe took Landon's arm to slow his approach to the door. "She's exhausted, and still battling walking pneumonia," Joe told him. "I haven't been able to convince her that not eating and sleeping through this isn't a good idea. Can you maybe get her to rest, even for a little while? I promise to keep you two updated should anything change here."

"I'll try my best."

"Thanks," Joe said.

Landon found Lizzie waiting by the elevators.

"I still don't feel like eating," she began.

"I know," he replied, as he kissed her. "But you need to try. Did you bring your prescriptions with you? Won't help anything if your case of walking pneumonia turns into full-blown pneumonia."

Lizzie narrowed her eyes. "Landon Kendal, are you *handling* me?"

"If it means keeping you from running yourself into the ground? Absolutely," he answered without hesitation as he pressed the call button for the elevator car. "I am taking you to my house, and I am going to fix you a meal. After that, we can both catch a nap – we could both use one," he added, seeing her jaw set stubbornly. "And then we will come back up here. Deal?"

She glowered for a moment, brushing past him to get into the waiting elevator.

"Fine," she muttered. "But I don't want to be gone more than three or four hours, tops."

"I'll make sure of it," Landon replied, as they rode down to the first floor and walked out toward the main exit.

***

Donny leaned back from his keyboard and smiled. Just a few more details to tweak and it would all be ready. The love of his life would get the surprise of her life come Memorial Day weekend. Still smiling, he logged off and headed for sleep.

***

Nathan sat in a chair beside Bella's bed, holding his son in his arms. "I am still blown away by this," he told his wife.

"Me too," Bella answered as she yawned.

Marianne, the nurse who'd helped during delivery, tapped on the door, then entered. "Hi guys! How are we doing in here?"

"Great," Nathan replied, smiling.

"I'm exhausted," Bella told her.

"Understandable," Marianne said. "I suggest that you try to get as much sleep as you can while you're here. I can take the little guy back to the nursery for a while so you can rest."

"Can I stay?" Nathan asked her.

"You can, if you like. We can bring in a sleeper chair. I will warn you though, they aren't the most comfortable things after a while."

"Baby, go home, get some real sleep," Bella told him. "You and I both know once we get him home real sleep may not happen for a while."

"I don't want to leave you."

"What are you going to do, watch me sleep all night? Go, honey. I'll see you in the morning."

Nathan handed the baby to Marianne, who headed back to the nursery. Then he walked to the bed and hugged and kissed Bella. “I love you. See you in the morning; I will be back by nine.”

“I love you too, Nathan,” Bella managed through a suppressed yawn. “Like she said, we need all the sleep we can get. Something tells me we’re going to go without for a while.”

Nathan chuckled. “Probably. But we will be sleep-deprived together.”

***

Silence filled the car as Landon drove the fifteen minutes to his home in Pantego. Lizzie stared out the window, mindlessly viewing the surroundings. Finally, she spoke. “I still can’t believe this is happening, Landon. Dad’s always been this robust, lively guy, larger than life to me, almost bulletproof. He's only fifty-six."

Landon pulled into his driveway, put the car in park, then took her hand. "I wish there was something I could say or do that would make it better."

She sighed. "I know. I appreciate you being here with me through it."

As they walked into his house, he asked, "Anything sound good?'

"Something simple," she answered.

"How about an omelet?" he offered.

"That will work."

"Great," Landon smiled. "Have a seat, it won't take me long. Coffeepot is just over there, or if you feel like something stronger, the wet bar is in the living room."

"Bathroom?"

"Down the hall to the left," he pointed.

Lizzie nodded and headed down the hallway. Closing the door behind her, she moved to the sink to splash cold water on her face. She lifted her head and met her reflection in the mirror. “I look as wrung out as I feel,” she muttered as she noticed the deep shadows under her eyes. She dried her face, went back to the living room toward the bar Landon had mentioned, then thought better of it and made her way to the kitchen for a cup of coffee instead. She poured, added cream and sugar, and Landon handed her a spoon. “Thanks,” she said, and sat at his kitchen table. “Nice place, by the way.”

“Thanks,” Landon smiled. “It’s the house my mom and dad bought when we moved to Texas.”

“You’ve never told me about them.”

He shrugged as he flipped her omelet over. “Not much to tell, really. We settled here when I was eight, Mom died when I was ten. After that, well… let’s say Dad had a rough time of it and leave it at that. He passed away in 2002.”

“You have any brothers or sisters?”

“One. Little sister. She’s two years younger than me.”

“Where does she live?” Lizzie asked.

“Not far from here, actually,” Landon stated. “She’s been a nurse for some time now, but lately she’s talked about switching careers. You’ll have to meet her sometime. I think the two of you would like each other.”

He put her omelet on a plate and handed it to her. “There you go, ham and cheese. Want some toast?”

"This is plenty, thanks." Then, "I'm not going to be able to eat this whole thing. Would you like half?" she offered.

"Sure." He got up and brought another plate to the table, and she maneuvered half the food over to him. As he sat back down and picked up his fork, he asked her, "What about you, Lizzie? Any brothers or sisters?"

"Nope, only child," she said as she reached for the pepper. "Which makes all this harder. My mom and I had a huge blowout a little over a year ago and we haven't spoken since. I've always been closer to my Dad; he's who I turn to when I need to vent, or whatever…," Lizzie's voice trailed off as the tears threatened again, and she took a deep breath to steady herself before she continued. "So, I will be there for him, the way he's always been there for me." Her motions were deliberate as she seasoned her food then started to eat, and Landon could tell she was forcing herself to take each bite.

She noticed him watching her, and grimaced. “Sorry. I just have zero appetite.”

“I know,” he answered gently. “Do what you can.” After a few more minutes, she yawned.

“Let’s go crash for a couple of hours,” he suggested. “At least try to rest before we head back up there. What time do you want me to set for the alarm?” He held out his hand to her, and together they walked down the short hallway into the bedroom.

“What time is it now?”

“Midnight. How about five o’clock? I know you said you didn’t want to be gone more than four hours, Lizzie, but we also need some sleep.”

“Five is fine. Which side is yours?” Lizzie asked as she moved past the king-sizde bed toward the master bath.

“The left.”

“Good to know.” Then she stopped. “Dammit.”

“What?”

“My suitcase is in my car at the hospital.”

“And?”

“I don’t have anything to sleep in.”

“Here,” he offered as he opened a dresser drawer, then moved to his side of the bed to set the alarm clock. “Pajama bottoms, shorts, couple of t-shirts. Take your pick.”

“Thanks.” She rummaged and decided on a pair of shorts with a drawstring and a faded green but extremely soft shirt. Lizzie changed in the bathroom then made her way to the bed’s right side and climbed in.

"You good?" he asked her as she snuggled close so she could lay her head on his chest. She yawned in response and was asleep in moments.

Landon stayed awake a while longer, just to savor the feel of her in his arms before he too drifted into sleep.

***

She pulled up her notes and cross-checked them against what she'd just found. *Yep, that's her. Well, well, well. Nina Kennedy just booked herself a little getaway.* She smiled. She loved Puerto Vallarta, and that was as good a place as any to get to mark another name off the list. Humming to herself, she opened the booking site she frequented and made special travel plans of her own before she called it a night.

***

Nathan couldn't sleep. The euphoria of being a father meant adrenaline continued to surge. He had called all three of his sisters on the drive to let them know, and when he arrived home, he emailed them pictures of their brand-new nephew. Within moments, Jandy called him back.

"Nathan, he is so beautiful," she gushed.

"I know, right? He got his momma's looks."

"Oh, honey," she chuckled. "I wanted to offer to come up and stay for a week or so, if you need me to."

"I'd love that, and I am sure Bella would appreciate it too, but let me ask her."

When he finally wrapped up the call, he went to lie down but found his mind was still churning. He wandered down the hall to the nursery and stood in the doorway, surveying the landscape in which their child would begin his life. “We have a son,” he said softly to himself, and he felt his heart might burst.

Eventually he retreated to the master bedroom, got comfortable, dozed off, and dreamed of playing catch with Charlie someday.

***

Lizzie jolted awake at the screech of the alarm. “What the hell?”

Beside her, Landon chuckled sleepily. “You did say five o’clock was okay.”

“What’s up with that alarm? Thing sounds horrible. Like it’s been run over or something,” she groused, rubbing her eyes.

He roared, pulled her close and kissed her on the tip of her nose. “How did you sleep?”

“Pretty good, actually. Glad you talked me into getting some rest. Thanks for that.”

“How about some coffee to go?”

“Sounds good, meet you in the kitchen.”

Fifteen minutes later they were in Landon's car, heading back to see Lizzie's dad. She absentmindedly played with her college ring as she steeled herself for the return trip.

Joe met them just outside Frank's room. "Nurse said Dr. Adamal would be by shortly to check on Frank and update us," he announced. "I'm going to get some coffee, be right back."

"Did you stay all night?" Lizzie asked him, noticing that he looked completely worn out.

"Yeah," he admitted as she hugged him. "I stayed. Couldn't sleep anyway." He glanced past her shoulder, and his eyes widened a bit. She turned to follow his glance and saw two officers coming down the narrow hallway – the head police chaplain and the Chief. As they approached, the Chief said, “Here, Joe, thought you could use this,” and handed Joe a cup of coffee.

“Thanks, Chief, I sure can.”

“Chief Collins, thanks for coming,” Lizzie greeted him as he stepped to her side to give her a hug.

“How’s he doing, Elizabeth?”

“Last I knew, no change,” Lizzie told him. “Joe stayed with him overnight so I could get a bit of sleep. The doctor’s supposed to be making rounds soon though.” She turned to Landon. “I’m going to go see Dad for a bit.” And she touched his hand briefly before walking into the room.

As she moved toward the bed a wave of intense sadness washed over her, buckling her knees a bit. She took a deep breath to steady herself, then pulled a chair up beside him, sat down, and took his hand.

"Daddy," she began, voice breaking. "I love you Daddy. If you can hear me, please squeeze my hand. Just squeeze it, Daddy. Please."

But no response came, save the cadenced, subtle noises of the machinery surrounding her father, keeping his body going. She sat, his cool limp hand tucked into her warm one, for what seemed an eternity before a soft rap on the door beckoned her attention.

Wiping tears from her face, she cleared her throat. "Yes?" she called, her voice husky with grief.

Landon cracked the door and poked his head into the opening. "Dr. Adamal's here, Lizzie. Needs to talk to you." She glanced at his face, hoping to see something in his countenance that meant good news, and saw no sign.

"Oh," she responded, and with that one syllable she realized what was coming. She stood, leaned over Frank and kissed his check. "I'll be right back," she whispered, and walked out into the hall.

Dr. Adamal stood in the foyer with Landon, Joe, Chief Collins, and the chaplain. "Miss Zimmerman," the doctor intoned gently. "I think it's time to go over some things. If you will please follow me?"

The group moved just down the hall towards an area with seating. Then Dr. Adamal cleared his throat. "I have looked at all of Frank's tests, and all the readouts since he got here. The surgery stopped any more blood leaking into the brain, but the swelling hasn't gone down..." He paused.

"Go on, Dr. Adamal, just say it." Lizzie said dully.

He sighed. “I don’t know if your father has any sort of living will in place, but regardless, as his next of kin you become the decisionmaker about his care since he’s unable to make them himself.”

“Okay. What do you need?” she asked.

Dr. Adamal hesitated, trying to choose his next words carefully.

“Miss Zimmerman –,” he began but she cut him off.

“Please, call me Lizzie.”

“Okay. Lizzie. Here’s the situation. All our results have come back the same – no brain activity. There’s just… there was too much damage done. Breathing, the heartbeat, that’s all because of the machines at this point.”

“He’s gone, isn’t he?” Lizzie asked directly.

Dr. Adamal looked into her eyes. "Yes," he answered, knowing he couldn't spare her the pain.

"Then I need to let him go, don't I." It was a statement, flat, without emotion.

"It's completely your decision whether or not to turn the machines off."

She reached out to either side of her to take Joe's and Landon's hands in hers. "May we have a moment, please?"

Dr. Adamal stood. "Sure. Take all the time you need. I will be on rounds all morning, but just have the nurses page me if you need me. And I'm so sorry, I wish I had better news for you than this." He left the room, closing the door gently behind him.

"Well," she whispered, overwhelmed. Then, "Joe? Thoughts?"

"I love him, kiddo, you know I do. He's a brother to me," Joe managed before his voice broke a little. After a moment or two, he continued, “But him hooked up like that? That’s not living, Lizzie. Your dad’s always been active, energetic, a larger than life kind of guy. He wouldn’t want this.”

“I agree,” she managed as fresh tears began to trace her cheeks. “It hurts like hell, I don’t want to let him go, but that’s not Daddy in there.”

Chief Collins leaned forward. “What can we do to help you, Lizzie?”

“Um, can you guys help me line out the service arrangements? Color guard, bagpipes…” She swallowed hard, trying to focus. “I don’t know where to start.”

The chaplain nodded. “We can absolutely handle that part for you. It would be an honor. And anything else you need, Lizzie, just tell us. You’re not alone.”

“Let’s go find Dr. Adamal,” she replied, eyes closed for a moment to try to stem the tide of emotions crashing down on her. “And I need to call my section chief and let him know I won’t be back for a week or two.” She released Joe’s hand to dry her face with the tissue the chaplain handed her.

Landon’s grasp on her hand tightened in silent support as she stood and led the group out the door toward the nurses station. When asked, the nurse confirmed that Dr. Adamal was still on rounds nearby. “We’ll be in with Dad. Could you please ask the doctor to join us?” Lizzie asked. The nurse nodded somberly; she’d seen the chart and knew what was coming.

“Thanks.” Lizzie turned and made her way back to her father’s side, resuming her place in the chair and once again taking his hand in hers.

"I'll start making some calls," the chaplain said to Joe and Landon.

"And I'll give you some privacy," Chief Collins told them. He shook hands with Landon and Joe, then he and the chaplain headed for the elevator.

"Well…," Joe let out a deep sigh and looked at Landon. "Let's get this over with." He and Landon filed into Frank's room. Joe pulled up a chair on the other side of the bed from Lizzie, while Landon walked to her and put his hand lovingly on her shoulder.

Within a few minutes, Dr. Adamal appeared. "Yes, Lizzie?"

"We talked about it, and we agree this…," she pointed to the machines, "this is not what Daddy would want. Leaving them on like this to keep him here would be selfish. Turn them off, please. Let him be at rest," she finished as she began to sob.

Dr. Adamal fought back the lump forming in his throat enough to say, “Okay, Lizzie. I’ll be right back.” He stepped out again, returning with one of the nurses assigned to Frank’s care, and they each took up stations– him where he could see the monitors, the nurse at the equipment’s controls. He nodded solemnly, and one by one the machines were stopped.

“I love you, Daddy. *I love you*,” Lizzie repeated, clutching his hand. The beeps representing her father’s heartbeats sounded less and less regularly, until they ceased completely.

CHAPTER FIFTEEN

Six days later.

Lizzie stood in her father's living room, hands on hips, uncertain how and where to begin. Figuring out the best starting point to handle his estate was proving to be more difficult than she'd imagined. She'd known that the service arrangements could get complicated, but the police chaplain had assisted every step of the way.

Now she was down to the things only she could do –informing his Visa card company, the cable company and others of his death, deciding what to do with the house, with all his clothes… It was too much to tackle at once.

As she wound her hair up into a ponytail, she relived some of his memorial service. Two days ago, she'd stood in the family room just off the main chapel with Joe and Landon on either side, waiting for the moment that the funeral director would escort them in to be seated. *It still doesn't seem real. None of it. I keep expecting Dad to call me just anytime now*, she'd thought to herself. Hearing a familiar voice, she had turned to see her section chief and her partner David entering the room, both dressed in their best Seattle PD dress uniforms. David picked her up in a bear hug and said, "I'm so sorry, Zim." It undid her. Once she'd composed herself, she insisted they sit with her, Joe, and Landon.

Then she noticed someone else had walked into the room, and her mouth dropped open. Her mother Linda was standing there, tears flowing freely. "*Mom*," Lizzie managed before they came together in a long embrace.

The director standing patiently with his arm extended brought them back to harsh reality. They'd moved into the chapel and

Lizzie was amazed to see it was filled almost beyond capacity with people also mourning her loss. She counted twelve different police departments represented, as well as state troopers and sheriff's departments from several counties in attendance. The moving show of support from their brothers and sisters in blue had her in tears again before she reached her seat.

The dialogue and motions of the service itself she could not completely recall; emotions swirling had rendered that part hazy, just little snippets here and there that floated up into clarity. The Lord's prayer. Chief Collins standing at the podium. An ocean of dress blues going past as people paid their respects. The dignified honor guard solemnly maneuvering the casket into the hearse. Looking out the window of the limo as the procession made its way to her father's gravesite. Bagpipe strains of "Amazing Grace" wafting through a crisp April morning, a final prayer, and condolences from the Chief as he handed her the flag that had draped her father's casket during the service.

She'd placed a single white rose on the casket once most of those in attendance had returned to their cars, and she stayed with her father while his body was lowered into his grave. Only then was Landon able to convince her it was okay to leave.

Next came the gathering back at her father's house; the chaplain had been gracious enough to arrange enough food to feed a small army. Eventually the crowd had dwindled until only Landon, Joe, Linda, David and her section chief remained.

Her chief had hugged her. "We're going to head back, Lizzie. But you take as long as you need, you hear? I mean it. Come back when you're ready."

"Yes, sir," she'd answered.

Linda spoke next. "I'm flying back tonight with them, honey. But I have two suitcases of clothes for you. When David called me about your dad, I figured you would need more, so we went by your place and grabbed some things for you."

"Thanks, Mom. I never thought of that."

"Lizzie, did you want to stay here tonight, or my place? Your call," Landon chimed in.

"I don't think I can stay here yet," she admitted. "Not yet. Maybe in a day or two."

They'd put the food away and made sure the house was locked. Landon went with Linda to transfer the suitcases over to his car while Lizzie talked to David. "Tank, can you watch my house for me until I get back?"

"Sure, SWG, no problem," he'd said on purpose to elicit a smile. It worked.

Linda walked back over to Lizzie. "See you when you get back?"

"I'd like that, Mom."

Lizzie hugged her and David one last time and waved as they got into the rental car with her boss and drove away. Then she slung her arm around Joe's shoulders. "What now?" she'd asked. "And – how are you holding up, Joe? I know he was your best friend."

Joe shrugged. "Yes, he was. I'm all right, Liz, I promise." His cell phone rang. "Wallace," he said, then, "Hey there. Really. Okay, I'm on my way." He hung up. "Just caught a break on a case I've been working for eight weeks."

She hugged him. "I understand that feeling. Go. We'll have dinner or something in the next week or so, okay?"

"You got it, kiddo." And he shook Landon's hand before leaving.

Landon looked at her. "How are *you* doing, Lizzie?"

"Exhausted," she'd replied. "I made it through today, but I have no idea how. It still doesn't seem real to me, Landon."

He'd driven her back to his house, where they had spent the night and the next day just being together. She'd seen a little bookstore not far from Landon's place, and they'd stopped in. They met the owners - Rick Conner and his fiancée, Faith Thomas - and after chatting with them, Lizzie and Landon wandered through the aisles of Book Keepers hand in hand before walking up to Mama J's for a meal. It was a welcome break between the heartache of the funeral and the mountain looming known as settling someone's estate. Parts of it were easy –

Frank had a simple will in place leaving everything to her. Other things were more complex – sell the house? Keep it and rent it out? What should she do with his car?

With effort she returned her focus to her current situation, surveyed the contents of her father's living room, and sighed. I w*ish Landon was here right now,* she realized. *He'd know the best place to start.* But he was in Los Angeles dealing with one of his importing contacts and wasn't scheduled to be back until tomorrow night. *Get back to basics, Liz,* she told herself. *One step at a time. Maybe light cleaning first? THEN tackle the place, room by room, from the back of the house forward.*

Sighing, she flipped on the TV for some background noise as she began to dust. But the noon broadcast caught her attention as the anchor relayed the story of a private plane crash in West Palm Beach, Florida over the weekend. The two victims in the crash had been identified as Fort Worth real estate mogul Jeff Hartford and Crystal Lee Hartford, his wife. *I feel for their family,* she commiserated as she shook her head sadly and continued her work.

***

Nina Kennedy smiled as she lounged in the warm sunshine. *I so needed this,* she thought to herself as she stretched her frame like a satisfied cat before rolling onto her stomach to continue her sunbathing.

Her killer observed the behavior from the second-floor breezeway and nodded in satisfaction. Nina wouldn't be leaving her lounge chair any time soon.

Turning, she made her way to the elevators, then to the fourth-floor suite that Nina had booked. Once she made sure she wasn't being observed, she slipped on her surgical gloves, slid the master keycard she'd lifted from the housekeeper's cart into the lock, and entered the room, closing the door swiftly but quietly behind her.

As expected, she found Nina's insulin in the mini fridge, and replaced the vial with an exact replica that contained a much more dangerous and fast-acting substance. Then she left the suite and headed down to the pool for some sunbathing of her own.

***

Charles Daniel Thomas has a set of lungs on him, that's for sure, Nathan thought as he prepped the bottle. He'd taken a shift so Bella could soak in the tub for some down time. He sat in the rocking chair in the nursery with their son and fed him, pausing occasionally to burp Charlie gently.

Jandy flying in to help the first week had been both useful and very appreciated. The idea of giving this tiny creature a bath, for example, had terrified Bella and Nathan both; neither one had spent much time around infants before. But Jandy had shown them how, and their confidence levels had been bolstered a great deal.

“Everything okay in here?” Bella asked as she stood in the doorway in her robe.

“Perfect,” Nathan grinned. He looked down to see Charlie had fallen asleep. Moving as steadily and as quietly as he could, he got up and settled the baby into the crib, then walked over to his wife.

Now Bella smiled as she wrapped her arms around Nathan. “I think he’ll be asleep for a couple of hours,” she said. “And the baby monitor is turned on, in case he proves me wrong. How about we go make lunch?”

Hand in hand they wandered downstairs. “I was thinking grilled ham and cheese,” she suggested.

“That sounds great,” he told her. “I got this. You take a break.”

“I am okay with that,” Bella grinned, but she moved to the fridge first to retrieve the ham, butter and cheese for him before she settled onto the barstool closest to him. “I’ve been meaning to ask you, honey. What do you think about all this? Do you… feel any different?”

“Different? Hmm,” he pondered the question as he spread butter onto bread slices, assembled the first sandwich and placed it into the hot skillet. “Kind of. I mean, I didn’t go through any of the physical changes you did. But it’s a whole new level of responsibility. You know? Awe-inspiring and a little intimidating all at once.”

"Yeah," she sighed. "That makes me feel better. I hoped it wasn't just me feeling overwhelmed a bit."

"No, baby, not just you," Nathan assured her. "But like Jandy said, there's really not a complete how-to manual for this. We will learn it together as we go." He kissed her gently, then pivoted to flip the sandwich over so it could brown on the other side. Moments later he plated it and presented it to her with a small flourish. "Madam, your meal."

Bella laughed. "Why thank you, kind sir."

He made his sandwich and was just about to sit down beside her when his phone rang. "Thomas."

He listened, asked two questions, and nodded as he followed up with, "On my way." Nathan hung up the phone and looked at his wife.

"Go," Bella urged. "I've got this. Be careful, and we'll see you when you get home."

"I love you, Isabella Rose Thomas."

"I love you too, Nathan Thomas. Go. Be safe."

He kissed her, then grabbed his sandwich off its plate. "Guess this is takeout."

***

Lizzie sat on the side of Frank's bed, tears brimming. While trying to organize what to do with his clothes, she'd found a box. When she opened it, she'd been overwhelmed and had to sit down.

Inside was everything she'd ever given her dad, all the way back to the hand outline Thanksgiving turkey picture she'd done in kindergarten. Dried macaroni noodles covered in glitter and glued to construction paper, strange little structures made from wooden ice cream sticks, her A-B honor rolls through elementary, pictures of her in her softball uniform when she was nine, school pictures, every birthday and Father's Day card she'd ever sent. It was all here, tucked with great care into the box.

She also noticed he'd continued the trend more recently. Her high school, college, and police academy graduation announcements were in the box too, in pristine condition. The most recent addition had been the picture taken of the two of them at her promotion ceremony when she made detective a little over two years ago.

"I can't take much more of this today," she mumbled out loud. If she found just one more sentimental thing, she'd crumble completely. She swiped at her cheeks to dry them, then stood up. Time to call it a day and head back to Landon's place; she still wasn't ready to spend a night here.

She realized on her drive to Landon's house that she needed a distraction for the evening. Lizzie glanced at the clock in Frank's car – six-thirty p.m. *Hmm. Book Keepers doesn't close until eight. Maybe I can find a good book to get lost in tonight.* The idea appealed to her. Hot bath, simple dinner, and curl up with a book.

She parked on the street in front of the bookstore and as she moved toward the entrance, she noticed Faith coming down the sidewalk. "Hey Lizzie!" Faith said warmly. "Nice to see you again. How have you been?"

Lizzie burst into tears.

Alarmed, Faith quickened her pace to close the distance between them. "Oh God. Are you okay?"

“Not really,” Lizzie managed.

“Here, come with me. It’ll be okay.” And she led Lizzie into the store. Rick looked up, saw Lizzie’s distress, and raised an eyebrow at Faith. She shook her head to wave him off, then inclined it toward the back of the store and the lift. He gave the ‘thumbs up’ in return, knowing whatever was wrong Faith would try to fix if she could.

“You look like you could use a drink and someone to talk to,” Faith told her as they stepped into the elevator. “We have a full bar if you want, but we also have coffee and tea.”

“I’m so sorry to put you through any trouble,” Lizzie responded as Faith opened the lift gate and they stepped out into Faith and Rick’s home above the store.

“Oh, honey, it’s not any trouble. Okay? You can share or not share as much as you like, and you can stay as long as you like." Faith led the way across the room and into the kitchen. "Now, alcohol, coffee, or tea?"

"Hot tea actually sounds really good. Thanks." Lizzie sat at the kitchen table. "Beautiful home, by the way."

"Thanks." Faith set the cup of tea down in front of her and handed her a spoon. "Sugar bowl is there," she pointed at the middle of the table. "Let me get mine poured right quick, and then we can talk."

Lizzie added sugar to her cup, and Faith joined her at the table moments later, armed with a box of tissues. "So, Lizzie. What's going on? Anything I can do to help?"

Lizzie took a deep breath and told Faith about all of it. Her engagement breaking up and losing her best friend in one fell swoop. Losing her dad, trying to figure out what to do next, feeling absolutely overwhelmed by it all. That she had forgotten what it was like to have a female friend to confide in since Jessica had betrayed her. That she had not realized how truly alone she felt until Faith greeted her so kindly.

"Don't get me wrong, Landon is great," Lizzie added hastily. "But it's just not the same as having a best friend to talk to about stuff."

"I understand, Lizzie, I truly do. I'm close with my two sisters, but I've never really had a best friend either. And, you and I have some things in common. My first marriage ended because I caught my ex with someone, too. Then he died unexpectedly, and I had to handle his estate."

"So, you've lived parts of this," Lizzie confirmed.

"Yes, I have. In my case, I threw myself into work, shut myself away in my house when I wasn't at my office. After a year of that, I talked myself into braving the world long enough to find something new to read. That's all I was planning on. And I walked through that door downstairs and found the love of my life."

Faith took a sip of her tea, then continued. "As far as the estate stuff goes. I've been there, and so has Rick. We'd be willing to help, if you need us or have questions." Now she smiled at Lizzie. "It also sounds like you have a really good guy in Landon; sounds like he really cares about you."

Lizzie sighed. "Yeah, he does."

As they talked more, they found other shared interests, and discovered they had birthdays eleven days apart. By the time Rick came upstairs from closing the store for the night, they were giggling about something like a couple of schoolgirls having a sleepover. He approached the doorway to the kitchen cautiously.

"Everything okay?" he asked them. "Do you need privacy?"

"No, babe, it's good," Faith answered, with Lizzie nodding in confirmation. "We're finding out we have a lot in common." And she patted Lizzie's hand and smiled. "Hey Lizzie, you said Landon's gone until tomorrow night, right? Stay and have dinner with us," Faith prompted as she stood and went to the kitchen cabinets. "I put a pot roast on this morning."

"*That's* what that is," Lizzie responded. "That smells amazing. I haven't had pot roast in forever."

"Oh, now, see? There you go. You two were destined to be friends," Rick quipped as he walked over to help Faith set the table. "Because Faith makes the best pot roast on the planet."

Lizzie laughed, her first genuine one in a week. "You know what? Yes, I'll stay for dinner. Thanks."

Faith and Rick brought food to the table and as everyone filled their plates Rick said, "So, Lizzie, what do you do?"

"I'm a detective with Seattle PD."

"Cool! How long?"

"Well, I've been on the force almost nine years now, coming up on two as a detective."

"You like it?"

"I love it," Lizzie answered sincerely. "It always feels good to catch the bad guy. Plus, my dad was a detective here in Fort Worth almost all my life, so I consider it the family business. I've never wanted to be anything else."

"My brother, Nathan, spent a couple of years as a Virginia state trooper before he joined the FBI as a profiler," Faith chimed in. "We have three generations of police in our family history, and from the time he was small, it was all Nathan's ever talked about for a career."

The small talk continued as they finished the meal. Lizzie glanced at her watch. "Oh, good Lord, it's almost ten o'clock already! I'd better get going." She stood. "Thanks again, guys. For dinner, and for listening, Faith. I really appreciate it."

"Anytime," Faith told her. "Matter of fact, I can come over Saturday, help out at your dad's, if you need. Is nine o'clock all right?"

***

She'd shadowed Nina at the pool, then watched her from across the restaurant during the evening meal. *Tsk, tsk, Nina.*

Easy on the daquiris. You know you're not supposed to drink those. Ah, well, guess you'll just need a bit bigger insulin dose than usual before bed. She barely contained a chuckle at the thought.

When she observed Nina's departure toward the elevators, she smiled and ordered coffee and dessert as an early celebration gift to herself. She took her time and enjoyed each bite before paying her tab and strolling leisurely to the elevators. Arriving at the fourth floor, she returned to her room and set her timer for two hours, then entertained herself with a movie.

When the timer sounded, she checked her watch. *Midnight. Not too many people will be up and about this late.* She left her room, slinking down the hallway until she came to Nina's door, then knocked softly with gloves in place again and waited. No response.

Once again, she quietly let herself in, and found Nina sprawled on the bed, lips a deep shade of blue, eyes wide and vacant behind the film that accompanied death. The succinylcholine had worked precisely as expected. She picked up the offending vial, set Nina's pilfered vial of insulin in its place, added a bowtie candy wrapper to the nightstand as a finishing touch, and returned to her room triumphant. Before she settled in for a good night's sleep, she crossed off Nina Kennedy's name in her notebook. *Almost done,* she thought as she drifted off. *And then I can be with Donny all the time.*

***

On the west side of Fort Worth, Texas, the grandfather clock in Bruce Richards' living room solemnly announced the arrival of two a.m. March the seventeenth as the Raven put his finishing touches on the scene. As was his custom, he left his hobby kill token on the TV tray next to the recliner. *Thank God for chloroform*, he thought as he arranged Bruce's unconscious body in the recliner. *Big bull of a man like this I'd have had trouble going one on one with.* But chemicals had evened up the size and weight imbalance.

He stepped back for just a moment while he loaded one round in Bruce's own handgun, a Beretta .380. *Gotta admit, this is not my favorite part,* he mused grimly. Blood spatter was never fun to deal with. But he'd learned very early on in his career that black clothing made that part simpler to conceal. And over time he'd discovered that in situations like this one, unlikely tools came in handy.

He knelt beside his bag and took out his full-face shield, settling it into place before placing the gun in Bruce's right hand and using his own gloved ones to guide the pistol up to its intended target area – Bruce Richard's right temple. A gentle squeeze of his gloved right index finger over his victim's right index that lay on the trigger, and it was done. He stepped back, removed the face shield that now was covered in a fine mist, and placed it back in his duffel bag along with the top layer of rubber gloves. Then silently he made his way to the back door, listening intently for a moment.

Good, it's still going. Better chance no one heard the shot, he smiled to himself as he confirmed the kegger next door was still raging, complete with music almost cranked loud enough to rattle windows. Slinging his bag over his shoulder, he crept out of the house, locking Bruce's back door behind him. He peeled off the second set of gloves, shoving them in his pocket as he moved swiftly around the side of the house furthest from the party and disappeared into pitch black.

CHAPTER SIXTEEN

True to her word, Faith met Lizzie at Frank's house promptly at nine a.m. Saturday as they had agreed. "Morning," she said brightly as she followed Lizzie up the front steps and into the living room. "Where would you like me to start?"

"And me," Joe called out from the sidewalk, startling them both. "Sorry if I scared you. Thought you could use more help, kiddo." Then he held up a box. "And donuts, of course," as they all walked into the house.

"Thanks, Joe. I'd like you to meet my friend, Faith Thomas. Faith, this is Joe Wallace, Dad's best friend and former partner when Dad was a detective."

"Hi," Faith smiled.

“Nice to meet you,” Joe smiled and shook her hand. Then, “So. What she said. Where do you need us?” to Lizzie.

She sighed. “Well, I got the cleaning part done. Now I guess we start boxing stuff up. I went and got some packing supplies yesterday.”

“I can start in the kitchen,” Faith offered. “You grab newspapers to wrap dishes in?”

“Sure did, they’re on the kitchen table.”

“Nice!” And Faith grabbed a still warm glazed donut as she traveled to the kitchen to get started.

“What can I do?” asked Joe.

“I still need to figure out what to do with his clothes,” Lizzie replied. “So, I thought we’d start in his room. And I wanted you to go through his personal effects with me, Joe. I think there are some things he would have liked you to have.”

Joe paused a moment or two to collect himself before saying “All right,” in a gruff voice.

By noon, Frank’s room had been tidied, bed linens stripped and run through the washer and dryer, and clothes and other items destined for donation had been packed up neatly. Lizzie had talked a reluctant Joe into keeping her father’s Saint Michael medallion. “Thanks,” Joe finally managed, as he looped the length of chain around his neck and tucked the medallion underneath his polo shirt. “This means a lot. He wore it every day. But you already knew that.”

“Yep,” she confirmed. “That’s why you should have it.” She absentmindedly tugged at her ponytail, then said, “Well, what next?” as they headed for the kitchen.

"You two okay with pizza? I can call one in, shouldn't take long to get here," Joe suggested.

"Sounds good to me. Faith?"

"Yep, pizza works for me too. Hey Lizzie," Faith pointed into the dining room as Joe walked away to make the call. "Things were getting a bit tight in here so as I got each box done, I labeled it and moved it in there."

"Good idea. How's it going in here?"

"Almost done, actually. I have one more box for the countertop stuff like the toaster, and after that, the food pantry and the silverware drawers are all that's left. I'm thinking by two o'clock, at the latest, the kitchen will be complete."

"Thanks, Faith. I really appreciate your being here," Lizzie began. But she was interrupted by an incoming call, and she beamed as she noticed the number. “Hey Landon,” she said as she answered. “What’s up?”

“Checking on things there. How’s it going?”

“Pretty good, actually. Got Dad’s room completely done, Faith’s almost done packing up the kitchen. That leaves the guest bedroom and bath, the living room, and his office.”

“That’s good,” he encouraged. “And you sound better, honey. More cheerful. I’m happy to hear that.”

“Yeah,” Lizzie sighed. “I’m getting there.”

“Well, I just wanted to let you know I should be done here about six, and I was wondering if you wanted to meet back at my house, then go to dinner?”

“Sure, I’d love that.”

"Okay. I'll call you when I leave the office."

"Bye." She hung up the phone and turned to see Faith watching her. "What?"

"Girl," Faith said. "You *glow* when you talk to him."

Now Lizzie grinned mischievously. "I do, don't I?"

***

"I think we found something," the lead mechanic called out to NTSB agent Tom Sharpent. Nodding, Tom crushed out his cigarette and walked back into the hangar serving as the investigation's main hub of operations.

"What do you have, Jude?"

"This," the mechanic pointed grimly. "Elevator controls. What do you not see?"

Tom gazed intently at the exposed mechanism. "Hmm," he murmured. "We seem to be missing the bolt connecting the cockpit control cables to the elevator's bell crank."

"Exactly," Jude confirmed. "And the horizontal stabilizer remained intact at impact. See how there's no warping on any of this that would indicate the bolt broke or worked its way loose? Didn't shear off, and didn't just fall out; this is self-contained, we'd have found it when we opened this up. I think it was removed and not put back on. Either overlooked during maintenance, or not put back intentionally."

They walked over to the table where the Hartford's Cessna's maintenance records and flight logs were stacked. Jude reexamined the maintenance notes, then tapped the pages. "Tom, there's nothing here at all about the elevator control areas ever requiring servicing above a perfunctory visual examination. The last time these records even *mention* the elevator controls was two months ago, during recertification inspection."

"You think that this was deliberate?"

"I do," Jude replied.

Tom frowned. "But even with elevator failure it is possible to land safely. Difficult, but not impossible. How many flight hours did Hartford have again?"

He flipped through pages until he found his answer. "Wow. Okay. He'd only gotten certified for solo flight twelve days before the crash. Still brand new at this."

"Man," Jude took off his ball cap and scratched his head. "Bad timing."

"Yeah," Tom agreed. "And something tells me whoever removed the bolts knew enough about Jeff Hartford to know he didn't have enough experience to handle it well if something major went wrong."

"But wait," Jude exclaimed. "Even brand-new pilots perform a 'full and free' check before they take off. It's a basic step, no matter what type of aircraft they're flying. Instructors drill it into their students' heads."

"You're right." Tom's brow furrowed in concentration. "And if this happened deliberately, whoever messed with this would have known that. So – How the hell did they do it and it still pass the check?"

"Substitution?"

"What do you mean?"

"It's like this," Jude explained. "It just needs to get through the preflight check, right? It could fall apart right after, wouldn't matter, because it was operational during the check, so the pilot wouldn't have known anything was wrong until *after* takeoff."

"What are you getting at?"

"What if somebody took the bolt out and replaced it with something else, something that would hold together just long enough to make it *seem* like everything was fine until the pilot really moved the controls around?"

They walked quickly back over to the exposed bell crank. "There," Tom pointed. "What is that?"

"Some sort of residue?" Jude said and shook his head, then looked at Tom. "But I can tell you this much. I've never seen anything like that in an elevator setup before."

"Get samples, let's get it tested," Tom instructed.

***

Louisville, Kentucky. The 137th running of the Kentucky Derby. That's where her preliminary research so far indicated

Theresa McNamara would be on May seventh. *Huh. I've never been to Kentucky before,* she mused. *Cool! I get to go somewhere else new for this one. And then, I'll finally be done, and I can move on and build a future with Donny.* She smiled warmly at the thought, then straightened her shoulders and kept digging into her next target's background.

***

"How did today go?" Landon asked Lizzie as she sat down in the chair that he had pulled out for her.

"It was, well, not fun, but good," she said. "Having Faith and Joe there really helped a lot. We got a lot done."

"Have you thought more about what to do with his house?"

"Not yet," she admitted. "But if I can get that figured out, some other answers will fall into line, like what to do with the furniture." She picked up her fork and started in on her salad. "Besides, I still have his office left to go through. He had years and years of stuff accumulated in there; probably the only room in the whole house that he ever showed packrat tendencies." She laughed lightly, shaking her head at the memory. "Knowing Dad, he probably has some work-related papers stashed away somewhere, so I really need Joe there for that part so I know what I can shred and what needs to go back to police headquarters with him."

"Sounds reasonable," Landon replied. "When will that part happen, you think?"

"Not until Thursday. Joe's working until then."

"Could I interest you in a mini-getaway, then?"

Lizzie smiled. "What did you have in mind?"

Landon took her hand. "How about the Florida Keys? We could fly down tomorrow, come back Wednesday night."

She tilted her head, considered. "Deal."

***

Joe Wallace was frowning as he looked through the open unsolved murder file of Ramon Garcia. Physical evidence was pitifully scant, making it hard to gain any traction. His desk phone ringing broke his concentration. "Wallace," he barked.

"Hey Joe, I've got Ramon's wife here at the front desk, she wants to talk to you, get an update."

Joe sighed, running his free hand through his hair. "Okay, please tell her I will be right down." He hung up the receiver and closed his eyes, counting down from ten.

Christ, I hate this. I hate having to tell someone who is grieving that there's been no progress. As he mentally reached 'one', he sighed again, got up, and headed to the first floor.

Isabel Garcia stood, watching him approach after the elevator doors opened and he stepped out. Joe extended his hand. "Mrs. Garcia," he said. She clasped his hand in both of hers.

"Any word, Detective Wallace?" she asked, with hope undimmed even though six months had passed since Ramon's death.

He sat down next to her. "No breaks so far, Mrs. Garcia. Believe me, I want them as badly as you do."

"I have faith in you," she told him earnestly. "I know you will find who did this. I know the answer is somewhere."

Joe felt strangely comforted by her unwavering faith, even though as a seasoned detective he knew that sometimes the truth never did come to light in a case. “I hope you’re right, Mrs. Garcia. I want to be able to find the truth for you. There’s just not much evidence to work with.”

She nodded, pulling a peppermint candy out of her purse. “Would you like one?” she offered.

“No thanks,” Joe said.

She shook her head sadly. “So many little things I am still getting used to. Did you know, I could not have these at all when Ramon was alive?”

Joe was confused. “Why?”

“He was deathly allergic to peppermint,” Isabel said. “He couldn’t be around it, in any form. I couldn’t even keep any in the house.”

Something prickled in the back of Joe's mind.

He made his goodbyes, promising to reach out with any new information. Then he headed upstairs and thumbed through Ramon's case file. Running his finger down the pages, he came across the supplemental details section of the coroner's report. When he re-read the inventory list of the victim's personal belongings he swore under his breath. It was right there in black and white, seemingly innocuous.

"Peppermint candy wrapper, tied into a bow, front pants pocket."

"Son of a bitch," Joe said aloud. "This wasn't a copper theft. He was targeted."

Another realization hit him squarely between the eyes and dropped his jaw wide open. *I've seen another scene recently with a bow-tied wrapper in it…*

He pivoted to his file cabinet, pulled out the last three cases he'd caught. He skimmed each one, looking at his notes, official reports, photographs of the scenes. And swore aloud again. Bruce Richards' presumed suicide last Thursday. On the TV tray next to the body, readily obvious now that Joe knew what to look for, was a peppermint candy wrapper, tied into a neat little bow and perched on the remote control.

Joe picked up his phone, dialed, and waited. "Boss," he said to his squad leader. "You got a minute? There's something I'd like to show you."

Ten minutes later he in was in the boss's office, walking him through what he'd discovered. "I'd like to drill down further into the lives of these two," Joe concluded. "This doesn't feel random to me. My gut says there's a connection between the two victims that leads back to one killer, we just have to find that connection."

"I agree," the squad leader said. "Also think it would be good to talk to some of our neighbors about any like cases, see if anything pops."

"On it, boss," Joe answered, getting to his feet. "I'll keep you posted."

***

Lizzie sighed and her fingers interlaced with Landon's as they strolled along the beach in Key Largo. "This feels familiar," she announced as she nudged him playfully.

He grinned. "Just about the same timing, too," he told her, inclining his head toward the water where a breathtaking sunset was underway.

"Yep. Hard to believe that was almost a year ago."

"Agreed," he nodded. "I will be honest, Lizzie. From the moment I met you, I'd hoped we'd be walking hand in hand like this for years to come."

She stopped, jaw slack, pulse quickening. *Oh, hell,* she almost said out loud, but caught herself.

"Landon. What are you saying?"

"I'm saying I fell in love with you the moment I saw you dive into that resort pool in Grand Cayman." He saw her turn pale, and hurriedly said, "Okay, sorry, that freaked you out. Too soon?"

"Um…," she stuttered, mind racing to try and find the right words. "Umm… you're not about to…. you know… are you?"

"Propose?" Now Landon was shocked. "No. Not tonight, at least. I'd be lying if I said I hadn't considered it already. But from the look of sheer panic on your face, my assumption that now would be way too soon was right."

"I'm so sorry," she managed. "I care about you, deeply. I just… I'm still making sure how I feel before I say something like that to you. That's a big deal to me. I've only said it once before to a man that wasn't family, and, well, I told you how that turned out."

Landon cupped her cheeks with his hands and lowered his lips to hers in a tender kiss. "I know, Lizzie. I know how badly you got burned. And I didn't tell you I love you to rush you, or make you feel guilty. If you don't feel it, don't say it. I just couldn't hold myself back from saying it any longer."

As she stepped into his arms, he rested his chin on the top of her head, and said softly, "I will wait as long as you need."

Lizzie let go the deep breath she'd been holding and relaxed in his embrace. "Okay."

As the sun gave itself to the western horizon, they made their way back to the hotel room with few words spoken. When she joined him in the king-sized bed, she held out her arms to him. "Be with me," she said simply.

Landon paused only to turn out the light before he moved closer to fulfill her request.

***

"What on earth?" Jude muttered.

"What?" Tom asked.

Jude held up the tweezers. "This was shoved in the bolt hole, along with whatever left this residue."

"That looks like…" Tom started to say.

"Some sort of candy wrapper," Jude finished. "Tied in a bow."

CHAPTER SEVENTEEN

Joe was waiting for Lizzie at Frank's house when she pulled into the drive on Thursday. "Morning," she called out.

"Hi, kiddo," he said, then sighed. "Last room to go, huh?"

"Yep."

"Figured out what you're gonna do with the place?"

She wound her hair into a ponytail so it would be out of the way. "Not yet." Then, "Joe, you okay? You look distracted."

"Lot going on right now," he confided. "Can't say much, active investigation, but it seems two of my cases are connected, just gotta figure out how."

"Wow," Lizzie replied. "Good luck with that." They walked into Frank's office and took in all the stacks and boxes.

“Did your dad ever throw anything away?”

“Looking at all this, I’d say no.”

“Where do you want to start?”

“Well,” she paused, thinking. “I will start with firing up his computer, see if there’s a file on it somewhere that makes sense of all these stacks.” As she sat at the desk she continued, “What I need you to do is start going through boxes, see if there are any work-related papers that need to return to your office.”

“On it,” he told her.

Joe moved to the nearest box, opened it and began scanning contents while Lizzie waited for her father’s computer to wheeze to life.

“I didn’t think anyone could have a slower desktop unit than mine back in Seattle, yet, here it is,” she groused, drumming fingers on the wood beside the mouse as she waited.

Joe chuckled, then said, "Wow, Liz. There's stuff in this box from the day he made detective back in 1983."

She smiled. "Honestly, it doesn't surprise me. Dad was pretty good about clearing out certain things, but when it came to this room, I truly cannot remember a time it *wasn't* stacked up like this."

Her forced patience was finally rewarded with a sign-in screen. "I *used* to know for sure what it was. I hope he didn't change it," she murmured, and typed 'FWPDProud76' into the password field. To her delight, Frank's desktop display swam into view.

A file folder, named "LIZZIE – Please Read" and located dead center of the screen, immediately had her undivided attention. Curiosity bursting, she moved the mouse to hover over the icon, and double-clicked. Inside the folder were two files – one Word document, one Excel. She opened the Word file first, noticed it was created on March 8th. *The last time he texted me,* she realized.

"*Lizzie,*" it read, "*If you are reading this, I didn't see them coming. Use the Excel file to put a stop to it. Be careful - and remember how much I love you. Dad.*"

"Joe!" she exclaimed, and her tone caused him to double-time it to her side.

"What's wrong?"

She pointed numbly at the screen.

"What the hell?" Joe exclaimed, his eyes going wide.

Hand trembling, Lizzie opened the Excel file, and scanned its contents. Three columns. The first held eighteen rows of initials. Column two had "N" or "?" running downward for eleven rows, column three contained dates, but also only for the first eleven rows. Across the top of the first column was a seven-digit number.

"What *is* this?" she asked Joe.

"I don't know," he told her grimly. "But I intend to find out. Print a copy of that for me, would you?"

Frank's printer grumbled and shook but finally produced the desired report. Joe snatched it and studied it for a moment.

"This," he tapped his finger on the seven-digit number. "This looks like it *might* be a case file number from back before the system conversion, but I'd have to log in to the database at work to make sure. That would be faster than wading through all this," he concluded, sweeping his arm out to indicate their surroundings.

"I agree," she said. "Want me to come with you?"

"Nah. This shouldn't take long, if my hunch is right."

"Okay. The note he left, Joe. It sounded like he thought he was in danger somehow. Do you think Dad's stroke might have actually been, you know…," she fumbled for words, "…not natural?"

"No idea," he told her honestly. "I had the same thought. Here's the thing. If he was right, and someone *was* after him, I just don't see how they could have gotten close enough to him without him noticing anything. Your dad was always very aware of his surroundings. But," he continued as he held her gaze, "I've got some good contacts at the coroner's office, so I can damn sure ask. You could call Dr. Adamal too, get his opinion, to help us figure this out."

Lizzie nodded, pulling out her phone. "I'll try him now. See you when you get back."

"Okay." Joe moved toward the front door, then stopped and turned back to her. "Frank didn't spook easily, Lizzie. Something about this is very wrong. I don't like it. Lock the door behind me. All right?"

She swallowed hard. "All right."

"It may be nothing," he offered. "But let's play it safe, just in case it's not."

***

Tom Sharpent tore open the envelope with the lab results, skimmed them, then headed down the hall. "Jude," he called out as he went into the breakroom. "Lab report's in."

"What was it?"

"Graphite."

The seasoned mechanic tilted his head and considered it. "Okay, yeah, I can see that. Very brittle unless it's mixed with something. You get a section of graphite that roughly matches the diameter and length of the bolt, swap it out where the control cables attach to the bell crank. It'll hold together long enough to get through the preflight check, although it would probably crack pretty good. Then once the plane's in the air, now you add a bit of resistance on the elevator, and yeah, the next few motions would have snapped it like a twig." He leveled his gaze at Tom. "That's a smart bastard right there. I don't envy anyone trying to catch this guy. Not one bit."

"Me either," Tom shook his head. "Me either."

"So, are you bringing in the FBI?"

"Yep," Tom confirmed. "A deliberately sabotaged plane, with a calling card left behind, absolutely moves to their turf now."

As he left to go make the call, he paused and said, “Jude, can you get a hold of some graphite? I want to run some simulations, test our theory, see just how long it takes the graphite to fail.”

***

“Nathan Thomas,” Nathan said briskly, once his unit secretary routed the incoming call to his cell phone.

“Agent Thomas, good afternoon. My name is Tom Sharpent, and I’m an investigator with the NTSB. Got a downed plane here I think you guys are going to find very interesting.”

Nathan listened with eyebrows raised as Tom filled him in, then said, “Let me check, hang on a sec,” and pulled up his work calendar. “West Palm Beach? I can be down there this afternoon. Where would you like to meet?”

***

Joe was about to enter his search parameters when he noticed new email. He opened it and found three responses to his original query. Three separate confirmations of other cases in the North Texas area involving bow-tied candy wrappers at the crime scenes; one in Waxahachie, one in Benbrook, and one in Decatur. He followed up with the points of contact, asking if he could arrange a visit to discuss their case files. Within a half-hour, he'd made appointments with each, starting in Decatur at eleven-thirty a.m.

He called Lizzie on the way to his car. "Hey, kiddo," he said when she answered. "I got some leads on the current cases I'm working, need to follow them up."

"It's okay," Lizzie told him. "I get it. You gotta work your actives, absolutely."

"Tell you what. Go to the courthouse, to the clerk's office. Unless a case has been sealed it should be part of the public record. You can put in a request for that number and get a copy of the case file, if it is in fact a case number like I think it is. It may take a few days, but it'll have everything in it – court transcript, the works."

"I'm on it, Joe. I'll let you know what I find out."

"Ok. Let's touch base tomorrow night?"

"You got it. See you then."

"Yep. And Lizzie – be careful."

***

Donny opened his door, trying his best to smile as she walked in. "What's wrong?" she asked, moving to him quickly.

He ran his hands through his hair. "This," he walked over to his answering machine and pressed the play button.

"Donny, it's Phil. I wanted you to hear about this from me first. Tell All Weekly somehow found out about Mary, and they're planning on running it on Monday. I'm trying my best to block the story. I'll keep you posted. So sorry, man. Call me."

"Who's Phil?"

"My agent," Donny sighed heavily.

"Let me get this straight. Some half-ass gossip rag dug up 'dirt' on you from *over a decade ago*, and they're going to publish it? Why?"

"I honestly don't know." His shoulders sagged.

"What happened to her wasn't your fault, Donny. I know you think it is, but it's not. It's not. Donny. *Donny, look at me*," she said forcefully as she put her hands on either side of his face and made him make eye contact. "She chose to shoot that speedball.

Not you. I know you feel guilty about her death. I get that. But when it's all said and done, baby – the choice was hers, and she made it."

"But if she hadn't met me..."

She cut him off. "NO. You don't know that." Now she gentled her tone and wrapped her arms around him. "You've carried this for so long, Donny. Carried this…this shame, this guilt with you. But you didn't cause this."

After a moment, she stepped back. "Now. I need a shower. Care to join me?"

"I need to call Phil back, see if there's anything I can do to get ahead of this," Donny answered, bitterness rising. "This could wipe out my business. No one's going to buy insurance from a guy they think killed somebody."

"It'll be all right, baby. You'll see." She patted his cheek then headed upstairs while he called Phil back. As he and his agent lined out next steps, Donny started to take notes, then threw the pen down in frustration – it was out of ink. He held his phone to his ear with his shoulder as he waded through drawer after drawer looking for a replacement.

"Dammit. Hang on, Phil, gotta find a pen that actually works around here." He looked around, noticed her purse sitting on the couch. *Man, I hate going through other's people's stuff, but this is important, I'm sure she won't mind.* He dug through, found a pen that was hooked onto the front of a little notebook, pulled both out. As he slid the pen downward to remove it from its cap, he fumbled and dropped it all. He swore, bent to retrieve the book that had landed and come open, and froze once he stood upright again. The page the pen cap had bookmarked contained some sort of weird list. As he scanned the page, he could feel the color leaving his face. “Phil, let me call you back,” he said softly, and hung up, not bothering to wait for Phil to agree.

It’s a list of names, he realized. *All numbered, and some are marked out. Hey, I’m on here…*He struggled to process what he was seeing, but in his core an overwhelming sense of dread was building. *And the number beside my name was changed? What the hell is this?* He activated his phone’s camera, snapped several pictures, then hastily placed the book with its pen back into her purse.

Donny took a sharp breath in, listening intently. *She’s still in the shower. Good.* Trembling, he moved to his desk, where he'd be able to see her come downstairs, and looked at the pictures he'd just taken. He could clearly see that the numbers besides his and another person's name – Samuel Norton - had been swapped out. *Samuel Norton, Samuel Norton. Where do I know that name from?* He racked his memory but couldn't place the man. *All these other names sound familiar, too. Where do I know all these people from?* "Something tells me I need to figure it out, and soon," he whispered to himself, as he heard the shower upstairs turn off. *Game face, dude,* he told himself. *You do NOT want her knowing what you found. Let her think it's still all about that damn story coming out.*

***

"You must be Tom," Nathan said, extending his hand toward the man that met him at his car.

"I am. Nice to meet you, Agent Thomas," Tom replied as he shook the hand Nathan had offered. "If you'll follow me please. Jude's set up some simulations for us to test our theory out."

"So, you said you found some sort of wrapper?"

"Yep, and I'll show you where."

He led Nathan into the hangar and directed him toward the elevator assembly. "See the hole right there?"

"I do," Nathan replied.

"It was tucked in there, along with what we believe to be a piece of graphite. The tests we're about to run should bear out what we think happened."

"Not accidental, then, any of it," Nathan stated solemnly.

"Not in my view, and I've been investigating crashes for fifteen years now. But finding something left behind deliberately, that makes it *obvious* it's been tampered with? This is a first for me."

Jude strolled up and was introduced to Nathan. "Now then," Tom announced. "Your test ready to run?"

"Yep, right this way, gentlemen," Jude swept his arm out to his right. "We've brought in an identical setup from another Cessna, so we can run tests on both of them, just to eliminate any chance the downed plane's parts had any sort of fault."

"Sounds thorough," Nathan observed.

Jude grinned. "Want to make sure we're right, definitely." He handed Tom and

Nathan safety glasses then slipped on his own pair.

They began with the new Cessna parts. Jude very carefully removed the bolt and replaced it with a similarly sized section of graphite. “First,” he directed, “the standard ‘full and free’ check.” He maneuvered the controls as a pilot would during the procedure, while Tom and Nathan eyed the bolt substitute carefully.

“There,” Tom pointed. “It’s already cracked. See it?”

“I see it,” Nathan confirmed. “Didn’t take much, did it?”

“Now,” Jude intoned, “We are going to simulate the wind resistance on the elevator at takeoff speed.” He nodded to the tech standing at a nearby control panel, who turned a knob slowly, and the machinery they’d set in place to recreate the force of wind against the elevator during climb replicated the conditions perfectly.

"Okay," Jude said. "Moving elevator controls as the pilot would at this point." He pulled on the handles and Tom and Nathan were both surprised to see the graphite shatter completely within just a few moments.

"Wow. That took a lot less time than I thought it might!" Tom exclaimed. "Okay then, let's test it again on the elevator assembly from the Hartford plane."

The two assemblies were switched around, and the test sequence was run again. Once again, the graphite rod failed at a spectacular rate.

"Pretty conclusive, I'd say," Jude pronounced once they were back in the small office area. "So, what comes next?"

"We'll need to pull any surveillance video from the hangar the Hartfords used to store the plane," Nathan answered.

"Thought you might say that," Tom swiveled in his chair to the table against the wall and picked up a disc as well as a copy of his own report. As he turned back toward Nathan he said, "Here you go. I had them send me the last two weeks' worth. I haven't reviewed it yet."

"Great, thanks. I'm going to head back to my office to check it out."

"Anything else you need, Agent Thomas?"

"Yep, one thing – please call me Nathan."

Tom and Jude chuckled. "Anything else?"

"Nope, this is good for now. I'll be in touch once I've seen all the footage."

"Good luck, Nathan."

***

She frowned. "Donny, did you hear me?"

He came out of his reverie, blinking, a deep scowl marring his handsomeness. “Sorry…What did you say?”

She set down her fork. “I asked you three times to pass the pepper.”

“Oh. Here.”

“Thanks.” She chewed thoughtfully as she watched him pick at his pasta. She could feel the tension rolling off him in waves and damned if she knew what to do about it. *I know he’s upset, but I refuse to spend our whole weekend this way,* she grumbled to herself. The phone ringing broke the heavy silence between them.

“Hello,” Donny said abruptly, then, “Hey Phil. Hang on a minute.” He covered the receiver and told her, “I’m going in the other room.”

“Fine,” she grumbled as he stalked away, then she dropped her fork with a clang, irritated with him and herself equally. *Get a grip*, she scolded internally. *This is a big problem for him, and he's really freaked out about it. Quit being a selfish bitch and be more supportive.* But the diva half of her snarled at that directive.

She waited, fingers tapping a staccato rhythm on the table's surface, growing more impatient with each passing minute. When Donny finally did return, his features were hardened in resolve. "I'm flying out to meet Phil this evening," he announced curtly. "Should be back in a day or two."

"What about our plans?"

He looked at her, but she felt like he was staring through her. "Sorry, but I have got to get this damn gossip mag off this story. That means an in-person consult with Phil and his team of lawyers."

"Okay, so, guess I am going back to Texas then."

"If you need to, sure."

Her temper began to get the best of her. "Do you even *care* if I leave?"

"Right this minute, I have to focus on keeping my life from falling apart over a ten-year-old tragedy. I'm sorry my crisis ranks higher than whether or not this screws up *your* day," he snapped with a voice dripping sarcasm, and she could see his temper rising to meet hers.

"Fine. I'm out. Don't have to tell me twice." She stormed into the bedroom, gathered all her things, and slammed his front door as she left.

The tears formed and fell as she sped away from him to return home, and the look of relief that crossed his face once she was gone was obvious. He threw the deadbolt on his front door, and with shaking hands pulled his cell phone out and called Phil back. “It worked,” he said. “Now what?”

“Dude, you have *got* to show the police what you found,” Phil replied. “As soon as possible, man. Cause from what you described to me it sounds like you stumbled across a hit list.”

“I don’t know,” Donny hesitated. “I mean, it can’t possibly be that. There’s got to be some other explanation.”

“At least Google the names that have been crossed out, man,” Phil urged. “If you don’t find anything bad, then yeah, maybe there’s another explanation.” He paused. “But if you find bad stuff, then I’m telling you, go to the cops with it.”

“Let me search and see what comes up,” Donny decided. “And Phil? Don’t mention this to anyone.”

"You got it. Be careful, Donny. Let me know what you find out."

CHAPTER EIGHTEEN

Lizzie and Joe continued going through Frank's office a day later.

"How did your trip to the courthouse go?" he asked her.

"Well, the clerk was able to confirm what you thought. That seven-digit number matched an old case number in the archives. She said it would be a few days before the copy was ready to be picked up though. What about your actives? How's all that going?"

He ran his hands through his hair. "Definitely all seem connected," he said after a long pause. "They gave me copies of their case files. Manner of death was all over the place – gas explosion, accidental drowning, car wreck. But every single scene had the same weird little item in it."

"Gonna call in the FBI?"

"Gonna have to, I think. At least for a profiler consult. Because right now, there is absolutely nothing else tying these cases together."

"Sounds intense," Lizzie said. "Hey, if you need to focus on that, I can keep doing this stuff, it's all right."

"I hate to let you down, Liz, but yeah, I think I might be putting in a lot more time at work the next few days," he muttered, despondent.

She patted his hand. "No worries, Joe. It's the job. It's what we do. I get that."

His cell rang to life, and she announced, "Duty calls," in her best squeaky voice to make him smile. He shook his head at her and chuckled as he answered his phone.

***

Donny blinked rapidly, trying to tell himself it was coincidence, that he was just punchy after staring at his computer screen for almost thirty hours straight. The first three names he'd searched on his computer had returned results, all right – including obituaries. And the further down the list he went, the more death announcements he'd found.

As he walked to his wet bar, he frowned as the enormity of his discovery began to sink in… then he stopped mid-stride as the memory swam clearly to the forefront of his mind. Suddenly it was all crystal clear. He knew every single name on the list now, and he knew exactly why they'd seemed so familiar to him.

"Oh, my God," he whispered in horror. "*It can't be…*"

Shaken to his core, he poured out a double shot of whiskey to calm himself as his mind raced ahead to figure out what to do next.

***

Nathan Thomas sat in his office late in the afternoon of March twenty-eighth, twirling his pencil as he watched more of the hangar's surveillance video. The first week of footage had been fruitless. He clicked 'pause' and stood up to stretch a bit.

His desk phone chirped, signaling an intercom call from Charlotte, the BAU's unit secretary. "Hey, Charlotte," he said.

"Line one, a Detective Wallace with Fort Worth PD," she announced.

"Thanks, patch him through," he told her, then "Thomas," when Joe came on the line.

"Agent Thomas, Joe Wallace here. Have you got a minute? Need to run something by you."

Nathan listened intently and made notes as Joe described the reason for his call. But it was the last thing Joe said that caused him to almost drop the receiver in disbelief.

"I'm sorry, can you repeat that last part?"

"I said, the only thing these cases have in common is a bow-tie candy wrapper."

"That's what I thought you said, Detective Wallace." He paused, mind whirling at the implications. Then he said carefully, "I'd like to come down, see these case files in person. I think they might be connected to one I'm already involved in."

The exclamation on the other end told Nathan that Joe was just as surprised as he was. They arranged to meet at Fort Worth police headquarters the next morning at ten-thirty a.m.

Nathan placed the receiver back onto its cradle, ruminated for a moment, then pressed the intercom button for Charlotte.

“Hey,” he said when she answered. “Get me a full background on Jeff and Crystal Hartford, if we haven’t started that already.”

“How far back?” she asked.

“As far back as you can,” he answered.

“How fast do you need it?”

“I’m flying out to Dallas first thing in the morning.”

“I’ll see what I can do,” she admonished, “but I probably won’t have it all before you go.”

***

Donny stopped pacing as the wall clock clicked to midnight. He’d decided. He’d go to the authorities in the morning, share what he’d found, and then.... well ... after that he wasn’t sure, but he felt the need to be prepared for anything. He packed two suitcases, then set his alarm for seven a.m. and fell into a very troubled sleep.

***

Nathan arrived at Fort Worth's police headquarters as scheduled, shook Joe's hand, and took a seat in one of the visitor's chairs across from Joe's desk. They'd just started talking about the Ramon Garcia case when Joe's phone rang. "Hang on a sec," he told Nathan, then picked up.

Nathan watched as some color leeched away from Joe's complexion. *Man, whatever he's being told, it's big*, Nathan mused silently. Joe asked several questions as he furiously scribbled notes, then hung up and looked at Nathan.

"How do you feel about taking a trip with me to Colorado?" he asked.

Nathan raised an eyebrow. "What's in Colorado?"

"That was Detective Molina with Vail PD. Seems they have a guy at their station right now with what sounds like some sort of hit list, and he told them it involves an old case down here."

"What does that have to do with us?"

Joe's jaw set. "Everything. Five of the names on the list we already know about." And he waved his hand over the case files spread in front of them.

There was a moment of silence as they both contemplated this revelation.

"Let me make a call," Nathan offered. "I can line up transportation through the Bureau. It'll be faster." At Joe's nod, Nathan pulled out his cell.

“You do that, I’ve got to go fill in the Chief. Be right back,” Joe replied as he stood and headed toward the door.

Within ten minutes an intrigued Chief Collins had joined them in Joe’s office. “Walk me through it, please,” he instructed. So, Joe read him in on the five cases in North Texas, then Nathan took point, describing the Hartford plane crash and its peculiar called card.

When he finished, the Chief sat quietly for a moment before speaking. “Get up there as quickly as you can, Joe. In the meantime, I’m going to personally make a call to the clerk’s office. We need that file *now.*”

“Sir, I’ve already made arrangements for us to use a Bureau plane. It’s standing by at Meacham Field,” Nathan told him.

“Come see me when you two get back,” Collins answered.

The small jet streaked across the sky, and by twelve-fifty p.m. had taxied to its assigned stopping point at Eagle County Regional Airport. Detective Molina was waiting for them in his unmarked police unit. Handshakes and introductions made, they settled in for the thirty-five-mile drive to police headquarters.

***

Lizzie paused, stretched her aching back and took a drink of water. As she sipped, she counted boxes left to go through. “About twenty. Not bad,” she confirmed. Her growling stomach reminded her that lunch was overdue. As she headed into the kitchen to make a sandwich, she noticed movement on the porch. Landon greeted her with a kiss when she opened the front door.

"Hi, baby," she said, surprised but confused. "Thought you were working today."

"Oh, I am," he told her. "But I wanted to bring you lunch, see how it was going over here." He held up a distinctive orange and white bag. "Burger okay?"

"From Whataburger? You bet!" She grinned. "After all, it's a Texas institution. We don't have any in Seattle. That was one of the things I missed the most when we moved up there."

He laughed. "Then I chose wisely. I got you a bacon cheeseburger, no onions, with mustard."

"With fries?"

"Of course, with fries. Got to have fries too, that's a given."

Lizzie beamed.

They sat at the kitchen table and unpacked the bounty. As they ate, Landon asked, "Lizzie, when do you have to go back to Seattle?"

She frowned as she chewed and swallowed. "I had five weeks' worth of vacation going into this, and then my boss texted me and let me know I also had a week's bereavement. I've used up…," she paused, calculated in her head, then finished, "about two weeks of vacation so far."

"How much more do you have to do here?"

"Well," she sighed, "there are some things I can't do until I get the death certificate copies. Hopefully that won't take much longer. I'd like to get everything wrapped up, and *then* go back."

"Have you considered staying here?"

Lizzie stared at him blankly. “What?”

Landon took her hand. “Stay here. You can live here in your dad’s house, or with me, or your own brand-new place, whatever you want to do. Don’t go back to Seattle. Stay. Let’s try living in the same city for a change.”

“Landon,” she murmured quietly as she tried her best not to feel cornered. “That’s a huge step.”

“I know,” he confessed. “Please at least think about it.” He glanced at his watch. “I have to get back, I’ve got meetings all afternoon.” He leaned over and kissed her, then let himself out, leaving a very conflicted Lizzie at her father’s kitchen table.

***

“Agent Thomas, Detective Wallace, meet Donny Atherton. Donny, Agent Thomas is an FBI profiler and Detective Wallace is with the Fort Worth police department," Detective Molina announced. "When I called and talked to Detective Wallace about what you told me, we thought it was best for him to hear what you had to say in person."

Donny shook their hands and tried his best to smile, but Nathan and Joe could both plainly see the man was devastated.

"You need some water, or more coffee?" Molina asked Donny.

"More coffee would be great, thanks."

"Let me get some in here, and then we can get started, all right? How about you two?" he asked the newcomers.

"Coffee, please," Joe chimed in.

"I'll take a water," Nathan answered.

"I'm on it," Detective Molina said, and stepped out of the room. In a few minutes he and another officer returned and handed out the beverages.

"You ready, Donny?" he inquired.

Donny took a sip, nodded his head, let out a breath. "Let's get going," he muttered.

Detective Molina reached forward and turned on the tape recorder. After stating the names of all in attendance for the record, and the nature of the interview, he looked at Donny. "Mr. Atherton, please relate to Agent Thomas and Detective Wallace what you shared with me earlier."

Donny sighed, then started from the beginning, recounting how he'd met her and the relationship that developed.

"And Donny, what happened recently that made you come in to speak to the police?" Molina prompted.

Donny slid his cell phone across the desk to Joe. "These are some pictures I took, of a list I found in her purse."

Joe reached into his jacket pocket and pulled out the printout of Frank's list he and Lizzie had stumbled across. He smoothed it out beside the image on Donny's phone, compared them, and swore softly. "Looks like these two are a match," he announced, gesturing to the other three to see for themselves. Nathan and Detective Molina nodded their assent.

"What is that?" Donny pointed to the paper Joe had produced.

"It's a printout of an Excel file my former partner built and was working on," Joe told him. "I think Frank realized something was going on and was investigating it on his own time."

"Frank *Zimmerman*?" Donny asked, incredulous.

Joe's eyebrow shot up. "You know him?"

"He's on this list. He testified."

"Testified?"

"On the murder case I was a juror for back in 1987. That's how I know all these names," Donny stammered, pointing at the cell phone. "One of the original jurors got pulled off the panel right before the trial started, and I was the first alternate, so I got called up."

Now he stood and began to pace. "When I saw the list, it confused me. So, I started researching. Six people on that list are dead. I found their obituaries. The names all looked familiar, but I couldn't figure out why until a day or so ago. But that's what it is. That murder case twenty-four years ago."

Donny sat again, rubbing his hands over his face. "I realized that, and I decided I didn't want to look any further, and I came to the police station."

Joe leaned forward, staring at Donny intently. “Donny,” he said gently, “Do you remember who the defendant was?’

“Yes. I’ll never forget his name as long as I live, because I thought he was innocent. The other jurors wore me and Theresa down after four days and got us to change our votes. He was on trial for murdering his girlfriend. His name was Harold Kennard.”

Joe blanched.

“What?” Nathan asked.

“One of Frank’s first cases as a detective,” Joe explained. “The real killer confessed in 2008, and we confirmed it with DNA testing in October of that year, but it was too late. Harold was killed in prison in 2002. Frank felt so guilty about it he went back to walking a beat.”

“Aw, man,” Detective Molina shook his head in sympathy. “Rough.”

Nathan waded in. “Donny, you said you looked up some obituaries. Did any of the dates of death match any of the dates here on Frank’s list?”

Donny studied the paper for a moment. “The judge, DA, and defense attorney dates listed here all match what I found, yes.” Then his eyes went wide. “Wait. There’s *eleven* dates listed here...she’s... *she’s killed eleven people?*” He looked from Nathan to Joe to Molina, pale and panicked. Overwhelmed, Donny put his head down on the table while Joe compared the two lists again.

Nathan cleared his throat, then spoke gently. “Donny, I know this is hard, brother, and I’m sorry, but we need her name, and where she is,” he urged. “We need to find her before anyone else on this list dies.”

"Sarah," Donny said as he lifted his head, tears running down his cheeks. "Sarah Edwards. She told me she lives in North Texas. Never told me her address. She never wanted me to come down there." He wiped his eyes. "Now I know why," he finished, then fell silent, staring despondently at the table.

Detective Molina turned off the recorder and moved his head slightly, indicating he wanted to speak to Joe and Nathan outside. "Donny, we'll be right back, okay?"

Donny nodded, still silent.

"Holy shit," Joe exclaimed once he, Nathan, and Molina got into the hall.

"Indeed," Molina replied. "Feel sorry for him, man." He shook his head, then looked at Joe and Nathan. "So. What happens now?"

"It's higher than eleven. There are three names here on Frank's list with no dates, but we know they died," Joe pointed out, looked squarely at Nathan. "Because their active case files are what you and I started to cover this morning."

"I think he needs to come into protective custody," Nathan stated firmly. "If she even *thinks* he's seen that list, she won't hesitate to kill him."

"Agreed," Detective Molina said. "From the sounds of it, he's the only one that's seen her and lived so far."

"And we need to start working that list, pronto. Any names *without* death dates from Frank's list. That's who we need to focus on saving now," Joe added. He turned to Nathan. "Your resources can probably work that part faster than ours can."

Nathan nodded in agreement. "Meantime, can you guys research and verify what Frank's list shows against the list Donny found? And let me know locations. We'll have to pull copies of those files, too."

They hammered out a few last points, then stepped back into the room. Donny hadn't moved. Now he raised his eyes slowly as they filed in.

"Donny," Nathan spoke carefully. "Donny. This probably hasn't occurred to you yet, but the numbers being switched beside your name and Samuel Norton? My best guess is, she came to Vail to kill you. But she fell for you instead, and so she skipped your name and moved on down her list."

Any color that had hope of remaining in Donny's face was chased away by Nathan's statement.

"What that means," Nathan continued, "is that we believe you're still a potential target. If she gets any idea at all that you've seen that list, we believe she'll try to take you out. I want to take you back to D.C. with me, put you into protective custody, just until we can catch her. Do you understand?"

"I understand, Agent Thomas," Donny replied, crestfallen. "I kind of thought that myself, so I packed a couple of suitcases, just in case."

"We can get going whenever you're ready," Nathan assured him.

"I'd like to make one stop first," Donny said sadly as he pulled a small box from his pocket. "To return this engagement ring I bought her. I don't need it anymore."

CHAPTER NINETEEN

"Dammit."

She'd gotten over her mad by the time she'd walked into her apartment, but she figured she'd give him space for a day or two, let him get back from meeting with Phil and the lawyers, before she called and apologized.

Now she faced the prospect of leaving her fifth voicemail for Donny in three days. She'd tried texting, too. No answer from him, at all, which wasn't like him. Her shoulders slumped. *Man, I really screwed up*, she thought bitterly, eyes welling. *He needed me, and I was a coldhearted selfish bitch.*

She left her message, asking again for forgiveness, asking again for him to please call and at least let her know he was okay. She sighed heavily and started to put her cell phone back into her purse.

And then, she noticed it.

Her notebook didn't look right. She could see the pen.

She always put it in the interior side pocket, with the pen facing inward, so that it would be out of the way. Always. She hated to admit it, but it was an OCD trait of hers, a compunction she'd never been able to overcome. So too was her penchant for lining up a pen cap exactly with any writing or inscription on the pen's surface. But as she looked more closely, she saw that wasn't right, either. The pen had been turned; she could see the inscription on it from here.

Her knees buckled and she fought to keep her breathing level. No one else had been even close to her purse, except Donny, in the last few days…

Oh, my God. He found the list.

Her mind whirled, the fine red mist of rage beginning to cloud her vision. When the hell would he possibly have had a chance to find it without her knowing? She paced, eyes closed, trying to remember, then stopped as it hit her. “While I was in the shower,” she stammered. “Bastard must have gone through my purse while I was taking my shower.”

She snatched up her phone, dialed, and waited. When it was answered she snapped, “I have a huge problem,” then relayed her discovery.

“Okay, not good,” came the reply. “Here’s what needs to happen next.”

She listened, then argued for the next several minutes before hanging her head in defeat and muttering, “Yes, I understand. I screwed up. I’ll fix it.”

"Call me back when it's done," was the last thing she heard before the call disconnected sharply.

She walked into her kitchen, wrapped her phone in a dishtowel, and smashed it beyond recognition with a hammer. Then she reached around behind her microwave and removed the small manila envelope taped to the wall. Opening the envelope yielded her strongbox key, and she moved with purpose into her bedroom.

Two hours later she paid cash and left the salon, her new look a pixie-cut brunette to match her new identity. Her driver's license and other documents proclaiming her to be Susan Edwards had been shredded at the apartment, the tiny pieces joining the ruined remnants of her phone in three separate trash receptacles along her route. Tucked into her purse was a brand-new burner phone as well. Before she went through airport security on her way to Vail, she made a trip to the ladies' room and put in the contact lenses that changed her eye color from emerald green to the deep blue shown on her new driver's license.

***

After flying Joe back to Meacham Field, the Bureau plane took on more fuel and set a course for D.C. Donny sat quietly, hands folded in his lap, staring at the sun refracting through the clouds.

"Donny," Nathan said softly. "I'm going to need to get her phone number from you."

"Why?" Then realization dawned. "Oh, so you can track her down. I've seen that in the movies," Donny explained. "Didn't know if that was a real thing, or not."

"It's a real thing."

Donny passed his phone over and turned back toward the window.

"One last thing for now," Nathan informed him. "Did you tell anyone else about what you found?"

"My agent, Phil Tucker. But he's a good guy, he won't say anything." Donny turned back to Nathan, noticed his expression, and made the connection. "Jesus. You think she'll go after Phil?"

"I'd like to have local police contact him to check on him, at the very least. I'd rather be safe than sorry," Nathan answered. "Where does he live?"

"Suburb of L.A. called Northridge."

Nathan pulled out his laptop to make the request as their plane continued traveling northeast.

***

“Hey Joe. What are you doing here?” Lizzie asked as she let him into Frank’s living room.

“Need to talk to you, kid. Where’s Landon?”

“Traveling again, won’t be back until tomorrow sometime. What’s up?”

He sighed. “It’s big, Lizzie. Come take a look at this.”

“Joe,” she began, “does this involve your actives? You probably shouldn’t be reading me in, if it does…”

He held up a hand to stop her. “It does, but Chief Collins has already cleared me bringing you into this. It’s all connected, Lizzie, all of it.”

Joe saw her confused look, and chuckled. “Come let me show you, it will make more sense.”

At the kitchen table, she watched as he laid out pages before them. “You already know what this one is,” he began, pointing to the list they’d found on Frank’s computer.

She nodded.

“Well, check *this* out,” he announced, and set a printed copy of Donny’s picture beside it.

“Holy hell,” she breathed, eyes darting rapidly between the two pages. “Where did you get this?”

“Guy up in Vail, Colorado. Donny Atherton,” Joe pointed out his name on the list. “Came across this list in his girlfriend’s handbag, of all places. Agent Thomas and I went and interviewed him, and now he’s headed to D.C. to go into protective custody until we can track her down.”

“What do you need me to do?”

Joe smiled. “I was hoping you’d say that. What we need is to cross-check the names on your dad’s list against the ones on the list Donny found. Verify deaths, get locations.”

“That will happen faster than you think,” Lizzie chimed in as she stood and led him into Frank’s office. “I was constantly on Dad to clear his computer’s browser history on a regular basis so his computer would run faster, but he never would do it. Every single time I brought it up he’d say, ‘That’s just dumb. What if I need to find something again?’ So, whatever he looked up, I bet we can see pretty easily.”

As Lizzie moved the mouse around to try and rouse the old desk unit from sleep mode, she said, “So. What do all these people have in common that they are all on these lists?”

“Harold Kennard.”

She stiffened as she turned to him, her eyes wide. “The case Dad couldn’t get over.”

Joe held her gaze. “Yeah. Donny was a juror. Every single name on this list was connected to that case.”

***

She climbed out of her rental car, strode to Donny’s door, knocked and waited. No answer. Fuming, she paced, then knocked again. ‘This is useless. He’s gone,” she muttered under her breath.

“Can I help you?” came a voice from her right.

Mrs. Kelley, the shriveled busybody. Great, just great.

“I’m good,” she answered. “But thanks.”

She walked back toward her car, keenly aware of Abagail Kelley’s intrusive stare as she did so.

"Do I know you? You seem familiar," the old lady persisted from her rocking chair.

Oh, hell. Can't have that, can we?

She opened her driver's side door and leaned in, retrieving her purse as she formulated her next few movements. Then she straightened, closed the door and strolled toward Donny's neighbor's front porch. "Hi, Mrs. Kelley, how are you?"

"Sarah? Is that you? You look so… different. Forgive my saying so, dear, but you were much prettier with blond hair," Abagail announced primly.

She laughed. "I got bored, needed a change. Hey, do you mind if I use your phone? Mine's almost dead, forgot to charge it."

"No problem, dear, come on in," Abagail lurched to her feet and motioned toward her door, delighted to have some company. "We can have some lemonade and catch up. Haven't seen you in quite a while."

Wow. Dotty old bird doesn't remember me being here four days ago, she realized. *Do I* really *need to do this? She won't remember seeing me today anyway.*

But a clear, firm voice in the back of her mind stated what she already knew. *Better safe than sorry.*

"That sounds nice," she told the frail old woman, as she counted down internally. *Few more steps, get inside the house, get this done quickly.* As she climbed the porch steps to follow her host into the living room, she slipped the syringe of succinylcholine meant for Donny out of her purse.

***

"Hello?"

"Hey, honey," Nathan said. "How's Charlie?"

"Down for a nap," Bella answered. "But he fought it a bit. Where are you?"

"Well, it's been a long day. Dallas, then Vail, now back at the office."

She heard the strain in his voice. "Rough one, huh."

"You could say that. I have a few more things to line out before I come home. Just wanted to let you know I'm safe, I love you, and I will see you tonight."

"I love you, Nathan. See you soon."

Donny smiled at Nathan as the agent ended the call. "How many kids do you have?"

"Just the one, so far. But he's awesome," Nathan grinned.

Donny's smile faltered. "I've been thinking about kids lately, a lot. I wanted them with her." He shifted in his chair. "I'm… it's just… I cannot get my head around it. You know? Like it's a dream, or some sort of messed up, awful joke. I finally found the woman of my dreams, and she's a serial killer. It feels weird to even say that," he finished, bitterness in his tone. "How do I ever get past this?"

Nathan's expression became solemn. "I know. I'm so sorry, man. I wish there was something I could do to make this easier on you."

"Pinch me. Hell, hit me. Wake me up, please," Donny responded, the grief stark in his eyes.

Another agent poked his head in Nathan's open doorway. "We're ready," he announced.

"Thanks, Mark," Nathan said, then turned his attention back to Donny. "You ready? Transport's waiting."

Donny ran his hands across his face then back through his hair. “I suppose so. Where am I headed?”

“Secure location, very comfortable, and the agents can get you whatever you might need during your stay there, all right? I’ll be by in a couple of days to check on you and update you.” He clapped Donny on the shoulder. “I know you don’t believe this right now, but everything is going to be all right.”

Donny looked him squarely in the eyes, and softly answered, “Nathan, I appreciate the sentiment. I do. But, no, it’s not. Not for a long time. Maybe never,” then slowly turned and walked out to the hall where his escort waited.

***

She drove back to the airport, mind churning with frustration. *Where the hell could Donny be?*

His agent in L.A. He and Donny were tight, almost family. Maybe he'd know something. And she knew for sure she had more than enough ability to make him share any information he had.

Her lips curled in a predatory smile. *Next stop, Los Angeles, and one Phil Tucker.*

***

"Thomas."

"Hey, it's Joe. I'm here with Lizzie, Frank's daughter. She's a detective too, and I got my Chief's clearance to read her in. Let me put you on speakerphone."

Nathan heard a few scraping noises, then, "Can you hear us?" in a slightly tinny voice.

"Yep, what did you find?"

"Well," Lizzie began, "Judge Copeland's obituary mentions he died up in Alberta, Canada. Some place called Sunburst Lake.

Livingston and Singletary were both local, Joe's already got those files in hand."

Joe picked up the thread. "Sam Norton died in Austin, Texas, and Monica Stewart died out in L.A. McDaniels, he was the one in Decatur, so I've already got that file too, as well as Ramon Garcia's."

Lizzie finished with, "Selma Frazier, according to Dad's research, died up in New York, and the Eric Nibless death was in Wyoming. I remember hearing about that one when it happened because it was all over the news. They were saying it was a hate crime."

"They were right, just not the way they thought," was Nathan's response. "Who does that leave to track down?"

"Well, let's see, we also already know about the Hartfords, and Bruce Richards. Donny's with you. So, that leaves..." Joe glanced at the list. “That leaves Nina Kennedy, and Theresa McNamara.”

“What about Marie Turnbill and Charles Maxwell?”

Lizzie spoke up. “Agent Thomas, Dad had ‘N’ beside those two names. Looking at his browser history, I can see their obits. Marie died of cancer in 2003, and Charles was killed by a drunk driver in 1990. Lee Kim didn’t confess to the murder until 2008, and it wasn’t until after that point that all these other deaths happened. I think Dad’s take on it was, those two predate and aren’t involved here, so he marked them ‘N’.”

Silence radiated from Joe’s cell phone for a moment, then they heard Nathan say, “I agree. I think they were included on your dad’s list since they were both part of the jury, and he was researching the whole case. They don’t appear on Sarah Edwards’ list at all. Which tells me she did her homework first, then made her list. She *already knew* they were dead."

***

Both her postman and the Meals on Wheels delivery team figured Mrs. Abagail Kelley was just napping when they came by the next day and received no answer to their repeated knocks on her front door. It wasn't until her grandson, Lucas, arrived in early evening to take her on her weekly shopping trip that her body was found.

***

"Coming." Theresa McNamara opened her door and stood, looking politely at the young man with the serious expression. "May I help you?"

"Theresa McNamara?"

"Yes…" She was thoroughly confused.

He showed her his badge. "My name is Nathan Thomas. I'm with the FBI. May I come in and speak to you a moment?"

Ten minutes later they sat in Theresa's living room, her pale and shocked, Nathan calm and patient as she processed the news she'd just heard.

"Let me get this straight. You're saying some random woman is killing anybody who was involved with a case in Fort Worth over twenty years ago? Why?"

"That's what we're trying to figure out, Ms. McNamara," Nathan said gently. "And I don't wish to frighten you, but I think you need to know the truth. So far, only two people on that list have been confirmed as still being alive. One of them is you. I'd like to keep you that way, so, I'd like you to come in and let us place you in protective custody until she's been captured."

"This is unreal," she gasped in disbelief.

"I can understand why you'd feel that way," he told her.

"You realize the biggest race of the year is coming up, right?" she pointed out. "I can't miss that. We've worked all year toward that!"

"I know this is not good timing. Believe me, I wouldn't be here if I didn't think the threat to you is very real. I wouldn't be surprised if she tried something *at* the Kentucky Derby. Which is why I cannot in good conscience allow you to go."

"I've worked my ass off, *for years*, to be taken seriously as a jockey, to reach the top level of my sport," she snapped, eyes blazing, fury radiating off her tiny frame. "And now you want me to just run and hide and throw all that away because some lunatic is running around?"

Nathan's cell phone interrupted. "I am so sorry, one moment," he murmured as he answered the call. "Thomas." He listened, jawline setting like granite, then said, "Thanks. I appreciate you letting me know. Tell them to run an extended toxicology screen; something tells me we might see very interesting results. I'll be in touch."

He turned to Theresa and spoke, all subtlety gone now. "That was a detective in Vail Colorado, where Donny Atherton lives. His perfectly healthy next-door neighbor was just found dead. And we think this 'lunatic' did it. She wasn't even *involved* in the case, Theresa, she just happened to live next door to someone who is. Now, will you *please* help me help you live through this?"

The revelation shocked Theresa into silence for a long moment. When she did lift her head to look at Nathan, it was with resignation. “I’ll pack a bag,” she said wearily. “Hopefully you can catch her before the Derby.”

***

Back in her kitchen in Texas, she took deep breaths and tried her best to regain her composure. Phil Tucker hadn’t been home either and she’d barely managed to contain the beast raging inside her on her return flight to DFW Airport. Her temper had finally overcome her self-control and she’d smashed very dish she owned right after she’d slammed her door and thrown her suitcase. *Careful where you step, dumbass,* her mind taunted as she moved to the pantry to pull out the broom and dustpan.

She swept up the jagged bits, only half paying attention, her system still surging from the adrenaline overdose the rage had released. Robotically she moved the broom back and forth, scooping broken pieces into the dustpan, dumping them into the trash, until at last the mess she'd made was gone.

Done acting like a child? Good. Now focus. There's still a name on the list you need to handle. Might as well finish what you started.

She willed away the last dregs of anger and moved to her computer to finalize her trip to Louisville. As she did, she was interrupted by her cell phone ringing. She glanced at the screen and scowled before answering.

"What?" she snapped.

"Did you handle it?"

"He wasn't home. But that nosy bitch, Mrs. Kelley, was, so I had to handle her."

She jumped and pulled the phone away from her ear as the loud, angry shouting barreled toward her.

“What in the hell were you thinking? That was never part of the plan.”

“She recognized me! And don’t you dare take that tone with me, it’s not like you’ve never fucked up.”

The clipped, icy tone she heard next told her she’d overstepped. “I told you, several times, not to take the list with you. You chose not to listen. Now, stand down. You’re done, understand? I will clean up your mess.”

“But…”

“Do we need to have this conversation in person?”

She sulked. “No.”

“Then do what you’re told.” And the call ended.

She weighed the phone in the palm of her hand for a moment before throwing it as hard as she could against the rough brick of her fireplace. Then she burst into tears.

She felt used up and utterly alone. There were only two people in the entire world she would have trusted enough to reach out to for comfort – one was Donny, who she felt certain was lost to her now. The other one had just treated her like she was disposable.

As she sobbed, something inside her soul that had been fractured long ago shattered beyond repair, and by the time her tears subsided, she'd latched on to her new course of action.

She moved to the bathroom, splashed cold water on her face, then stared unseeing at her own reflection.

"Time to get to work," she announced in a venom-filled voice. "If I can't have my happily ever after, then neither can anyone else."

***

CHAPTER TWENTY

"Hello?"

"Miss Zimmerman?"

"Yes?"

"This is Mr. Stevens," came the reply, and his face came to the forefront of her mind. The funeral director that had been so helpful and sympathetic.

"Hello, Mr. Stevens, how can I help you?"

"I wanted to let you know we finally got the death certificate copies in. I also got a call that your father's headstone is ready; they will be placing it at his gravesite in the morning."

"I can come get those copies today," Lizzie informed him. "And I appreciate you letting me know about the headstone. I'll go see it tomorrow afternoon."

"If there's anything else you need, we're here to help. And once again, I am so sorry for your loss." With that, the kind old man gently disconnected the call.

Lizzie took a moment to let it all wash through her consciousness. Another moment of finality, of physical confirmation that it wasn't a bad dream. Her dad was truly gone. A solitary tear traced its way down slowly before landing on her shirt, but its brethren soon began to follow. *I'd give anything to be able to hear his voice, just one more time...*

Her cell interrupted with a shriek. "Hello?"

"Baby. Are you okay?" Landon's voice, filled with worry, caressed her across the miles.

"Yeah," she sniffled. "Just… the death cert copies are ready, and they're going to set Dad's headstone tomorrow morning."

"Oh," she heard him say in understanding. "And it feels more real now."

She nodded. "You get it."

He sighed heavily. "Been there. I know exactly how you are feeling right now."

"When are you coming back?"

"My flight lands at six p.m. tomorrow."

"I'll meet you at the airport."

As they ended the call, the uninvited witness who'd tapped into their conversation smiled, and it was dark and feral.

"No, Lizzie," she murmured softly. "No, you won't."

***

"Hey, Nathan, it's Joe."

"What's up?"

"Your guys can stop searching. We found Nina Kennedy. She was a court reporter assigned to Judge Copeland. She was supposed to come back to work two days ago. But her family called in last week, said she was found dead in her hotel room in

Puerto Vallarta. Something about a bad batch of insulin, maybe."

Nathan let out a low whistle. "Where is the body now?"

"It was transported up here, Nathan, but it's already been processed through the coroner's office and released to the family. Her funeral is Friday."

"Ask them if they ran extended tox screens, Joe."

"I already did. They didn't see anything strange. Nothing presented except an abnormally high insulin level – not even any marks of any kind that would indicate a struggle. Nothing. That's why they signed off, let the body go to the funeral home."

"Dammit," Nathan exclaimed. "There's really no way to prove it was something else that killed her."

"I know," Joe agreed, feeling as frustrated as Nathan sounded. "That just leaves two people alive out of that whole damn list. Donny, and Theresa."

"Well, they're both safe, we've made sure of that," Nathan said firmly. "Now we just need to catch her, then figure out the best way to get her to admit what she did." He took a deep breath, then continued, "Problem is, her name's not Sarah Edwards. My guys hit a brick wall there. Need to look at that case with a magnifying glass, Joe. The killer's got to be connected in there somehow."

"I've spent the last hour reviewing it. That's the other thing I called to tell you. I have an idea of who she might be," Joe said slowly. "We'd have to show a picture to Donny, see if it is who I think it is."

"How fast can we get a picture?"

"Let me get back to you."

***

Within four hours, Joe had located an old photograph, and had scanned and emailed to it to Nathan, who in turn rendezvoused with Mitch, the FBI's resident computer genius.

"Hey Mitch," he said as he walked into Mitch's lab. "Glad I caught you. Got a minute? I could really use your help here." Nathan explained what he needed, and Mitch grinned.

"You kidding me? I can have that for you first thing in the morning. Geez. I thought you were gonna ask for something difficult."

"Thanks, man. I appreciate you. See you in the morning." And Nathan headed toward the elevator to start his journey home.

Bella rushed over as soon as she saw him come through the front door. "You look exhausted, baby," she gasped, noting the shadows under his eyes.

"It's a big one," Nathan said, and sighed. "You know I can't get into specifics, but man, there's this one guy I really feel sorry for. His whole world's been turned upside down."

He set his briefcase down and took his bride in his arms, taking comfort in her warmth.

"Where's Charlie?" he murmured against her hair.

"Sleeping. And he should be down for the night. You know, I could use some soak time. Sounds like you could too, baby. Join me?"

Nathan smiled. "You always know just what I need. Lead the way, my love."

***

Donny lay on the unfamiliar bed in the unfamiliar room for the third night in a row, staring at the ceiling fan. He'd processed a lot of the grief from his system; what was left was a dull ache, an emptiness that he feared he would never be able to overcome. He briefly considered traveling out to the living room and pouring a drink but realized it would solve precisely nothing.

He took a long, slow, deep breath, closed his eyes and deliberately relaxed his body. Sometime after one a.m. his restless mind finally followed suit enough to let him sleep.

***

Lizzie rose around ten-thirty a.m. and stretched her frame languidly. "Huh. I hardly ever sleep in," she mused as she noted the time on Landon's alarm clock. "Must be getting comfortable here." That offhand observation immediately brought Landon's proposition to mind, and she bolted upright.

She frowned. He'd rattled her with that one, no question. She knew that for them to make a serious relationship out of what they had they'd have to eventually remove distance from the equation. But she had honestly not expected Landon to bring it up with her in the middle of navigating her dad's estate.

What do I really want? Lizzie asked herself.

I have no idea, was the response.

"Ugh," she muttered. "I can't do this without caffeine." She moved, still yawning, toward the kitchen to remedy her lack of fuel. A few minutes later she sat at the table, taking the first sips of clarity-giving liquid as she mentally lined out her day's activities.

But the previous question refused to go away, and she realized it wouldn't unless she gave it some serious thought. A spark of an idea appeared, and she dialed Faith's number.

"Hey there, it's Lizzie."

"Hey you!" Faith answered. "What's up?"

"Do you have lunch plans today?"

"I had planned on eating at my desk, but I can already tell I am really going to need a break from this spreadsheet. What did you have in mind?"

"Well, I could use your advice on something."

"I'll help as much as I can. There's a bistro six blocks from the office. Let's meet there. Say, noon?"

"Great, I'll see you then, Faith."

Whistling, Lizzie picked up her mug and headed for the shower.

***

Nathan made the two-hour drive to Donny's location almost on autopilot. He knew there was a good chance what he had to share would cause the man more damage. But it couldn't be helped. Donny had become the key to unlocking his suspect's identity.

He pulled up in front of the bungalow, shifted the car into park, and mentally prepared himself. Then he clambered out of the vehicle and headed toward the door, badge in hand and photo ID on a lanyard around his neck. Even though he recognized the man keeping watch, protocol dictated a proper vetting.

"Morning, Agent Lewis," he said, offering both the badge and the ID card for scrutiny.

"Hey there, Nathan," Aaron Lewis replied.

"How's he doing?"

"Restless, and still shaken up, though he's trying hard not to show it," came the reply. "He's in the living room."

"Thanks, Aaron." And Nathan stepped inside.

***

Faith had already grabbed a patio table by the time Lizzie arrived. They exchanged hugs, ordered their food, then Faith said, "Okay, spill. What's going on?"

Lizzie filled her in on Landon's request.

"Wow. That is a dilemma," Faith exclaimed, then took a sip of her iced tea. "What does your gut tell you?"

"I am so churned up," Lizzie admitted. "I mean, I am still trying to decide how I even feel about *him*, much less packing up my life and moving two thousand miles to attempt *us*."

"I do understand that," Faith commiserated. "When Rick and I met, we only lived two blocks apart. Even after I realized I loved him, it still took me a while to take that next step and move in with him - and that was just two blocks down. I was terrified. Felt like I was giving up my sanctuary."

"Exactly," Lizzie chimed in. "And it's more than that. I've built a life up there. I love my job. My house up there, not so much, after what Jeff pulled. But still…," she trailed off, shrugging her shoulders. "I've lived up there since I was twelve. It's become more like home than down here. Especially since Dad's gone now."

They paused the conversation as the waiter presented their meals and topped off their teas. Then Faith said, "Look. I know it feels like you need to decide something right this minute. But you really don't. The last thing you want to do is rush into something, right?"

"Right."

"And there's a lot of different parts involved here. Not just moving, but – what to do with your house up there, and how quickly you'd be able to get hired on with a police department down here. Things like that. Those things can take a while. So," Faith continued, "if it were me, I personally would go back, as scheduled. Once you feel like you're ready to make the change, start putting out feelers down here with local police forces, set that part into motion. It makes it easier to relocate when you've got a job lined up already, trust me."

"Good point," Lizzie acknowledged.

"So, what else have you got going on?"

"Well, Dad's headstone was supposed to be set in place this morning. That's my next stop. I want to take some flowers and see how the design we chose turned out. After that, I've got some down time until Landon's flight gets in at six."

"My afternoon is going to consist of wrangling a big gnarly Excel file into submission," Faith quipped.

"Ouch."

"I know, right? Speaking of which," Faith glanced at her watch, "I probably ought to head back in a few minutes. I wish I had more time to stay and visit."

"It's okay," Lizzie told her. "Maybe we can get together, do a double date, before I head back to Seattle?"

"Rick and I would like that!" Faith smiled. "Let's plan something for Monday night. You guys talk about it and let us know when and where to meet you."

***

Donny's face was still pale as Nathan prepared to head back to the office.

"Are you okay?"

"Really? The girl of my dreams has killed several people, and I am in protective custody. How would *you* be, in my situation?" came the acidic reply.

"You got me there, man," Nathan answered softly. "Dumb question. Sorry."

Donny shook his head, and his shoulders slumped. "Me too. It's just… it's hard. Still doesn't seem real. But it's not your fault." He closed his eyes, took a deep breath, then exhaled. "So, Nathan, what comes next?"

"Well," Nathan replied, choosing his words carefully, "Once we have her in custody, we'd work on building our case. She'd be brought to trial in federal court first. After that, each state in which a crime occurred would have the option to also pursue filing criminal charges and setting a trial."

"Will I have to testify?"

Nathan figured it was better to be direct; the man had endured enough surprises. "Yes, most likely you will be subpoenaed to testify."

Donny's eyes clouded a bit at the answer, but he nodded his understanding. "Just so I'm prepared. I figured that's the way it works, but I wanted to make sure." Then, "How quickly would all that happen?"

Now it was Nathan's turn to sigh. "It really just depends. For multiple count cases" – he winced internally when he saw Donny flinch as if those words had physically struck him – "it can take months to get ready to go to trial."

"Would I be hiding out the whole time?" Donny asked.

"Probably not," Nathan assured him. "Once we're certain she has been apprehended and that she was working alone, it should be safe for you to return home. It would be a different story if, say, the Mafia were involved."

"You think others were involved?"

"We don't have any evidence of that, but I'm not ruling anything out just yet. Not until we know more."

"Fair enough. Thanks, Nathan."

"I will keep you updated, all right? With any luck, you will get to go home soon."

He extended his hand to Donny, they said their goodbyes, and Nathan walked out to his car. "Take care of him, Aaron," he called out.

"Will do, Nathan."

Before he started down the driveway, he tried to call Joe to give him an update. But cell phone reception was poor, so he decided to wait until he was closer to the city.

***

Lizzie parked her car and slowly made her way up the gravel path before veering to her right toward Frank's grave. The bouquet of wildflowers in her hand had caught her attention at the market; her father had always loved wildflowers.

She strolled slowly among the beautifully carved reminders of departed souls until she finally reached her destination.

"Wow," she breathed. "It's beautiful."

The pale gray granite had been etched for all time with the design she'd selected. Her father's name was prominent, of course, the black inset a sharp contrast, but the calligraphy that composed the rest had been masterfully done as well. The date of his passing had been labeled "End of Watch" at her request, in deference to their shared career path, and his badge replicated onto stone reflected expert craftsmanship and amazing attention to detail. The entire surface had been lovingly polished as a final touch.

She sat down, very carefully laid the wildflowers on his grave, then reached out a trembling hand to the stone, and let the tears fall.

Time seemed to come to a stop as she grieved. The next awareness she had was someone standing beside her, offering her a tissue.

“Miss Zimmerman?”

Lizzie glanced up, accepted the Kleenex. “Thanks… Can I help you?”

“I work here at the cemetery. I knew your father’s stone was being placed today, and I know how emotional that can be, so I thought I would check on you."

"I appreciate it. You're right, this is tough."

"Yeah," the woman sighed. "I lost my dad a while back, so I know exactly what you're going through." Her face took on a pensive look for a moment, then she said, "Would you like some help up?"

"Sure, thanks."

As Lizzie dried her tears with her right hand, she reached out her left hand toward the woman, who gripped her firmly around the wrist, and before Lizzie could react or even pull herself upright, she felt the sting of the syringe in her deltoid.

"Ouch! What are you…? What …" Lizzie's words trailed off as she fumbled to speak, the sedative working quickly to render her pliable and unable to stand up or get away.

“So, *Lizzie*,” her assailant hissed, “how about we go somewhere else where we can talk more freely?” She reached down and heaved Lizzie into a standing position, slung Lizzie’s arm around her shoulders, and maneuvered back toward the gravel path to the car she’d parked just in front of Lizzie’s. A groundkeeper passing by called out, “Is she okay?”

“She’s really shaken up. New headstone,” she explained. The groundskeeper nodded solemnly in acknowledgement and kept walking.

Lizzie tried to form a plea for the man to help her, but it wouldn’t come. Her instincts screamed she was in big trouble, but her muscles wouldn’t cooperate. She felt drunk, like she was encased in a thick liquid; she could hear everything, see everything, but it was hazy, and her comprehension and motor skills were severely compromised.

With a bit of effort, the mystery woman got Lizzie into the car and strapped in tightly. "Now," she said gaily, "just a bit more. Wouldn't want you to notice where we're going." Another brief sting, and darkness took hold. Lizzie's head drooped to her chest.

Prize in hand, her attacker closed the passenger door, got into the drivers' seat, and drove away, smiling in triumph.

CHAPTER TWENTY-ONE

Landon settled into his seat for the return flight to DFW. As usual, he texted Lizzie to let her know his status, then turned off his phone and opened the magazine he'd bought before boarding.

***

Nathan checked his reception again. "About time," he muttered, and dialed Joe. "Hey," he said when Joe answered. "We have a positive identification on the picture you sent. Good call."

"Okay," Joe replied. "I've already built an all-points bulletin to distribute down here, I was just waiting to hear from you before I released it."

"Send it out, and send me a copy," Nathan prompted. "I will make sure it circulates nationwide."

"Will do," Joe answered. "I'm gonna call Lizzie here shortly, let her know the latest."

***

The first sound to pierce the veil of oblivion Lizzie was cocooned in was a text notification. Then her phone rang repeatedly before it faded back into quiet. But it sounded like it was miles away…

"*Ohhh*."

With a groan, Lizzie came back into awareness. Her brain still felt fuzzy, as if she'd gone without sleep for days. She blinked rapidly and shook her head, trying to move away from the fog toward clarity.

When she tried to reach up to rub her eyes, she found her wrists had been secured by zip ties to the wooden chair she sat in. Leaning forward and looking down she could also see similar zip ties around each ankle, holding her in place. She strained against her restraints, to no avail, then gave up and leaned back again as a mild wave of nausea hit her. Taking deep breaths in through her nose and blowing them out through her mouth gradually eased the seasickness.

As the fog continued to clear, her eyes focused, and she began to take in her surroundings. “I don’t know this place,” she slurred, tongue thick against her teeth. “Where am I?”

From behind her, a humorless chuckle echoed that made her flesh crawl.

“Does it matter, really?”

Lizzie cleared her throat and found her voice. “Who are you?” she demanded.

“Now, now, Lizzie, no need to take that tone,” came the mocking reply. “But you’re right, we’ve not been properly introduced. How tacky of me.”

As she spoke Lizzie could tell she was moving around to the right. Her peripheral vision caught the same cue, and Lizzie turned her head toward the voice's location.

Her assailant moved directly in front of her now, pulled up a chair and sat down facing her, and for the first time Lizzie got a good look at who had attacked her. The woman was approximately Lizzie's height and build, with spiky brown hair, cut pixie-style, and serious gray eyes she could tell were measuring her up.

Those serious eyes took on a more menacing look as the woman leaned forward and announced, "Lizzie Zimmerman, my name is Samantha Kennard. And we're here today because your father helped kill mine."

"Harold Kennard," Lizzie replied, her voice tinged with sympathy. "He died in prison, was later proven to be innocent. That case broke my Dad, you know. When he heard the real killer confessed, he was never the same."

"That case broke *your* dad? That's rich. You have no fucking idea. That case *killed* mine, not to mention shattered our family. I know what happened to your father," Samantha's tone was pure ice with an undercurrent of disdain. "Believe me, he got off easy. You're lucky he stroked out before I could get to him."

"So why are you bothering to talk to me? It's revenge you're after, isn't that right? So, what are you waiting for?" Lizzie's head raised and her eyes flashed in challenge.

"I have to say, I admire your spirit," Samantha countered with a grin. "Let's just say I've been mostly alone on this journey and it's been no fun at all keeping all my success to myself. Besides," she checked her watch, "your boyfriend's plane should be landing in about forty-five minutes, and I really think he ought to join us, along with that old partner of Frank's. What's his name again? It's Joe, isn't it? Joe Wallace?"

"Why would you bring them into this?"

"Oh, honey, I didn't. You did. They're going to die along with you because of *you*, not me."

"Leave them out of this. You're pissed at my dad, and the judge, and everybody else connected with your father's case. I get that. I understand it. But leave Joe and Landon alone."

"They mean that much to you?"

"Yes," Lizzie said earnestly. "They really do."

"I thought as much," Samantha's eyes gleamed. "Which is why I am going to make sure they die first, in front of you."

Now she rose, amused as Lizzie struggled again to free herself. "But until they get here, I've been dying to brag a bit."

Keep her talking, Lizzie told herself. *More talking equals less action and that buys some time to figure out how the hell to get out of this.*

"Well, it's not like I can run off anywhere," Lizzie quipped, trying to look and sound as defeated as possible. "Go ahead."

"Do you know what it's like to have your whole world torn apart? To be ripped away from your dad?" Samantha began.

"Actually, I do," Lizzie answered honestly. "My mom moved me over two thousand miles away from my dad when I was twelve."

Samantha paused, nodding slightly in acknowledgement. "But your mother was still alive, and you could still see him if you wanted, and I'll bet your trips to see your father didn't involve being groped by creepy, overeager prison guards during the 'mandatory pat-down' process. Perverts." She shuddered involuntarily at the memory before she regained control.

"My mom had been dead for two years when Dad started dating Rosalyn. She was a nice lady. I remember hoping she would become my stepmom. But they used to fight a lot. The night she died, Dad had gone over to her apartment to make up with her after one of their big fights, and he found her body. He's the one that called the cops. But that didn't matter. In their eyes," Samantha flushed with anger, "in *your dad's* eyes, he was at the scene, so he was automatically guilty. Your dad never even *bothered* to look at anyone else."

She paused and took a drink of water.

"We had no family in Texas, so I got shuffled off into foster care when he got arrested and I floated in the system, being bounced from place to place until my great Aunt Beatrice finally came down from New York and got me and took me to live with her. I was fifteen at that point."

"Wait…Didn't you have a brother?" Lizzie asked, confused.

Samantha grimaced. "He bailed on me, lying about his age to join the Army. His unit was ambushed in Iraq in 1991." A cloud of emotion rolled across her features. "Anyway, Aunt Beatrice could be a mean old bitch sometimes, but she taught me the value of patience and planning and how to do top-notch research. So, when Lee Kim finally confessed to killing Rosalyn, I decided payback was way overdue for everyone who participated in sending Dad to prison."

Samantha paused to check her watch. "Good, we still have about thirty minutes before I call the boys to come out and play."

Distract her from making those calls! Lizzie's mind raged.

"Samantha," Lizzie queried, "refresh my memory about Lee Kim again?"

"Stupid bastard was looking for a fix and went to the wrong apartment," Samantha spat out. "Rosalyn came home, saw a strange man rummaging through her place, she confronted him, and he grabbed a knife from her butcher block set and stabbed her to death. My dad's life, my life, was ruined because he went to the wrong floor of the building." Her face twisted in anguish.

"That sucks."

Samantha laughed harshly. “That is a severe understatement.”

Lizzie changed track. “How long did it take to track everyone down? I mean, twenty-four years between the case and now, that’s a long time, and not everybody stays in the same place their whole lives.”

A note of pride crept into Samantha’s voice as she answered. “Parts of it were a complete pain in the ass,” she admitted. “Like Ramon Garcia. Very common name, so that one took a while. But a pompous jackass like Judge Copeland? So simple a toddler could have found him. A man like that, with that much power, no way he would have retired anytime soon. He got off on it all too much. That’s how I chose the way some of them would die,” she told Lizzie, almost as a confidence between friends. “I used their little quirks against them. The

Judge was a serial skirt-chaser and had a severe God complex going. I lured him somewhere private, made him think he was finally going to get me into bed, then made damn sure his final waking moments were spent lying on a wood floor in the middle of nowhere like a nobody."

"Clever," Lizzie observed. "But wouldn't an autopsy have shown it wasn't natural?"

"Potassium chloride. Great stuff, and metabolizes quickly," Samantha revealed. "Now, take Monica Stewart. She was the jury forewoman. Even way back then she was one of those better-than-thou types just because she had money. Total bitch."

"She fell down the stairs, right? I remember seeing news coverage. Something about she tripped?"

"She didn't trip," Samantha sounded offended. "I snuck into her hotel room and sabotaged the heel of her shoe. I'd practiced with it and I knew odds were good it would break as she came down the stairs. And I was right," she said triumphantly. "Boom! Three steps in, down she tumbled. It was glorious to see."

"You were there?"

"Hell yes! No way I was gonna miss seeing Miss Ice Queen break her stuck-up little neck. I was in the crowd below and had a front-row seat for it. It was delicious," Samantha's lips curved into a radiant smile as she relived the memory.

"So, what happened with the skier?"

Lizzie's question caught her off guard, and she turned pale. Pain skittered across her visage before she very carefully set her mask back into place.

"Donny was supposed to be before Monica," Samantha said quietly. "But once I met him, I.... I...," her voice failed her.

"You fell in love with him," Lizzie finished gently.

"Yes. Yes, I did." Samantha shoved the heartache back down, squared her shoulders. "So, I decided to move him farther down, and Samuel Norton came next."

"How did you kill him?"

"It was super easy, actually," Samantha grinned. "Stubborn old coot had been a chain-smoker for years, and he had advanced emphysema as a result. Plus, he had sleep apnea. Doctor ordered a CPAP machine for him. I just made sure it had a hell of a lot of liquid nicotine in the water well, was all." Her smile faded slowly. "I almost regret that one. He was funny, real straightforward, authentic. Didn't pull any punches. What you saw was what you got, and he didn't give a damn what anybody thought. Kind of reminded me of my dad."

***

When he didn't get an answer or a return call, Joe drove to Frank's house. No Lizzie. His next thought was that she might be at the cemetery, so he headed there. As he pulled up close to the section that held Frank's grave, he could see Lizzie had driven Frank's car. He parked behind her, walked up to the headstone.

"Well, she's got to be here somewhere," he muttered, noting the wildflowers, as he turned and went back down the gravel path. He had just opened his driver's side door when a maintenance worker on a golf cart stopped beside him.

"We're closing and locking the gates here shortly," the man said. "If you know that lady who owns that car, you need to tell her to come back and get it pretty quickly, so it doesn't get locked in overnight."

"You saw her?"

"Yeah, about two hours ago. Her and the other lady."

"What other lady?" Joe asked, a sinking feeling beginning to form in his stomach.

"The one lady got out of that car, and she went to see the new stone," the man explained. "And then the other lady pulled up behind and went up there. Next thing I know, they're coming back down, and the first lady looks out of it; the second lady had her arm around the first lady's waist, like, helping her walk. I asked if she was okay and the second lady said yeah, she was just upset seeing the new stone. And she put the first lady into her car and drove away."

Joe's blood ran cold. His hand trembled as he reached into his car and pulled out the APB for Samantha Kennard.

"The second lady. Did she look like this woman?"

The man took the flyer and studied it with intensity. "That's her, but she didn't have blond hair. It's brown, and real short, like a…um… what it is called? A pixie cut!"

"Holy hell," Joe breathed as he snatched up his radio mike and called in to dispatch. After he relayed what was going on, he pulled out his cell and called Nathan as he walked forward to Lizzie's vehicle.

"Thomas."

"Nathan, it's Joe. Lizzie's missing. Samantha's got her."

"What?"

"Lizzie's car is here at the cemetery. I just talked to a groundskeeper that saw her being half-carried to another car. Showed him the APB, and he recognized Samantha, only he said she had really short brown hair…," Joe started to say more but his words tapered off.

"Joe! What's wrong?"

"Nathan," he croaked, "There's a bowtie candy wrapper tucked under the wiper blade of Lizzie's car."

"Text me Lizzie's cell number," Nathan urged. "If it's turned on, I should be able to triangulate her position for you." And he raced toward Mitch's lab.

***

Samantha checked her watch again and smiled coldly. "Almost time to send out the party invites."

"Landon and Joe weren't involved in your father's case," Lizzie pleaded. "Joe and Dad didn't even become partners until 1989. *Please*. I'll do anything you ask. Just leave them out of this."

Samantha studied Lizzie's face for a long time.

"You know what? I believe you," Samantha finally told her. "It's just that I don't care. If I don't get my fairy tale ending, no one else gets to have theirs, either."

Lizzie slumped forward, hot tears escaping down her cheeks.

"If you'll excuse me a moment, the cellphone reception in here sucks, and I want to make sure these particular messages are received. Be right back," Samantha taunted, waving Lizzie's own cell phone at her as she left the room.

***

Once his plane reached the gate, Landon turned his phone back on before standing to retrieve his bag from the overhead bin. It chirped, indicating incoming texts, and he smiled. It wasn't until he'd walked up the jet bridge and into the terminal that he paused to check his messages. When he did, his face drained of color and he felt his knees go weak. The next thing Landon was aware of was sprinting through the airport to the nearest exit to hail a taxi. A Yellow Cab saw him waving frantically and pulled over. The vehicle hadn't even come to a complete stop yet as he wrenched open the door and climbed in.

"2499 Northwest Dallas Street in Grand Prairie," Landon told the startled driver. "As fast as you can."

***

"Hang on a second, Joe," Nathan said, and Joe could hear him reading off Lizzie's number to someone. Then Nathan came back on the line. "Mitch is running it now."

Seconds became minutes that felt like hours until at last Nathan said, "Yes! Joe, you got a pen?"

"Ready," Joe replied. "Where is she?"

"Somewhere between the 2000 and 2500 blocks of Northwest Dallas Street in Grand Prairie," Nathan informed him. "That's as close as we could get. Her phone just turned off again."

"That's over in a big industrial complex about twenty minutes from here. I'm going to call Arlington and Grand Prairie departments on my way, since it straddles their borders, see if I can't get some help to meet me over there. That complex is way too big to search without more people," Joe explained.

"There's no way I can get down there in time to help you right now. But I'm on the next flight out. I'll call you when I land. Be careful, Joe, and good luck."

***

As soon as she heard the door close, Lizzie had begun wiggling the wooden chair arms back and forth as hard as she could. Finally, the left one seemed to loosen from the chair frame. *Just a few times more,* she thought to herself, *and maybe I can get it to break free.* Another two minutes passed but she was finally successful. She redoubled her efforts on the right side, but she heard the door open again and had to stop and hold still, praying Samantha wouldn't notice the damage to the chair.

"Not much longer, and our guests will be here," Samantha announced with delight. "Then the fun can really start."

Lizzie sighed. "I don't suppose I can talk you out of this. No one else has to die, you know."

"Oh, but they do. My party, my rules," Samantha's gaze was cool and level as she studied Lizzie's tear-stained face.

Lizzie heard the door slowly opening, and her heart leapt into her throat.

"Come on in, we've been expecting you," Samantha called out in sing-song fashion.

"What are you doing?" Lizzie heard Landon say.

"Landon?" Lizzie whipped her head around as far as she dared without revealing the true extent of her left arm's mobility.

"Hi, baby. You all right?" He moved over where she could see his face more easily, and Lizzie saw worry in his eyes, along with something else she didn't understand.

"Landon… Why are you so calm? Do you know who this is? Do you know what she's *done*?" Lizzie's voice pitched up on the last word, incredulous that he didn't seem fazed at all.

"Oh, see, there you go. I have such poor manners today," Samantha interrupted, a stealthy smile filling her countenance. "Lizzie Zimmerman, I'd like you to meet Lenny Kennard – my older brother."

CHAPTER TWENTY-TWO

Lizzie's hazel eyes filled with shock and horror, flitting back and forth between Samantha and Landon. Then she shook her head vigorously. "*NO*. You're lying. You said your brother was killed in the Gulf War in 1991."

"I never said that," Samantha calmly pointed out. "What I said was, his unit was ambushed."

Lizzie's jaw dropped, and for several moments she was at a loss for words. When she was able to finally compose herself enough to speak, she directed her conversation at him, not Samantha.

"Is this true?" she whispered. "Are you Harold Kennard's son?"

His shoulders sagged. "I am."

"You lied to me.... Have you *ever* been honest with me, *ever*? What, did you target me from the very beginning?"

"No," he said hastily. "We met in Cayman completely naturally, I swear to God. I had no idea whose daughter you were until I heard on the news you got shot, and even then, I wasn't sure. It wasn't until I saw your dad in your hospital room that I was certain."

"Did you have anything to do with my father's stroke?" she demanded.

"No. Neither one of us did," he replied.

"I can't believe I am doing this, but I will actually help him out here," Samantha chimed in. "Frank was supposed to happen right after Monica, but lover-boy here made me move him to the bottom of the list. For you."

"So, for me, you were going to what? Kill my dad last? That's very fucking chivalrous of you," Lizzie seethed. "You held me as I sobbed for him in his hospital room. You were by my side when they turned off the machines, and through the entire funeral service. Was all that just a big joke to you?" Lizzie was crying at that point but didn't even notice. "Did you get off on that, watching him die, watching my heart break, and me fall apart? I trusted you, Lan…Whatever the hell your name is. You make what Jeff did to me look like a fucking Boy Scout project."

"Lizzie, please know I never wanted to hurt you. I faked my death in Iraq to have a fresh start. I was tired of being called 'the killer's kid'," he pleaded, his face twisted in pain. "I was trying to build a normal life. That's all I ever wanted, ever, was a normal life. But this one," he thumbed toward Samantha, "would just *not* let things go, and if she'd done all this her way, she'd have been caught right after the first one. I couldn't let that happen, Lizzie. Don't you understand? She is my baby sister. I already bailed on her once. I couldn't do it again. I had to help her."

Lizzie's horror multiplied. "You… you… *helped her kill people*? You're honestly standing there and admitting to a detective that both of you are *serial killers*?"

Samantha laughed out loud. "Boy, you've kept her in the dark more than I thought."

"Shut up," he growled.

"What is she talking about?" Lizzie asked. "Or do I want to even know?"

"Later," he said, and he turned to his sister. "Why is she tied to a chair?"

"Oh, that. Yeah. I forgot to mention - If I can't be happy, neither can you," Samantha told him, now pointing a handgun at him. "I lost my chance at happiness with Donny. Now, you get to lose yours with her."

"Trust me, that ship has sailed," Lizzie uttered forcefully.

He winced, eyes filling with tears. "God, Lizzie, please no."

"Even if I *could* ever trust you again, the fact remains – I am a cop, *Lenny*, like my father before me. And it means something to me. Integrity means something to me. And you have none," Lizzie told him, chin raised, eyes glinting, her voice sharp and deadly as a blade. "Even if you'd told me up front who you really were, I can't get past the fact you helped her execute people based on some screwed-up sense of vengeance. Instead of helping her kill, the right thing to do was to stop her from killing at all. *That's* integrity."

She switched her steely gaze over to Samantha. "And it's a cowardly bitch that shoots an unarmed woman who's tied to a chair. You need to earn the right to take me out, and believe me, honey, you haven't. Untie me, let's see how good you are when your target knows you're coming. Let's do this right, and may the best woman win. Unless you're not brave enough to try me," she taunted.

"Oh, challenge accepted, and I'm gonna beat your ass," Samantha promised her. She put the gun in her waistband, pulled a blade, and stepped forward. As she leaned over to cut Lizzie's ankle restraints, Lizzie swung her left arm down, back then up and over in a windup motion as fast and as hard as she could, and the thick wood she was still strapped to made full contact with the back of Samantha's head. Samantha collapsed in a heap. Lizzie reached out, grabbed the knife, and quickly cut through her arm and ankle ties. The liberated chair arm nailed Samantha in the back as it clattered to the floor.

"Amateur," she snarled at Samantha, who lay groaning at her feet.

As she stood, Lenny stepped toward her. "Don't come near me," she threatened, backing away as she brandished the knife. He raised his hands as a signal of compliance and maintained his distance. She saw raw grief in his eyes. She didn't care.

"I'm sorry," he whispered.

"Me too. You had me completely fooled. I was almost ready to tell you I loved you," she snapped, and saw the grief deepen.

She circled around him to the table where her cell phone was, picked it up, and dialed Joe's number. "I need help," she said as soon as he answered. I'm at…" she looked at Lenny.

"2499 Northwest Dallas Street," he offered.

"2499 Northwest Dallas Street," she told Joe.

"I'm one block over, kiddo, be right there."

"Okay," Lizzie replied, and hung up the phone. She started to speak when she noticed movement ahead and to the right, and was shocked to see Samantha standing, holding the gun Lizzie had forgotten to clear and shaking with rage.

Lenny noticed it too and began moving toward Lizzie's position.

"Sneaky bitch." Samantha radiated fury as she touched the back of her head, winced, then saw her own blood on her fingers. "I knew I should have just killed you the first chance I got." She leveled the gun at Lizzie and just as Lenny reached Lizzie, she squeezed the trigger. He pivoted to shield Lizzie, and Samantha's shot struck him dead center of the chest. He staggered backward from the impact's force, eyes wide with shock, before falling to the floor.

"*No!!*" Samantha screamed in disbelief, then Lizzie watched as Samantha's body jerked once, twice. Lizzie swiveled her head toward the door and saw Joe, still in modified Weaver stance, smoke curling upward in seemingly slow motion from the barrel of his service weapon. Uniformed members of the Grand Prairie Police Department rushed in to secure Samantha's weapon and check her and Lenny's injuries.

Lizzie looked down at her feet. Lenny's mouth was working, trying desperately to form sounds. She knelt beside him and leaned in close so she could hear him.

"I…love you…. Lizzie," he managed. "You're the best thing… that ever happened to me." His brown eyes held hers, yearning, pleading.

She leaned over closer, and as she took his hand, she spoke to him, unfiltered, from her heart to his.

"*Landon. I love you too.*"

He smiled and squeezed her hand tightly for a moment, and then she watched the spark slowly leave his eyes and felt his grip relax in hers. The uniforms hustled her out of the way to begin CPR until the ambulance arrived. She stood there, numb, watching them work on him, knowing he was gone already.

Lizzie felt a soft touch on her shoulder and found herself looking at Joe when she turned her head. Without warning, she started to sob, and he pulled her into an embrace.

"Come on, kiddo, come with me," he murmured, and led her outside to his car. Two ambulances had arrived, and paramedics with gurneys rushed past them to try to aid whomever they could.

Joe gently ushered her into his passenger seat, and she buckled her seatbelt. Tears rolled unchecked down her face as she stared through the windshield, seeing nothing.

"I need to make a call, okay? I'll be right back," Joe told her, but she only nodded mutely in response.

He stepped a few feet away and dialed Nathan's number, but his call routed to the unit secretary, who informed him Nathan was already in flight to Dallas. Sighing, he walked around to the other side of the car and climbed in behind the wheel.

"Let's head to my office. Nathan's on his way," he suggested.

"Wait. Please," Lizzie implored softly. "I know he's gone. But I just have to see."

They waited, her staring at the warehouse door, until a gurney came rolling back out into the parking lot. They moved quickly to get loaded, the EMT's movements almost frantic, and she could see it was Samantha, most likely headed for surgery. But the other gurney didn't come back into view, and over Joe's police scanner she heard the call go out for the coroner's office to come to her current location.

It was the final confirmation she needed.

"We can go now," she whispered.

***

Two hours later, Nathan Thomas walked into Fort Worth police headquarters, and was directed to a conference room. Joe and Lizzie were talking quietly as he entered. Nathan noticed she wore the drab gray sweatpants and shirt that usually meant clothing had been logged into inventory as evidence.

"Nathan," Joe said in greeting, and shook his hand. "This is Seattle Detective Elizabeth Zimmerman, Frank's daughter."

"It's nice to meet you," Nathan told her. "I just wish circumstances were different. You all right?"

"No," she said quietly. "But maybe someday, I will be."

Nathan inclined his head to let her know he understood; he'd seen the exact same look in Donny Atherton's eyes just a day or two before. “Are you up for debriefing right now, or would you rather do it tomorrow?”

She straightened her shoulders. “I know we should get this done now, but to be honest, I am going to be more clear-headed tomorrow.”

“I understand completely.”

Lizzie reached into her purse and pulled out a set of keys. She worked a brand-new one off the keychain and handed it to Nathan. “This is the key to Landon’s….,” she stopped herself, and wavered a moment before forcing self-control back to the surface. “I mean, Lenny’s place,” she offered. “He gave it to me last week. I do have some personal belongings there that I need to retrieve, so I would appreciate being allowed to get my things out of there before it’s processed and inventoried.”

“We can do that here shortly, then we can take you home,” Joe assured her, as Nathan nodded in agreement.

She turned to Joe and asked, “Where’s my dad’s car?”

“When I realized you’d been kidnapped, I called Dispatch. They sent two uniformed officers, and I gave them the spare key Frank gave me a couple of years ago. I had them drive it back to his place for you.”

The three drove silently to Lenny’s house. Once inside, Joe and Nathan kept watch as Lizzie packed up her suitcases. They met the regional FBI crime scene processing unit as they stepped back out onto the porch.

“I’m going to stay here with them,” Nathan decided. “Get this part moving. Can we meet back at your office at three p.m. tomorrow?”

"Sure," Joe said. "I'm going to take her home."

When they arrived at Frank's house, Joe asked, "Do you want me to stay with you?"

She managed a wan smile that didn't reach her eyes. "I'm tough, Joe, I got this."

"I know you are, kiddo. See you tomorrow."

***

Thirty minutes in, Nathan was staring at a flashing red icon on Lenny's laptop. "Wow," he exclaimed, "That's some serious security." He called his boss and got permission for the idea that came to him. Once Steve Brown heard about the man's background and why Nathan wanted him involved, he agreed. Nathan's next call was to Rick Connor, his sister's fiancé – and one hell of a codebreaker.

"Hey, Rick."

“Hey, buddy! How’ve you been? Let me get Faith for you.”

“Actually, you’re the one I need to talk to.” And Nathan described the situation.

“On my way. I’m going to drop Faith at Frank’s house, then head to you. It sounds like Lizzie could use some company. And Nathan?”

“Yes?”

“Don’t touch another key, you could lock it all up.”

Nathan chuckled. “I promise.”

By the time Rick hung up the phone Faith was standing beside him, totally confused.

“Come on,” he told her. “I’ll explain on the way.”

***

After a long shower, Lizzie stood in her father’s kitchen, making tea, her mind churning a million miles a second. The doorbell pealing its single note broke her out of her reverie. She burst into tears at the sight of Faith on her doorstep.

Faith stepped over the threshold and wrapped her in a hug. "I'm so sorry, honey," she murmured as Lizzie clung to her and cried.

***

"Haven't seen this in a long time," Rick pronounced, rubbing his hands together in excitement. "It's a triple flip."

"It's a what?"

"Triple flip," Rick repeated. "The short and normal world definition is, three layers of fairly complicated encryption. I haven't come across this in five years or better. This is gonna be fun." He flexed his fingers, then began to type, working his way through the first layer in a few minutes.

"There's one down."

"How long do you think the other two will take?"

"Hour, maybe two."

"Seriously? That fast?"

Rick stopped typing and looked up at Nathan. "Dude. I'm offended you even asked me that."

The crime techs within earshot snickered.

True to his word, an hour and forty minutes later Rick gestured at the screen. "Voila."

As Nathan scanned the contents of the secret cache Rick had found, his eyes bulged.

"Are these what I think they are?"

"It sure looks like it," Rick's tone had turned serious.

"Holy shit. I need to call Mitch, send him these things, have him cross check…" Rick cut Nathan off.

"No need," he said, and reaching into his bag produced his own laptop. "Allow me."

Another hour proved out Nathan's suspicions. The encrypted files they'd found on Lenny Kennard's computer were all historical records of murder-for-hire contracts, most occurring internationally. The first fifty Rick cross-checked vetted almost immediately, including the kiddie porn distributor in Phoenix, the pedophile priest in Wicklow County, the sex trafficker who had died in Berlin, and the terrorist in Santiago.

A separate set of files contained the research on and kill methods of the Kennard victims Lenny had handled personally.

"Nathan," Rick spoke slowly. "Who the hell *was* this guy?"

"Definitely not who we thought, that's for sure."

“Well. It’s your case, bro, so I can’t tell you how to run it. But I see absolutely no value in telling Lizzie she was dating a professional assassin. It has nothing to do with her.”

“I agree, but I’m going to get Joe’s opinion on that,” Nathan told him. “He knows her better than anyone.” He stepped away and got Joe on the phone. Once he’d read him in, Joe’s answer was immediate and forceful.

“*No*. She doesn’t need to know any of that, Nathan. It doesn’t pertain to the Kennard case, and she’s been through enough. She’s devastated as it is.”

“Joe. Relax. I don’t plan on telling her. I just wanted your take on it. Glad to see we agree.”

***

The next afternoon Joe and Lizzie met Nathan again in the conference room, and the official debriefing began.

Lizzie started from the point when Samantha approached her at the cemetery and relayed the pertinent events all the way through the shooting.

“So, Landon Kendal was actually Lenny Kennard,” Joe confirmed.

“That’s right.”

“And he helped her kill people.”

“Yep. Here’s the thing. When she was bragging to me, she only mentioned certain people. The judge, Monica Stewart, Samuel Norton, Ramon Garcia.” Her brow furrowed. “I think they split the list up between them, and he didn’t just help her figure out the best way, he actually killed some of them too.”

Joe and Nathan exchanged glances.

"We were able to confirm that last night," Nathan informed her gently. "We've already secured their homes and picked up their electronics."

"Okay, so, what comes next?" she asked.

"I checked Samantha Kennard's condition last night, and again just before I walked in here," Joe began. "She underwent surgery. Currently she's listed as serious but stable. Her doctors expect her to make a full recovery."

"It will take a bit longer to retrieve all the case files, since the deaths occurred all over," Nathan pointed out. "Judge Copeland's in Canada will take the longest. Red tape. But, after that, we parse out the ones we know Lenny did, charge her with the rest, and include his murder, and your kidnapping and attempted murder," he finished, directing his attention to Lizzie. “Be expecting a subpoena to testify.”

“You don’t have to subpoena me,” she said. “I’ll gladly take the stand if it means that bitch won’t be able to hurt anyone else ever again.”

“You realize defense counsel may try to smear you, since you and Lenny were involved,” Joe mentioned as neutrally as he could.

“Let them try. I had no knowledge of who he really was and I damn sure didn’t condone anything he did.” Her jaw set stubbornly. “They can have at it. Can’t do any more damage than has been done to me already.”

The meeting was just about done when Lizzie remembered one final question she had.

"Something has been bugging me," she announced suddenly. "And I didn't get a chance to ask either one of them."

"What?"

"What the hell did the bowtie candy wrapper signify?"

"I did some research into the day Harold Kennard was killed in prison," Joe stated. "He was stabbed to death over a bag of peppermint candies; a new inmate arrived, tried to steal them, and Harold put up a fight. When they went to clean out Harold's cell, they found hundreds and hundreds of wrappers, tied into little bows."

***

A week later, Lizzie stood and stared at the newly turned soil of Lenny's grave. The prior body resting in that spot had been exhumed and positively identified as the real Landon Kendal, a platoon-mate of Lenny's killed in the ambush Samantha had described. Lenny had simply switched dog tags, and the mortar blast had rendered so much damage that normal identification processes hadn't been possible in 1991. Thanks to more sophisticated DNA testing, Landon's long-suffering family in North Carolina would now have closure too.

If she'd known for sure how she felt about it all, Lizzie might have had some final words to say over the man she'd fallen for that she thought she knew.

But her emotions were too tangled to be clear.

She stood a moment longer, then turned on her heel and headed back to Frank's car to begin her road trip home to Seattle.

EPILOGUE

Ten months later, Lizzie arrived as scheduled in front of the Earle Cabelle Federal Building in Dallas. Samantha Kennard's multiple homicide case was set to begin in US District Court at nine a.m. Lizzie originally wasn't supposed to testify until day four, but the schedule had been rearranged; the prosecutor had opted to come out blazing by presenting key material witnesses first.

She passed through the screening point without issue and made her way into the courtroom, taking a seat in the fourth row from the back. Just before the attorneys and defendant appeared, a tall, handsome man in a suit walked in, looking around nervously. He gestured to Lizzie, and she nodded, indicating the space next to her was available. He smiled and nodded his thanks as he sat down.

Moments later, the defense and prosecuting attorneys entered and settled in at their respective tables. The bailiff stood and announced the Judge's arrival, bidding everyone rise as His Honor worked his way to the bench and took his seat.

Next, Samantha Kennard was led in. Lizzie heard the man beside her gasp quietly.

She understood his reaction. Gone was the beautiful woman Lizzie had seen up close. Samantha looked haggard and haunted; clearly captivity had damaged her. Her hair had grown back out to shoulder length, but it was a dirty dishwater blonde, and only served to intensify the pallor to her skin, as did her dull gray suit. She moved in a slow shuffle toward the chair the guards indicated, the rustle of shackles her only noise. She sat listlessly, staring straight ahead, showing no emotion at all.

The judge looked out over the courtroom, nodded once, and spoke in a loud, warm baritone, asking the gallery to rise once more as the jury was brought in and settled.

The initial formalities came next – the reading of the defendant's name and the list of all charges leveled against the accused, followed by opening statements from the lawyers.

Then the US District Attorney rose, and announced, "Your Honor, the prosecution calls Elizabeth Zimmerman to the stand."

A grueling three hours later, she'd been released by the judge to exit the witness stand. Samantha's eyes had flashed only briefly with hostility at Lizzie before returning to a placid state. Under the District

Attorney's questioning the events she personally witnessed were laid out for the record. The defense team had tried viciously to undermine both Lizzie's testimony and her character, insinuating that witnessing her lover's death had unfairly skewed her prejudice against the defendant. But Lizzie kept her composure and never wavered, and at last the interrogation ended. She made her way back to her seat in the gallery on wobbly knees and sank gratefully back into her spot.

Next, the prosecutor consulted his notes briefly, then spoke again. "Your Honor, we'd like to call Donny Atherton to the witness stand."

The gentleman sitting beside Lizzie, who had smiled in understanding and sympathy at her as she moved past him to retake her seat, let out a long sigh, and rose. He too was sworn in, then asked to share with the court what he knew. He replayed his relationship with Samantha Kennard from the beginning up until he found the list in her possession. He talked about going to the authorities and sharing what he'd found and being put into protective custody. The entire time he spoke, Samantha's eyes never wavered from him.

Toward the end, the prosecutor leaned on the front of the witness stand, and said, "Mr. Atherton, is it safe to say you fell in love with the defendant?"

"Yes, it is. I did."

A murmur swept through the gallery.

"And Mr. Atherton, what were your intentions?"

Donny paused, looking down at his hands, and mumbled.

"I'm sorry, what was that?" the prosecutor prodded gently.

Donny raised his head again, and his eyes were brimming.

"I said, I had already bought her an engagement ring," he replied, in a heartfelt whisper that carried throughout the chamber as he finally looked intently at Samantha. "I was going to ask her to marry me."

A heart-wrenching wail escaped Samantha as she slid from her chair to the floor. Chaos ensued and testimony was suspended until calm had been restored. Samantha, silent again at last, sat staring forward as before, this time with tears flowing freely.

The defense opted not to cross-examine, and Donny was released from the witness stand. He exited the enclosure and walked quickly, without stopping, to the back of the room, never looking in Samantha's direction.

Lizzie slipped out of her seat and followed him. She found him sitting on a bench outside in the sunshine, working his tie loose, tears threatening to spill over.

He looked at her as she sat down beside him. "God, that was hard," he managed. "But I guess you'd know better than anyone exactly how I feel right now."

"I do know," she said. "We share the exact same heartache. They weren't who we thought they were."

"No, they weren't." He attempted a smile but didn't succeed.

"After what we just went through, I really could use some coffee," Lizzie prompted. "How about you?"

"Yeah," Donny said, wiping his eyes. "Lead the way."

***

Author's Note:

While both Federal and Texas criminal procedure dictate witnesses are not present in the courtroom during others' testimony, I opted to take poetic license in the Epilogue, because I felt it added more depth to the story's conclusion.